the Other Side of Dark

SARAH SMITH

ATHENEUM BOOKS FOR YOUNG READERS
New York London Toronto Sydney New Delhi

ATHENEUM BOOKS FOR YOUNG READERS

An imprint of Simon & Schuster Children's Publishing Division

1230 Avenue of the Americas, New York, New York 10020

ATHENEUM BOOKS FOR YOUNG READERS is a registered trademark of Simon & Schuster, Inc.

For information about special discounts for bulk purchases, please contact Simon & Schuster Special Sales at 1-866-506-1949 or business@simonandschuster.com.

The Simon & Schuster Speakers Bureau can bring authors to your live event. For more information or to book an event, contact the Simon & Schuster Speakers Bureau at 1-866-248-3049 or visit our website at www.simonspeakers.com.

Also available in an Atheneum Books for Young Readers hardcover edition

Book design by Lauren Rille

The text for this book is set in Adobe Garamond.

Manufactured in the United States of America

First Atheneum Books for Young Readers paperback edition November 2011

10 9 8 7 6 5 4 3 2 1

The Library of Congress has cataloged the hardcover edition as follows:

Smith, Sarah, 1947–

The other side of dark / Sarah Smith. —1st ed.

p. cm.

Summary: Since losing both her parents, fifteen-year-old Katie can see and talk to ghosts, which makes her a loner until fellow student Law sees her drawing of a historic house and together they seek a treasure rumored to be hidden there by illegal slave-traders.

ISBN 978-1-4424-0280-5 (hc)

[1. Ghosts—Fiction. 2. Supernatural—Fiction. 3. Race relations—Fiction. 4. Dating (Social customs)—Fiction. 5. African Americans—Fiction. 6. Orphans—Fiction. 7. Boston (Mass.)—Fiction.] I. Title.

PZ7.S65918Oth 2011

[Fic]—dc22

2010014690

ISBN 978-1-4424-0281-2 (pbk)

ISBN 978-1-4424-0282-9 (eBook)

KATIE

THE MAN IS HANGING FROM THE STAIRS AGAIN, which means it's going to be another bad day.

I slide past him without looking in his direction. He's just a shadow hanging off the stair rail, la la la, he doesn't exist, nothing to worry about.

Instead I'm thinking about Mom.

Maybe she'll come back today. Maybe this afternoon, when I'm home alone because Phil doesn't get home until six, maybe I'll finally hallucinate a knock at the door, and it'll be her, finally, her—

Part of me just says *I want to see my mom. I want to talk to her, I want to hug her, I want—*

Mom never liked me to read ghost stories, which is kind of ironic, but I read "The Monkey's Paw" in school. It's about a kid who dies in an accident, and his parents make a wish to get him back, and then late at night they hear this dragging, moaning thing knocking at the door? The thing is, Mom died in an accident too. Some guy hit her with his car. I can't look at her clothes or smell her perfume; I made Phil pack them away. She had a pair of red flip-flops I used to borrow all the time. When Phil gave them to me, I screamed and made him take them back.

Maybe the guy will still be hanging from the banister when I get back from school, and this'll be the day when he stops just hanging there and turns his purple face slooowly and starts pulling himself up the rope—

I'd rather see him than Mom. I want to see her. I don't. I don't know what I want.

I should introduce myself, like in a meeting of Ghost Seers Anonymous. Hi, I'm Katie, and I never see ghosts. None of the things I see are real. Nobody actually hung himself from the staircase in our two-family. I know this because I asked.

What I see are hallucinations. Hallucinations happen to lots of people, but mostly not to fifteen-year-old girls. Something bad has to happen to you.

What happened to me is Mom died.

A year ago today.

I could hang out with Phil, and we'll talk about how it's a year today, or we won't, and it'll be really awkward. Or I could sit in the school art room and draw and have Ms. Rosen, the art teacher, worry about what I might have to draw and tell me I have talent, but don't I want to draw something else?

Ms. Rosen is the worst, because she tries to understand and sympathize even though she doesn't know a thing about me.

She always wants to see what I draw, because she was a friend of Mom's and she used to admire my work back when I drew fluffy little kitties and princess outfits. I don't want to be sympathized with. I would rather be laughed at by half the school than understood by Ms. Rosen.

So where am I going to spend my time after school today when I don't want to be home alone?

Mom and I used to go to the park at Jamaica Pond. Back before everything happened. Back before there were any ghosts but Dad. Before.

Everything's all right in parks. Parks are sunny. Parks are full of swings and benches and green grass.

Nobody dies in parks.

When I get to the park after school it's sort of misty-foggy and chill, a northern light, with the trees making black blotches in the background. I chain my bike and sit cross-legged on a park bench with my sketchbook balanced on my knees. I lean back and let my mind and eyes blur: white space of the paper, pale gray water and field, black pine trees. I want to make something all pale smudginess, not an edge, not a line, something that will make people feel chilly and foggy and sad, like they're missing the person they love most. A picture about how Mom's not here. Not about her dying.

I uncross my eyes and look.

I'm not alone here. Out in the field a boy is playing with a dog, like they're both tired and cold and damp and thinking about going home. The boy is throwing a ball clumsily and running after it like someone told him he had to do it some more before he could go inside, and the dog is bored, sniffing at the bushes at the edge of the field, ignoring the ball and the boy. They both look lonely. I smudge them both into my drawing, using them to show the cold, the boy blowing on his hands, his shoulders squared against the damp, and the big white bulldog with one ear cocked toward the boy, sulking and muttering, *I don't see you, you're not the boss of me.*

"Bullet? Bullet! You bad dog!"

I was wrong about the dog belonging to the kid. The bulldog scrabbles stiff-legged toward a woman with a leash and whoofs up at her adoringly, and the two of them head away toward the baseball field. The boy looks after Bullet the dog, wishing for a dog so hard I can almost hear it, though the dog didn't even pay much attention to him.

Then, looking for something else to do, he sees me and shambles across the field toward me, kicking his ball.

He's older than I thought, a teenager maybe. As he comes closer I see his round face and thick eyelids. Mom used to work with Down syndrome kids. It makes my heart all pucker up, scared but happy, like he's a message from Mom. I smile at him and he smiles back, friendly but timid, like people usually pay attention to him only to make fun.

He's wearing the weirdest assortment of clothes, short wide pants and a thick jacket that looks made out of a blanket. No parka, no gloves. He doesn't look cold, but I can almost hear

Mom talking, like to one of her kids' moms: *Are you keeping him warm?*

Maybe I can just remember her today without wanting to burst into tears or scream.

"I'm George," he says.

"Hello, George. I'm Katie."

"Hello!" he says, grinning. "Katie." He looks at my sketchbook. "That's me. George." He hunkers down with his hands on his knees, looking at himself. He's nearsighted; he squints.

He has a nice face, kind of elflike: nice and a little unreal.

"Do you live around here, George?"

"Yes, I do!" George is an exclamation-point kind of kid.

"Do you like dogs?"

"Dogs don't play with me," George says. "Do you like drawing?"

"I do. I like it a lot. Can I draw you some more?"

He smiles all over at the thought of pleasing me, which is so nice of him. George is a good person to be with today.

He sits at the other end of the bench with the trees behind him. I outline him quickly, getting the proportions of his face right, then start on contour. The sun comes out through a hole in the cloud, turning the pines dark green and making blocky shadows. George is hard to draw; as the branches move and the light shifts, his face changes the way people's do in firelight or dreams, older and younger. The clouds trail like fingers across the sun, the light flickers; and behind George, as if there is someplace the strangeness of the light has to come from, instead of the nice quiet block of dark trees I want for contrast, my pencil began to draw a house.

A house in flames, all on fire, every window shrieking and fire-spiky and ghosting smoke and the roof sagging and beginning to fall.

Stop it! I jam the pencil into the notebook rings and look at the picture that should be for Mom, but now it's about death. On the paper George is a few years older. And he looks so scared. His face is toward me but already he is turning, twisting away, looking back toward the house. He is going to go back inside the house. He doesn't want to, but he's going to. And he is going to die.

I look up from the paper and see George posing for me, oblivious, and behind him I see the house.

It's right where I've drawn it, half-hidden in the trees. I didn't see it before. Now it's there. It has tall brick chimneys and pointed roofs that look like pine trees. Maybe it was beautiful once. But it feels as haunted and scary as one of my hallucinations. The windows gape and sag like dead mouths. Loose half bricks and broken roof slates litter the grass around it, as if it is throwing bits of itself away.

Part of the roof is just gone; through burned timbers I can see the sky.

But it hasn't burned all the way. Not the way it did in my picture.

Not yet.

"That's my house," says George, coming up behind me.

Oh, shit. "You live *there*?" Of course he does. With his clumsy clothes and his nearsighted eyes, my guy George is living in an abandoned house.

So? I practically hear Mom's voice. *What are you going to do about it?*

Today I should listen and do something.

"George, do you live by yourself? Who lives there with you?"

"I live with my grandfather. George Perkins is my name. I live at Mr. Perkins's house on Jamaica Pond."

Mr. Perkins's house. Some old homeless guy. I am practically channeling Mom. Do you have electricity, George? Do you have a toilet? Do you have a bed? Does your grandfather smoke in bed?

Because, George, I know how you're going to die, living in a place like that. I just drew it. You're going to get out of that house when it burns, but you're going back in.

"Is your grandfather—Mr. Perkins—is he old?"

George nods his head up and down, awed. "But Grandpapa will always take care of me."

Yeah. Sure he will. Until the fire. Then you'll go back in after him, and you'll die.

"George, would you like to go for a walk with me?"

"Oh, yes!"

The police station is just a couple blocks away, and I bet somebody there would like to know all about Grandpa and George.

"But I must be home before dark."

The shadows of the trees are stretching way onto the baseball field, but I can tell George he'll be back before dark and I won't actually be lying. He'll be back. In a police car.

"No problem, George. Let me get my bike."

I do the mother hen thing, shooing George back across the field, and grub in my pocket for my bike key and kneel down to unlock my bike. George rocks back and forth by the bench, looking at my bike as if he's never seen one before.

And then, then, I get it.

You would think I would have got it right away, being me.

I never draw things that are going to happen to people.

I only draw deaths that have already happened.

Way late, with the lock in my hand, reaching to pick up my sketchbook from the ground, I see George's feet. I see George's buttoned leather boots, and all around George's feet nothing but dead winter grass in the sun—

"George, you don't have a shadow."

"Oh," George says. "I forgot." And around his feet, like a stain, a shadow begins to spread, and spread, shapeless at first, and then it takes the outline of the shadows on the field.

My dead boy George, the newest of my hallucinations, stands in the middle of the field, in flickering light, with the shape of a giant tree shadowing all the ground around him, and spreading, and spreading. I stand up and back away. George calls out to me and holds out his hands, and I scream and I run and I leave him there.

Law

YOU DON'T LIKE MY FATHER and he probably doesn't like you. If you're a Republican, Southerner, banker, corporation lawyer, white person from old money, my dad wants your dollars. Dad is Mr. Big-Time Reparations. America was built on the black man's labor, says Dad, and we are owed.

He's an argumentative sort of man. He has words with his colleagues, other historians, his editors, his agent, his publishers, his publicist, and the people who interview him on TV. "My ancient African soul is grieving for my brothers," he says from out of the middle of his Brooks Brothers suit.

"Your father is a man of principle," says Mamma. "With all that that implies. Charlie is as stubborn as a mule, Law. Someday you'll be glad to have that streak in you."

His particular principle, right now, is I have to win the Walker Prize.

The Walker Prize for Rhetoric. It's about finding the next Martin, I guess, the next Barack. The next Voice of Our People.

African-American high school students from all around Boston write speeches, and the finalists deliver them at the African Meeting House or Tremont Temple. Old ladies wear their church hats and their best white teeth. Preachers come all the way from Chicago. Deval Patrick, the first African-American governor of Massachusetts, gives out the prizes. Dad's usually one of the judges. But this year, when he was asked, Dad said, "I'll excuse myself, since I hope my son will be competing. You do intend to compete, Lawrence?"

Mumble mumble, I say. By the way, Dad, my name's not Lawrence.

"It would be a great thing," Dad goes right on, "if a Walker were to win the Walker Prize. Heh, heh." Heh heh heh. Yes, Massa.

Malcolm could talk about reparations. "The only reason that the present generation of white Americans are in a position of economic strength is because their fathers worked our fathers for over four hundred years with no pay. Your father isn't here to pay. My father isn't here to collect. But I'm here to collect and you're here to pay." Even in this Age of Obama, people still talk about whether and what America owes us. Militant brothers and sisters put up websites and petitions: They want their forty acres and a mule, plus interest. Project 21, the black conservatives, go all contrary and Booker T.: No, suh, no way, they don't want no payment for being black, suh, they just want to join the Somerset Club. And they all cite Charles Randall Walker. The leading scholar of reparations.

My dad.

Dad has collected reparations all his life: guilt scholarship to Phillips Andover, full-boat to Harvard, Junior Fellow, and so on and so on, books and TV and NPR, he might be chairman of the department at Harvard someday. Reparations worked for him and he thinks they ought to work for me. Why shouldn't Charlie Walker's boy get some?

Except that Charles Randall Walker, Mr. Reparations, My Ancient African Soul, married Mamma.

Who is white.

I'm light enough to freckle. Can't dance, can't sing, can't play basketball, don't wear an earring or bling or a hoodie, as if Dad or Mamma would let me. Of course, nobody's in any danger of thinking I'm white. I've been stopped, I've been looked at. But am I black enough, do I have the race-man balls, to stand up there on the stage at Tremont Temple and talk about what white America owes me?

I feel less black than Eminem.

None of this gets me out of having to compete.

It's like the Walker Prize is what I owe my dad.

And two of my best friends are competing against me.

Mamma kicks off her shoes by the front door, shakes rain out of her hair, throws her jacket over the banister, tilts her portfolio against the wall. She's practically crying. She's been at another Landmarks Commission meeting. "How can they?" she shouts up the stairs. "Haven't they the slightest sense of history? Charlie, how can you agree with them?"

"Perkins was a Triangle trader, Susan." Dad stands halfway down the stairs, a big man even in his stocking feet. "That is the history you want to preserve. I would not give a cent for that building."

"Charlie, you know that's not the point."

"That is always the point, Susan," he says in the Voice. "You will not want Pinebank preserved when you read my next book."

"I don't care about your book, Charlie." This is heresy in our house. Mamma kneels down by the portfolio, unzips it, takes out a rolled-up cardboard poster, flourishes it like a sword, turns and marches into her office, and Dad and I hear pieces of masking tape being torn off a roll. The front window darkens.

What Mamma wants to preserve is a house called Pinebank, because Frederick Law Olmsted wanted it preserved. Mamma says "Olmsted, the greatest landscape architect in America" the way Muslims say "Muhammad, peace be unto him." Mamma has a signed picture of Olmsted in her office, and a bronze bust, and a drawing.

"And do you know what that hypocritical potato-mouthed Menino is doing?" she yells back at us. "He wants to hold the demolition hearing for Pinebank during Christmas week, when everyone is gone."

"I'll speak against keeping Pinebank, Susan," Dad shouts.

"You can't speak against Pinebank, Charlie. You cannot." Mamma comes into the hall, takes her jacket off the banister, and goes upstairs, wiping her eyes, pointedly ignoring Dad.

Dad goes into the kitchen, ignoring her.

Houses and history are what my family fights about.

Or at least what we say we fight about.

I'm supposed to grow up to be a historian. Dad always thought his son would be like him, and I guess he thought Mamma would be too. When he married her, she was in history and lit at Harvard, only gardening for fun and only helping her friends with their houses because she had an eye for restoration. Dad has a picture of her in his office, a graduate student sitting in the library reading. But she would spend her Saturdays tearing out walls and repairing horsehair plaster and doing plantings.

"Susan, what is this interest in manual labor?" he used to ask her.

I remember the exact moment when I started to disappoint Dad too. I was nine years old. It was summer, and Mamma had taken me to some friend's place in Nahant, an eighteenth-century house; Mamma was telling the friend how to restore the garden. The two of them were outside, talking, and I was in what had been the old kitchen. Big fireplace with a bread oven and a door to the right of the fireplace. I opened that door. And it wasn't a closet at all. On one side it was shelves, but on the other it was the chimney.

I could see the whole chimney, like a huge brick beehive. Beyond it I could see another wall, to another room, with the laths and joists all showing, and the bottom of the staircase going up to the second floor like a staircase turned inside out.

It was like I'd opened the door to the inside of the house.

I ran out past the stairs to make sure. That other wall was the Metcalfs' living room, it had to be. The brick fireplace in their living room belonged to the chimney. The ordinary wallpapered wall behind their TV was the same wall that I could see the secret rough inside of. I wanted to knock on the wall and run round fast enough to hear myself knocking. Everything was different, everything made sense, and this place I was standing in was the center of the puzzle where the pieces all interlocked. I ran back and forth and I stood in the door to the inside of the house.

And while I was standing in the kitchen, outside I could hear Mamma and her friend talking about a kitchen garden. And I realized: The house was in its garden and the garden was in the world and it was all the same puzzle. It all connected. I was standing in history.

I knew I was never going to be bored again.

My great spiritual vision, man. Did I tell you I was nine years old?

Did I tell you I'm a geek?

I would rather tell Dad I perform raunchy acts of sex with gerbils than tell him I want to spend my life being a historical architect.

Pinebank. I came across it when I was a kid, a couple of years after houses hit me over the head. Ever since, I go out there when I need to put my stuff in perspective. It started out a millionaire's country place—*the* millionaire, America's very first millionaire. Now it's falling to pieces in the middle of a city park. Good place to feel sorry for yourself. We're all going to die, the grass is going to cover us, all our troubles soon be over when we reach that Zion shore. Malcolm Forbes used to buy medals and prize cups out of pawnshops to remind himself that nothing lasts. Same principle.

Mamma wants Pinebank here because Olmsted wanted it saved for a restaurant in 1890, and you only have to stand near it to see why. The house rises at the end of a long winding path, on a promontory overlooking the lake. It has pointed roofs and it's surrounded by enormous pointed-topped pine trees. Olmsted might have made the path, must have done some plantings, but if the place were a parking lot instead of a park you'd still have that little rise, the mass of the chimneys over the lake, the sense that this house belongs right here. It's sweet as jazz, the way Pinebank sits on its land.

The Wednesday after Thanksgiving, I take my gang out to look at the place.

Brookline High runs on cliques. The kids who smoke by the bike racks, the kids whose parents will kill them if they don't get into Harvard, the newspaper wonks, the football jocks, the math nerds and dealers in mock oregano and people who know every line of *Battlestar Galactica*. Shar and Darryl and Bobby Lee and I are the Gang of People There's Only One Of. Shar and Darryl and Bobby Lee are stars. I'm just me. Son of a star.

"You should write your Walker essay about landscape," Shar says. "Landscape. Houses. What you like."

"Sure," I say, "talk about houses and history for the Walker Prize. That'll work."

"Ready-made audience, man," Bobby Lee says.

"For *historical architecture*? For the Walker Prize? In front of my dad?"

"So you will talk about reparations?" says Shar.

"I will not."

"Oh, sure you will not."

Shar da Cunha. Brazilian diplomat father, American mother who's a singer from Detroit. Perfect bronze skin, perfect African features, Shar would be in the Truly Stunning Black Girl Achievers clique, except that her blackness quotient is absolute zero. *Girlfriend, haven't you ever been given the Look? Haven't you ever been discriminated against?* Shar just laughs. In Brazil her mother's a samba heroine. Shar thinks reparations are funny.

"I will write about being African Brazilian but everyone thinks I'm African American," Shar says. "And Darryl will write too, yes, my hero?"

"Yeah," Darryl says, looking uneasy for a moment. "I'm writing about learning to read," and stops us all.

Darryl Muhammad Johnson. I've known the dude since we were both in third-grade Sunday school, and I swear he was six feet tall then. The man eats alligators for breakfast and can run like a bat out of Scripture. The Brookline football coach grabbed him off the METCO bus and had his future planned from now until his Super Bowl ring. Nobody cared that Darryl couldn't tell the difference between *B* and *D*.

Except Darryl. And Shar. And then Bobby Lee and me, once Shar shamed us into it.

Last summer, when he realized how much of a problem dyslexia was for him, Darryl went to see his coach and told him he couldn't play football until he learned to read. The coach personally got him a private tutor, but Darryl stuck up for himself and didn't play football this year. The dude loves football, and he's going to be really good, and he didn't play.

Darryl is my personal hero, for sheer spit persistence. I love that man.

And I'm going to compete against him.

"You're going to win," I tell Darryl.

"Your dad is the famous historian at Harvard," Shar says. "You talk about reparations. They give the prize to you. It's how things work. Darryl and I will get honorable mention."

"That's *not true*." I'm afraid it is. "I'm not going to talk about reparations. I'm not winning on Dad's back."

"Then you write about what you care about," Shar says.

Shar's mom is an entertainer. My dad is the Voice of His People. I slump at the back of the room in every class, drawing house plans and landscape plots. When I get called on I go *uh, uh, uh.* I am a nerd at something no one else cares about, and it's all I care about. My dad is a professor at Harvard, and I get Bs.

"I'm going to talk about killing whiteys," Bobby Lee says smugly. "They're giving the prize to me." Bobby Lee's our nod to multiculturalism; he's so white he fluoresces.

"No, man," Darryl says kindly, "you got to be a *star*, like a football *star*, or Mr. Reparations Junior here, or at least *pretty*. You just some no-ass cracker."

I clear my throat. "Hey, guys? You need to spend all afternoon circle-dissing? I want to put up a website, do *something* for Pinebank. I need your ideas. I need your help."

I'm no good at speaking. I'm good at websites, which are pretty much like house plans. Different pages, different rooms, different functions. Find a theme, link the parts, tie it together, a nice clean puzzle.

With a speech, you have to stand up for yourself. You have to know who you are.

I send my gang up the path ahead of me, watching how they see it, Shar in her pink coat and leather high-heeled boots, Bobby Lee the White Dwarf pointing his perpetual video camera, and Darryl, shaved head and gold earring, loping on ahead of them.

They aren't getting how good Pinebank is. All they're seeing is the graffiti and the fallen bricks.

"My neighborhood," Darryl says, "they tear down stuff like that and folks have a party."

"I could take some footage of Shar being eye candy in front of it," Bobby Lee says. "I get the angle right and nobody sees the house."

Shar poses, model-style, throwing out her arms.

"Yeah, but don't you see how the house is the right thing here and the landscape fits around it?" I ask them. "You have to see it. It's poetry."

"Poetry has a roof," Bobby Lee says behind his viewfinder.

"Maybe it's historical," Shar says, "but it is ugly, ugly, ugly."

Bobby Lee puts away his camcorder, pulls out his digital camera, walks back and forth looking into the screen, but not photographing.

"Look," I say. "It's one of the most historic places in Boston. Look at that white trim. First use of terra-cotta brick in the United States. Look at how it pins this whole part of the landscape. Frederick Law Olmsted said it was the best-situated house in America."

"Terra-cotta brick." Darryl snorts. "Man, you are weird."

"Guys, be serious. Please? What do I do to persuade Tom Menino to spend a couple of million dollars to restore it?"

"In this economy?" Shar shakes her head. Darryl and Bobby Lee nod, agreeing with her. Shar wraps her pink coat around herself.

"At least think about it, guys?"

"At Starbucks," Shar says.

We head back down the path toward the cars.

"You could blog," Shar says. That's how she's teaching Darryl to read and write; they do a blog together.

"Yeah, write about it," Darryl says. "Tell 'em *terra-cotta brick*." He chuckles like it's the funniest thing he's heard in his life.

"Tell a story," Bobby Lee says. "Make a movie."

"Show it how it used to be," Shar says. "Show it pretty."

"There's a story about the place," I say. "A mystery, about

some lost money. I could use that, I guess." Money would be good. Pinebank is going to cost millions to restore. "But my dad is set on having the house torn down. I can't do a blog and have him comment all over me."

"You need to kick your dad in the round ones, man. He is looming over you."

"What's your dad got against Pinebank?" Bobby Lee asks.

"I don't know. It's in his new book and he doesn't talk about his books while he's doing the first draft. The man who owned Pinebank was in the Triangle Trade, but if Dad was so worried about that, he'd tear down half of Boston."

"Your dad would do that," Shar agrees.

"What's that girl doing?" says Darryl.

There's a girl standing close by the house in the shadows under the trees. While we watch, she turns and begins to walk back down the path and then away from us, toward the baseball field, toward a bike chained to one of the park benches. She's making little shooing motions with one arm as if she's brushing away flies, and she's talking.

"Crazy Katie Mullens," Bobby Lee says.

"She is the one who—?" Shar says.

"Yeah," says Bobby Lee.

Katie Mullens. I had a big fantasy crush on her in seventh grade. She was a cute, curly-haired girl with a snub nose and lips almost wide enough to be righteous, and she was funny. We weren't in the same class, but one afternoon both our classes had gone up to the high school for something. Katie and I ended up in the atrium, and I talked her ear off about how they'd taken the old entrance to the building and built the new entrance around it, just like in this basilica I'd seen in Spain. She didn't laugh at me, unlike my friends, so I announced to Mamma I was going to take Katie Mullens to some seventh-grade dance—I don't think I'd mentioned it to Katie at the time. Mamma did a little checking and explained to me that Katie's mother was divorced and they lived in Whiskey Point, and didn't I want to take some other nice girl?

Whenever I talked to Katie afterward I felt stupid and powerless and as if I'd betrayed her. Robbed her of my wonderful dancing, I guess, and of knowing my amazing family. And having her ear talked off about houses. My first lost love: all in my head. Like so many others.

Then her mom died.

"Look at those legs," Bobby Lee says. "Shame she's nuts."

"Lay off, Bobby Lee."

Katie is talking to herself. She kneels down to unlock her bike. She's holding a sketchbook and she tries to keep hold of it, doing things awkwardly, as if she's in another universe and isn't paying attention to this one. She puts down the sketchbook—

And then she screams.

She screams, she yells out something, she jerks up and backs away from the bike and shouts something, and then she turns and runs back toward the path, away from Pinebank, toward us.

There's no way we're going to avoid meeting each other; we're standing right where the path goes down toward the pond. She sees us and stops in the middle of the path, facing away from her bike, panting. Terrified.

And embarrassed. That makes at least her and me.

"Oh, shit," she says.

"Are you all right?" I manage.

She opens her mouth. She closes it again, hard, and rubs her hand against her cheek. She's much thinner than she used to be, and pale in the cold. I want to take her to Starbucks and buy her cocoa and be braver than I was in seventh grade.

"I thought I saw something," she says finally. "A mouse."

"Oh." What am I going to say?

"Never mind." She turns and heads off down the path and the stairs toward the pond. I watch her. She stops at the bottom of the stairs, waiting for us to leave.

"She is so friendly," Shar mutters.

"She left her bike," Darryl says, "all unlocked like that."

Next to her bike, left abandoned by the baseball field, the pages of her sketchbook are flipping over in a breeze and loose pages are beginning to blow away.

"I'll pick those up for her. You guys go on, I'll meet you at Starbucks."

Shar gives me a look, but she and Darryl and Bobby Lee go off toward the parking lot, and I head across the field. I wedge the sketchbook under the bike and begin to pick up her drawings.

A boy in a field. She has the field by Jamaica Pond just right, the mist coming up from the water and the weird luminescence and the faded black of the trees. But she's left out the baseball diamond and the walkway, everything modern. In the middle of the field a kid is standing by himself. Behind him, at the end of the road, in the trees, is a house, just the suggestion of a building.

Pinebank.

But not this Pinebank. For two hundred years Pinebank has stood on the shores of Jamaica Pond, always the original foundations in the same perfect space. But not always the same house. Over the years Pinebank has burned and fallen and grown up again from its own roots: country cottage to wooden mansion to brick.

The Pinebank she's drawn is the wooden one, the one that burned in 1868.

Katie's drawing my favorite house?

I turn, and she's standing on the path, at the edge of the field, looking at me.

Most of the other loose pages have blown up against the fence by the baseball diamond. I gather them up and slide them back inside the cover of her sketchbook, all but the first, and wheel the bike back across the field toward her.

"You okay?" I say stupidly, and "Here's your pictures. You're drawing Pinebank?"

"I was just—drawing something. And then I saw . . ." Her voice trails off.

"A mouse?"

"Yeah," she says.

Well, that was that conversation.

"You're Lawrence Walker," she says. "From school."

Mamma and Dad flipped a coin for the right to choose my first name. Mamma won. (They couldn't agree on a name? They never agree on anything.) Dad says it sounds ridiculous for anyone to be named Law. Like a TV hero, he says. *Law West of the Pecos.* "Law Walker," I say. "Just Law. Is my name."

"I'm Katie Mullens," she says, as if I wouldn't know.

I know.

"You were drawing Pinebank?" I ask again.

"I was drawing the wind," she says, and suddenly she smiles and she's Katie from seventh grade. "The wind, the chill, it was all in the light. . . ." Her smile gets tired suddenly, as if she's remembering whatever happened.

"I like this." I show her the drawing of Pinebank. "I like it a lot."

"Oh," she says. "Yeah. That's nothing."

What am I going to do to keep this moment going? "Have you got any more like it? Of Pinebank?"

She considers, opens her sketchbook, folds it back and hands it to me. She looks at me defensively.

Katie must have read Seaburg's biography of Perkins. She's drawn the night the second Pinebank burned. It's in flames, five minutes from collapsing, and the boy's in front of it, the boy from the other drawing. He's almost leaning toward me out of the paper, I can hear him panting, and fire is flickering in his eyes, and he is terrified.

I know him.

It's the boy in the Seaburg biography. The boy who died when the second Pinebank burned.

What sort of person draws the past like that? Like it's alive and pains her?

I look up at her, Katie Mullens, who's crazy, but crazy in an absolutely unique and interesting way, and she's looking at me like she knows I'm going to call her a freak and that's everything she needs to know about herself. *Don't say a word about what I do.* Crazy Katie Mullens, who's got so thin and pale, with her long lovely legs and her green eyes.

Who can draw like Robert Johnson could play the guitar, by standing at the crossroads at midnight and giving her soul to the devil.

You think you're a freak, Katie? You're different, and I know different. I'm a nerd who can't talk about anything but terra-cotta, and not even my friends understand. I don't know what you're drawing when you're drawing Pinebank, but you're drawing houses.

I should have taken you to the dance in seventh grade. We could have been talking all this time.

Maybe, I think, maybe when all that happened to you, last year, maybe I could have been there.

"You want to get together after school tomorrow?" I ask. "Go get coffee in Brookline Village, something like that? Show me more of your pictures?"

She looks half-shocked. "Why?"

I'm way-the-shit too light: light enough to blush. "Hey."

She stares at me. For pity, her expression says, or to laugh at her?

Because I want to talk to you. "For coffee," I say. "If you want to, if you'd—I mean, you can *draw*. And I need someone to draw Pinebank, for a website I'm doing? Could I just talk to you about it?"

I feel like I'm asking her out. Or confessing. Or something.

She shakes her head, but "Sure," she says finally. "Okay. Sure. Why not. You can look at my pictures."

I get her cell number and give her mine, and walk her down the path toward Perkins Street.

KATIE

SOMETIMES PEOPLE WANT TO TALK WITH ME, you know? *Boy, that was really awful your mom dying like that, what's it LIKE?* What they really want to know is it'll never happen to them.

Guess what.

So why do I even bother talking with Law Walker?

Because he asked me. I'm pathetic.

Because he's good-looking and smart. I like his button-down shirts and his Buddy Holly glasses; he dresses so conservative and retro, he looks like Clark Kent. He has handsome hands. Because I'd like to be the sort of girl who goes out for coffee with a guy like him, even if I'm not. Because I'd like to be the sort of girl who's not crazy.

Because, even when I was standing there all shaking and stinky sweaty and realizing that I'd been hallucinating in front of him, I never, never once thought he was going to laugh.

Law must be crazy not to laugh at me.

"You want to get some ice cream?" Phil asks, breaking into my dreams of having a real boy ask me out.

After my shrink appointments, Phil always wants to take me out for ice cream or a pizza or something, like I've had an owie or a splinter in my finger and went to the doctor to take it out and was a brave girl. Phil doesn't know what to do to make things better, and it's sort of pathetic. Still, he's trying. Like Dad says, I should give him something to work with.

"Can we get sundaes?" I ask Phil, because I might as well let him feel he's doing something useful. Mrs. Morris, my shrink, tries to get me to talk about how I feel about Mom. She has plenty of theories about how I should feel, and how I should try to remember Mom, and I sit there while she talks and glare at her fat ankles and say *nada* for a whole hour.

Phil and I go out for ice cream first and have leftovers later for dinner (our cooking should be reported to the American Society for Prevention of Cruelty to Stomachs), and then I sit at the kitchen table and do homework while Phil grades papers. I should introduce Phil: Phil Stephens, high school English teacher. My stepdad, I guess. He looks like a pole with glasses and ears. He likes madras plaid, Mister Rogers sweaters, and sneakers. He's writing a book on Wordsworth. He's been writing it forever. He only talks to other teachers and only reads books that are out of print. Everyone at school used to think he was gay, or clueless, and he is clueless, but three years ago he saw Mom at PTO and though he'd known her for years as a friend, that night he sort of *duh*'ed and blinked once and asked her out, and that was it. They got married practically as soon as Mom checked with me.

Kind of sweet. Jimmy Stewart should have played Phil; he meant us to be a family from the beginning. It would have been nice. He can actually throw a mean curveball—he tried to teach me once—and I can see him with a boy of his own.

What he got was me.

What I think he's going to get, sometime, is Ms. Rosen, the art teacher. Ms. Understanding. They eat lunch together a lot, him in his flannel shirts and her with her gray hair and fluttery skirts and Birkenstocks and her endless doggy-eyed sympathy. *Poor Phil. Poor Katie.* If he starts dating her I will drive a fork into my brain.

"I need to do homework on my computer," I tell Phil, and go to my room.

Phil lets me surf the Internet without checking if I'm looking up suicide sites or being verbally molested by forty-year-old guys in chat rooms. Phil makes a big thing out of trusting me. Like I said, he's clueless. I should feel guilty, because I'm doing something in my room he wouldn't approve of.

I don't even need the Internet.

I don't need a computer.

I'm talking to Dad.

I would say "my real dad," except he's one of my hallucinations too. According to everyone who knew him, my real dad was the Wikipedia definition of "lout." He died in Afghanistan before I was a year old, and he and Mom had split before that. But when I was six or so, way before my other ghosts, I started pretending he came to see me. I still pretend. In my version of him, he's a sweetie. I ask questions, he has answers. I talk, he listens. He apologized to me for being a bad dad, even. It was a great apology, since I made it up.

"So, Katie," Dad says. "What's going on?"

I don't say anything for a while, and he listens to that. I think of telling him about Law asking me for coffee, but that's making too much out of it. Whatever Law wants, it isn't crazy me. I just hope it's a picture and not a laugh. Instead I tell Dad about George.

Look, I say finally, *you know you're not real. You and the other ghost roadkill I see.*

"You really think you're making me up?" Dad says.

I wish I weren't making Dad up. He's not like the others. If he got blown up or something, which I guess he must have, he doesn't look it. He looks normal. Like the kid George did, until the shadow.

I don't know how to say this the right way, not even when I'm talking to myself.

You're not real, Dad. I know that. But that kid, George? He felt . . . different. As if he'd really been alive.

"Sure he'd been alive. He's dead, right?"

"Dad, I *made him up*," I say out loud before I remember.

"Anything wrong, Katie?" Phil calls from the other room.

"Nothing, homework, never mind."

Dad has a lighter out; he's tapping out a cigarette from the same pack he's been smoking forever. If he were real, I'd be dead from secondhand smoke. He catches me frowning and shrugs.

"If you're making me up, how come I still smoke?"

Because in the one picture I have of you, you're smoking.

He lights his cigarette and points it at me. "Don't start. I got nothing to lose. But don't you start."

I'm not going to smoke. What's wrong with me, Dad? Why would I make up a dead kid with a tree for a shadow? And how come he has Down syndrome?

This has to be about Mom. Everything is about Mom.

"He's a mental defective ghost," Dad says.

You're not supposed to say that.

"What, ghost? Ghost," says Dad. "Bodily challenged. Boo. What you don't believe in, in spite of I come to see you every evening practically. Maybe you got to do something for him. Isn't that what people do for ghosts?"

I don't want to do anything for anybody. Why can't I be like other people? Why can't I still be somebody's kid?

He stands up and comes across the room to me. "Honey," Dad says. "Aw, sweetie. You see ghosts. It happens. It's what you do."

"I don't see ghosts."

He begins to flicker out, then goes solid again. "And what you do for me? I like your company, kid. I love you. Forever." He bends down and I can feel, on the top of my head, the lightest possible kiss, and I can smell the memory of a smell of tobacco. And then he's gone.

I told you he's nice.

But I don't see ghosts.

If I did, if I saw any ghost in the whole world, if any ghost in the whole wide dead world wanted to get in touch with me, it would be Mom. It would have happened. I would have seen her.

And I don't see her.

Not ever.

Law

A COUPLE OF YEARS AGO DAD WENT down to a history conference in Virginia, and he took me to introduce me round. For a couple of days, I got to go around with a graduate student visiting plantations, which Dad approved of because it would be a lesson about race history.

The lesson was going to be how plantation museum owners treated uppity black boys who wanted to study landscape and architecture. But I wasn't with Dad or anyone I knew, and the grad student wasn't going to rat me out, so after the first couple of assholes let off mouthfarts, I explored the benefits of disguise.

"I am Espanish. I have come from Espain to visit your so-beautiful plan-ta-thi-on."

Once I got over the guilt at sort-of-passing, I had myself a great time. Sorry, I did. The plantations amazed me. There's the big portico in front with the white pillars, and then there's the mingy mean house behind it, with the proportions all wrong: the great big reception rooms, the little dank earth-smelling kitchen, and the tiny cramped bedrooms upstairs. The floor plans are all obvious and rigid. And the descendants. A lot of these places are private museums, owned by the descendants of the original owners or a wannabe, some chinless white joy willing to own up to this house and love it and paint it and weed its historic landscape and show it to you. "Give me ten dollars and you can look at my private jail for the Knee-grows."

Houses are stories. The big hidden part of any house, bigger than the chimneys and the bearing beams, are the people who build them. House museums are those people doing a strip act for strangers. I could spend years around plantations. Sorry about that.

Dad would disown me.

In our house, Mamma's office and Dad's office face off on opposite sides of our front hall. Mamma's office is blueprints of houses, plots of gardens, shelves of books about historical plantings and house colors. The signed photograph and the bust and the drawing of Frederick Law Olmsted. A bowl of chrysanthemums. A still life of roses over the mantel. Mamma's company is called A House in Its Garden. I love her. I want to do what she does. But she couldn't be more white. And white isn't an option for me.

Across the hall, Dad's office. There are pictures of Dad with other famous people all over the walls. Here's his desk, where he writes the first draft of his books on the manual typewriter that belonged to Grandmam. Dad's secret vice: By the time the book reaches the publishers, it's a computer file, but that first draft, the one where he shuts his door and doesn't let anybody read it and lets his soul howl at the moon, he writes it on that sixty-year-old collection of stuck steel teeth and rubber platen and attitude. *Tut tap tat zzzr-ding*, late at night. Grandmam raised him all alone, her only favorite boy, and took in typing at night after her other job.

He said once that the sound of Grandmam's typing made him feel safe. It's hard to think what would make Dad feel unsafe. T. rexes in bedsheets and pointy hoods would just energize the man.

I look around Dad's office, with his fancy little computer on the computer desk and the old typewriter on the real desk, and his whitish-buff-leather chair that matches the sofa he picked for the living room.

It's the exact color of white skin. Just a few shades lighter than mine.

You'd think people would be careful who they show their houses to. There's nothing that's more your private business than where you live, what you fuss over and what you let lie; but people just bring it all out for you when they let you in their house, "showin' off now, here's my private life, here's my skinned-whitey sofa."

I don't look forward to telling either of them I'm hanging around with white Katie from Whiskey Point. Katie who draws houses. Katie whom I never forgot. I'd never tell Mamma that. I just hope Mamma's forgotten her.

Outside, we have a big portico and white pillars, and a magnolia tree in front. Right now it looks like any other tree without leaves, but come spring it's a little breath from the sunny South.

And there's Mamma's poster in the window. Mamma's poster, about the house that belonged to Perkins the slave trader: *Save Pinebank*.

Where do I belong in this house?

"A house is a history, right?" I tell Katie Mullens.

She's brought more pictures, a big flat portfolio wrapped in a trash bag. Starbucks smells like Starbucks's idea of Christmas: peppermint coffee, gingerbread coffee. Rain blows against the glass, hard as tossed pebbles, blurring the lights in the window of Chobee Hoy Real Estate across the street.

"What got you interested in Pinebank?" I ask her.

"Just the look." She shrugs.

"No, I mean, what got you interested in the history of it? Was it Seaburg's book?"

She looks blank. She has to have seen the book, but she's probably just skimmed it.

"What is the history of it?" she asks.

"The whole history of Boston, practically. The Perkinses were America's first millionaires, big politicos, like the Kennedys. Thomas Handasyd Perkins knew John Hancock and visited George Washington. He helped to found the Athenaeum and the Perkins School for the Blind. He lived forever, ninety when he died, saw Crispus Attucks's dead body when he was a kid and almost saw the Civil War. And the house? The house is great. What do you want for coffee?"

I see Shar sitting at the back of Starbucks, pink coat glowing in the Christmas lights, sipping a latte. No sign of Bobby Lee or Darryl. The usual contingent of other high school kids have either got their caffeine fix already or aren't here yet. Katie glances at the prime empty chairs at the front and then moves back toward the rear, Shar-ward.

"Uh-uh." I grab one of the chairs by the window and gesture at her to take the other. "These are ours. You want some coffee?"

She wants small, plain. I get coffee at the bar, and Shar passes me and drops her cup into the trash and raises eyebrows at me. I make a shoving move with one hand at her as I bring the coffees back.

"When Olmsted designed the Boston parks, he wanted Pinebank to be a restaurant and meeting place for the whole city. And it would be great, it's just so beautiful there, just so alive in that space. My mother's working to help save it, and I want to do something too, create a website about it, something that'll show people how great it could be."

"And I can help?"

"Those pictures you drew . . . I want to know if you could draw some more for me. Thomas Handasyd Perkins, the mystery of the Perkins Bequest, the fires. Making it visible. Could you draw me something like that?"

"I don't know," Katie says. She gets up, thinking, goes over to the bar to get sugar for her coffee. I look at her legs and take a deep breath.

"You just want me to draw the house?" she says, sitting back down.

Not *just*. "Like you did last time."

"Like what?" Her shoulders hunch up. I'm getting into difficult Katie territory.

"Like the picture of the house when it burned," I say. "It was amazing, what you did, making it look completely like the nineteenth century. And the fire—"

She moves her long hands in a kind of shrug, as if someone is going to blame her for something.

I've said something wrong and I don't know what.

"You don't want pretty pictures," she says. "You want *my* pictures. Let's get this over with. You want to see my drawings."

She pulls her beat-up portfolio roughly out of its trash-bag raincoat, moves our coffees aside, and opens up the portfolio on the table. She looks up at me like I'm another of whatever she was scared of in the field.

High school art at Brookline: still lifes, perspective, your friend's portrait, your own hand. Katie is way beyond that. The first picture is a bunch of daffodils, and it's pure jazz, a trombone solo on a spring day. There's Darryl on the bench, his face tense and coiled like a spring. And Dr. Petrucci, Uncle Brucie Buttrucci, the stupidest history teacher on the North American continent, with that pissy look he gets whenever anybody says something original.

"Petrucci always puts me in detention for drawing floor plans in class. You're good. I really want you to help me with this."

"You draw in class too?" she says, but not warming up.

"In Buttrucci's. Man knows nothing about history." And besides, if I do too well in high school, I'll get into Harvard. "Ms. Rosen must love you."

Katie frowns. She's wearing knee-high socks and one of them has fallen down around her ankle. She bends away from me to tug it up.

I'm doing something wrong and I don't know what. I turn over pages of drawings. Pictures of kids doing kid things. A boy stacking blocks; from his mouth and his laugh, you can tell he's looking forward to knocking them down. A couple of boys arguing with wild stubborn gestures; a girl singing with her mouth as wide open as if she's about to bite an apple. It takes me a moment to notice the slanted eyes, the stubby noses and wide faces; they're Down syndrome kids, like the Perkins boy she drew at Pinebank. There's a picture of him too, squinting into a winter sun.

"My mom was an art teacher. She taught art to special-needs kids," Katie says abruptly. "I go out and draw them sometimes. To remember her, sort of. Without remembering her, you know, the wrong way. I draw a lot of things. I can't help it."

"They're really good."

"They're—for her. About her." She says suddenly, "Stop now. Don't look at the rest, okay?"

But I turn the page.

There's the house burning and the scared Perkins boy. Next is an auto accident. Katie hasn't skimped on details. The guy was using a cell phone, and it drove right into the side of his face when he was hit. The third is a woman who jumped off something high. It must be a woman, because she was wearing high heels.

I can taste my coffee crawling up the back of my throat.

I look up at Katie, at her pale face and wild green eyes. She stands up.

"I guess that was what you expected?" she says.

"No."

She scoops and shuffles her other pictures toward her, pushing everything into the trash bag. "Your friends told you Crazy Katie Mullens draws scary pictures. And you saw one. So you had to see more, just to make sure."

"My friends didn't tell me anything. I remembered you from seventh grade. You could draw."

"Seventh grade," she says scornfully, as if it's a million years ago.

I look at her picture, really look at it, the pain in all those jagged, swirling lines. She's not angry at me. She's angry because her mom died.

She tries to grab the picture from me, and I reach out and take hold of her hand.

She's angry because she's scared of something.

"Stop."

I don't mean it as strong as I say it.

"You saw me freaking because of something I drew," she says, trying to pull away. "Congratulations, dipshit. Now I've performed for you, will you let go of my hand so I can go home?"

"Don't go."

She looks at me, the way she must look at everything. Scared and angry because her mom's death hurts her so much. Standing at the crossroads by the light of the moon. And drawing all those death scenes. And drawing Pinebank.

"That picture of Darryl," I tell her, "you've got him. And Uncle Brucie. And the daffs, the flowers. And the house—you've got Pinebank, too. I'm not trying to poke at you to see if either of us will scream. That other day? You looked really scared."

This is worse than asking her to a dance. This is asking her about herself. I'm still holding her hand, too.

Katie, at least you're not someone who won't tell his parents what he wants.

"Scared?" she says. "No kidding."

I've gone too far not to keep talking.

"Tell me why."

KATIE

LAW WALKER GETS ME TALKING. And I can't stop talking. I can go through entire hours staring at my shrink's fat ankles, not say a word, but—

"Mom had parked her car across the street and she was holding a bag of groceries, so she didn't see the car coming. The nozzle in the SUV was using his cell phone. So . . ." I shrug. "So now, every once in a while I have to draw something. Somebody. Who's. Dead."

The coffee Law bought me went cold so long ago I just twiddle with it and pretend it's warm, while I blow my chances with the only male human who's ever asked me out for anything.

"I mean, you know, things *happen*. And I can't help it. That's what's the matter with me. Things happen to people. And I could scream or cry, but I draw instead. So if I draw pictures, they'll probably be gross and no good for you."

Law just nods. He doesn't understand, really. He has his parents. Nothing has really happened to him.

"My shrink says drawing pictures is a way of dealing with

my feelings. I could think of so many better ways."

Law nods. "You draw dead people rather than missing your mom? Does it help?"

"That would be so nasty if it did."

"You want some more coffee?" he asks me.

He hasn't run. I don't know why, but hasn't run. I could almost laugh. "Yeah. Coffee."

"Sugar this time. Or cocoa?"

"Just coffee."

I toss it down and go on chattering, wired on caffeine. "I make up stories for them, for the pictures. The woman with the shoes? I was going to draw a picture of the rose garden in Knyvet Park, and then there she was on the sidewalk, and I must have heard about her on TV or something, but it was like I knew all about her and I was drawing her. She wore her coolest shoes to make her boyfriend sorry. She thought she was going to be a beautiful corpse and her boyfriend would be so sad, and then on the way down she decided he was a total loser and she should just move back to Memphis like she was going to do before she met him. But she died." She jumped from the roof and hit the sidewalk like a bag of ketchup. I am not going to tell Law that. "I—had to draw her to stop thinking about her. You know?"

Late the night Mom died, I took a flashlight and biked over to see where the accident happened. I wanted to be with her. Even though they'd mostly washed the blood away into the gutter, I could hunker down and see it in the cracks and edges of the sidewalk. It was worse than anything. I wanted to run back and tell Mom, *I saw the most awful thing, a terrible thing,* and have her tell me it was all right.

"What happened to the guy who hit your mother?" he asks.

"Not enough. He got probation and moved away. I hope he dies really, really painfully. I just can't think about my mom, Law. I just can't. I can't."

What do normal people say when they're having coffee with a boy? "Tell me about your family," I say.

Law swallows like he doesn't want to say something. "My mamma and dad?" he says. "This is nothing like what happened to you. But, I mean, they fight. All the time. It's worse now because of Pinebank. They're really cutting each other. My mamma lives in one half of our house and my dad in the other and they only get together to fight," he says. "And I draw houses. House plans. Houses that fit a place and make people happy. Like I could do something."

"Bring them back together?"

He makes a face. "Yeah. Hallmark After-School Special. Young Law draws a house and finds a home. I mean, I don't like my dad much. He and I fight all the time too. I think he's wrong and he thinks I'm Mamma's little Oreo. And Mamma's a snob. They both are. But I don't want to lose them."

He thinks for a bit, and then suddenly he smiles, half-sad, half all-over-his-face, fierce happy, and I fall in love with him just for that smile.

"The thing is," he says, "I just like houses."

I want to do for him whatever he wants, to see that smile. I want to draw him houses. But . . . "Law, thanks for not totally screaming and running. But my drawings are just creepy. You don't want me drawing pictures for you."

Law Walker leans back in his chair and looks at me.

"I do want you drawing pictures for me," he says. "If you can take it. If you want to."

Law, you don't know what I'll draw any more than I do. Take it seriously. I'm crazy.

But . . .

"Please?" he says.

I'm going to disappoint him and gross him out. . . .

"Okay," I say before I can be sensible and say no. "I'll draw Pinebank."

We don't say anything for a minute. We look at each other. He smiles at me. His face has wonderful planes. I think about asking if I can draw him.

That would be such bad timing.

"I want to ask you," he says. "You were drawing the boy? Why him?"

"I don't know." I think about George, the boy who doesn't fit. George is a story too, like the woman in Knyvet Park. My story, both of them, Mrs. Morris my shrink says. I have post-traumatic stress disorder and abandonment issues, says Mrs. Morris. Mrs. Morris knows everything. "George. His story is he was living with his grandfather. He had to go back into the house for something. Someone. I think for his grandfather."

I would go back for Mom. "Going back was more important than his life."

If I'd been in the parking lot with her, I would have saved her. I would have pushed her out of the way and had the car hit me instead.

Then she'd have been angry at me, and missing me.

Then I could haunt her, I think, I *would* haunt her, and weirdly, I begin to get so teary I can barely stop it. I miss her so much, and it's weird, because I know I make Dad up, so the real question is why I can't make up her or at least draw her and remember her and be haunted and happy.

I'm making George up instead of Mom.

Law hands me a handkerchief. "Here." I hide behind it and crumple it against my eyes.

When I look up, he's looking at me, almost as if he wants to put his arm around me. I'm making that up too, because no one alive wants to put their arm around me, and for good reason.

Law is saying something. "—what he went back in the house for?"

"Who?"

"George Perkins."

"He's just a story," I say.

"No, he's real. You must have looked at Seaburg a little at least, to know how to draw the second Pinebank. He's in Seaburg. But he didn't go back to save his grandfather," Law says. "His grandfather was dead years before the house burned."

"No," I start to say. *No, he says his grandfather looks after him.*

But I'm just making up George and his grandfather.

Then, again I understand, and I nearly scream.

Twice, in front of Law Walker, smart, good-looking Law Walker, who's listened to me and bought me coffee, in front of him I have to nearly shriek—

"You must have read enough Seaburg to know about him," Law goes on, not noticing, "and you needed to draw him, but why did he—"

George existed.

George was real.

My ears are ringing. This good guy I can never even think of being able to attract, not him, not any guy, because I'm going to throw *another* crazy fit right here, right now—

I'm not.

Not.

Not.

But I can hear Dad through the noise in my ears; I don't know whether he's a memory or he's here—

Didn't I tell you, kid?

You see ghosts.

I bite down on my tongue and somehow I manage not to look like a complete nutcase. Instead I just sort of breathe hard for a while, and then I ask Law to show me this Seaburg book I drew George out of. I'm figuring we'll go to the library.

But no.

Law's house is the *largest* place. It's one of those big, rich houses by the Reservoir: rest home, house of famous architect, Law's house. . . . He takes me there in his car, which is a teeny itsy two-seater, and we're jammed right together. Law spends the whole time we're going to his house talking about the car and the suspension and how fast it goes, which I guess is his way of covering up awkward silences. I don't say anything, because there's nothing but this big set of question marks in my head.

George Perkins.

George existed.

I can see ghosts.

Does that mean I'm not crazy?

Inside Law's house there's an enormous front hall, big enough for a fireplace and a couple of chairs and a Persian rug and the Walkers' Christmas tree, which looks like Mount Everest. The walls are so full of awards they stretch right up to the ceiling. Black awards and architecture awards. American Society of Landscape Architects, Martin Luther King Jr. Award, Preservation Design Award, Ebony Magazine American Black Achievement. Beyond the stairs there's a room with a big window full of plants and a couple of African masks over the fireplace, but right off the front hall, where other people would have living rooms, are two enormous home offices. His and Hers.

I'm not just guessing, because Law's mom is in her office, sitting cross-legged in one of the chairs by the window with her laptop in her lap. She's about fifty, wearing a black sweater and jeans and ballet flats, and she's keyboarding so fast that steam is practically coming out of her computer. She's white, which is sort of weird since Law isn't, but whatever. She holds up her hand for us to wait till she finishes, then keeps typing. I look around.

Her office is Martha Stewart perfect but not Martha Stewart scary. There's a big Victorian piano with claw legs, a couple of comfortable Victorian chairs by the window. Getting the sun from the window are Christmas cactuses in full Christmas-cactus-pink bloom, and on the piano there's an outrageous little Christmas tree made out of some kind of brushes spray-painted the same pink. The decorations are all antique glass balls and tinsel and my favorite Christmas decoration of all, a glass pickle. Mom had one. It was the only thing of hers I could bear to keep.

Law's mom command-S's, then looks up and smiles absently. "I despise Tom Menino," she says. Tom Menino is the mayor of Boston. Law introduces me as a friend who's helping him on a project. (I'm a friend of Law's? That sort of impresses me.)

"Hello, Law dear. How do you do—" She fumbles for my name and I realize Law hasn't told it to her. "Do you live in Jamaica Plain, by any chance? We need people to go door to door in Jamaica Plain to give out material on Pinebank. You have heard what that mumbling little hypocrite wants to do to Pinebank?" She runs her fingers through her blonde hair until it crackles like fireworks. "And the Landmarks Commission couldn't preserve jam. I am so sorry, you must never have heard of Pinebank. Would you like tea? Or hot chocolate? Something to eat? We have gingerbread."

I can immediately see where Law gets the smarts and the really caring about stuff and the fixing everything with food and the houses.

"My mom and I used to go to Pinebank," I say.

The phone rings, and Law's mom answers it. "Yes, Hugh, can you imagine it, *Christmas week*." She waves at us, shrugs, points to the phone.

"Mamma, would it be okay if we went into Dad's office to look at the Seaburg biography?" Law asks.

"Do it quickly, dear, he'll be home at five, and you know how he feels about *that book*."

Across the hall, across the divide between Law's parents, "Dad's office" is impressive: big desk, lots of awards wherever there aren't bookshelves; but I almost say hello to the woman typing at the desk before I realize Law doesn't see her. Law kneels down behind the desk to get a book from one of the lower shelves and I stare at my first actual, I-know-what-she-is ghost. She's fierce as a knife, with carved-looking curled hair and a dress that looks starched, and her fingers pound like rain on the typewriter keys. If you take a close look at her she's probably younger than Law's mom, but she looks a thousand years old. On the wall behind her are a couple of pictures of her with a boy who looks like Law but is stockier and much darker, who's got to be Law's dad, and a big photograph of her as an old woman, in some kind of ladies'-group robes.

This is the first ghost I've ever seen who didn't die horribly. (Don't ask me how I know she didn't. I know.) *Thanks,* I mouth at her. She looks up briefly, not approving of me any more than she approves of what she's typing. A woman with a lot of opinions, like Law's mom.

Law's dad married a woman like his mother. But now his mom and his dad live on opposite sides of the house.

Law hands me a big, thick book with a black and purple jacket. "Seaburg."

Black and purple, eeuw, two colors that completely don't go together, I would remember this book. I open it to the title page.

Harvard Studies in Business History. *Sure* I've read this book.

In Law's world, people actually read books like this. He is so out of my league.

I leaf through, looking for pictures. Law takes the book from me and shows me an old photograph. I know that roofline, those shutters, I know that window over the door. I drew them burning.

"That's the second Pinebank. Built 1848, burned in 1868."

You think I went online and Googled Pinebank and saw this before? Neither do I.

He pauses a moment, as if I'm supposed to say something, but I don't know what to say except *Normal guy, I see ghosts. Your grandmother's typing at the desk.*

Maybe seeing ghosts isn't going to be any more normal than making them up.

"So tell me about George."

"George was Thomas Handasyd Perkins's grandson. He had some kind of mental problem—"

"Down syndrome."

"—and lived at Pinebank. When the house burned, he ran back in, just the way you drew him, and they never found his body."

That sweet kid, who wants to play with dogs, who's proud of telling me where he lives. My George got burned alive.

"Nobody knows why he went back," Law says. "They figured it was because he was crazy."

"He just had Down syndrome, that's all."

I saw George's face, I drew it. George knew what would happen if he went back in. George wasn't stupid.

"Anyway, the Perkinses couldn't get over George dying. They abandoned the place and went off to Europe. Finally they rebuilt. Third Pinebank. Spectacular. The Perkinses' palace. Built of brick and terra-cotta so it wouldn't burn: first use of terra-cotta in the United States. Built between the actual existing trees. Famous architect, great building. But the third Pinebank was just never right. . . ." Law shrugs.

Haunted is the word, Law.

"The family didn't like living there. They bought another house on the North Shore and didn't know what to do with this one. Olmsted was designing the Emerald Necklace, the big parks system; he had the land all round it. He said Pinebank was the best-situated house in America, and he wanted it for the park restaurant."

Why did George go back into the burning house?

I could ask George.

"So the Perkinses gave Boston the land and the house. But there was a big kitchen fire, the restaurant never opened, and the house never quite made it as anything else. It began to deteriorate. Homeless people moved in and they set more fires and burned out the wood interior. Now Menino and the Parks Department want to tear it down.

"But Olmsted was a genius," Law continues. "He designed Central Park. He built the Emerald Necklace, the whole park system, from scratch. He built *rivers*. And I tell you, he had a reason for wanting Pinebank. Not only is it a great building, it gives focus to that whole part of the park." He sketches a circle with his fingers and jabs in the middle of it. "That piece of the Emerald Necklace would be nothing without it. Pinebank—It's just amazing, is all. I'm sorry. I'm geeking."

He's practically glowing, talking about that house.

There's the sound of a car turning in at the driveway. "Shh!" says Law. "Don't say 'Pinebank' around my dad."

"How come?"

He opens the book quickly and turns to the title page. *Merchant Prince of Boston: Thomas Handasyd Perkins, 1764–1854*. There's an inscription from the author. *To Charlie, faithful researcher*.

"That's why," Law says, stuffing the book back into its place. "Seaburg treated him like a Knee-grow. If Dad calls me Lawrence, don't react."

"You're named after Frederick Law Olmsted!" I may be dumb as a rock compared with Law's family, but—

"Dad hates Olmsted," Law says.

We make quick tracks out of his office and into the hall before he opens the front door.

Law's father is fierce-looking like his ghostly mother, with eyes that make you want to duck, and he's a huge man, like a statue of himself. "Good afternoon, Katherine," he says when we're introduced; this time Law introduces me by my name at least. Law's father has a voice like James Earl Jones, like thunderclouds and lightning. Out of the corner of my eye I can see his mother standing by the door to his office, smiling at him. He doesn't see her, but I think he feels her. His hand rests on the door frame just above her head.

I sort of know him, his story. He married a woman like his mother, but his mother loved him most and she's dead.

He starts asking me about my family. It's like a job interview with God. What does my father do, what does my mother do? When I tell him they're both dead, it's pretty obvious he doesn't approve. He definitely doesn't like it that Dad was in the army and Mom was a special-needs teacher.

Law rescues me. "Dad, Katie's doing a project with me." I can hear what he's saying: She's *just* doing a project with me. It's not like she's my *girlfriend* or anything.

As if I didn't know.

But "Are you on for the website?" Law asks while he's driving me home.

"I'm on."

He hesitates. "Do you mind not saying anything to either Mamma or Dad about it? Mamma would be cool with the idea if it weren't just now, but I'm supposed to be doing a big essay about something else, and they'd both be PO'ed."

Meaning his dad would hate Law doing anything for Pinebank. His dad even hates Law's name. Wow. *My* dad's better than that.

And Law's parents don't think I'm good enough for Law and don't care if I know it. I'm not, sure, but that's pretty annoying.

"What are you writing about?"

"I don't know yet." He looks anxious.

"Not Pinebank."

He shakes his head. "It's not that kind of essay."

"Will you drop me off by Pinebank? If I'm going to draw it, I'd better start getting ideas."

I'm not sure I'll see George. But he's there, just at twilight, on the baseball field, among the shadows of the long trees, a kid who doesn't cast a shadow throwing a ball that doesn't cast a shadow. The park lights are coming on. In the light he looks like just another kid, running a little awkwardly, dressed a little funny. In full shadow or full light he isn't there at all.

"George?"

He turns around and looks at me.

What is it I'm seeing, that sees me?

Ghost.

I see ghosts.

He sees me, and I guess he remembers what happened last time. He sees me and knows I'm seeing him, and I don't move or do anything for a moment, and his shoulders droop.

I wonder if people have seen him before, and turned away and ignored him because they were scared?

I'm scared. I'm trying not to think about it.

He's all indistinct in the fading light. He's like starting a drawing and not knowing what it's going to be a drawing of. Drawings aren't anything until the pencil marks go on the paper and they start being real. George is like the beginning of a drawing, not anything until he's finished, but something out there I am hunting for: something I have to find, something that's going to be.

He just looks at me, waiting to be disappointed.

He has the ball in his hand. It's a dark brown scuffed leather ball, sewn like a little football. He tosses it nervously, clumsily, and drops it.

I don't know what to say either. It wouldn't be polite to just start out *What did you go back for?*

"I'm sorry I ran away," I tell him, and he looks at me with his mouth open. *Oh.*

"I scared you," he says. "I'm sorry."

Well, yeah. But. "You didn't do anything wrong, George. It's okay."

I can see the shadow of Pinebank, just a suggestion of it, dark in the dark trees, with the dusk above the pond behind everything. As my eyes get more used to the light, I can see it's the house today, the ruined real house.

In the lights there's a new fence, lurid yellow plastic link fencing on high steel posts.

On the far side of the house, there's a Dumpster.

And the fence has a sign: PARK IMPROVEMENTS BY THE CITY OF BOSTON, THOMAS MENINO, MAYOR.

Law's mom got that right. They're going to tear it down.

I wonder what George is seeing. The house where he lives, a house with lighted windows, way out by a lake in the country away from Boston? His grandpa waiting for him inside? From where George is, am I something misty and faint? Am I a ghost?

I wonder what happens to a ghost when the place he haunts is torn down.

"George? Look at this." I point at the sign.

He comes back toward me and squints at the sign with his nearsighted eyes as if he can barely see it. As if he has to look at it through a hundred and fifty years. I wonder if he can read.

"That says somebody wants to tear down your house."

George giggles. "Houses don't *tear*. They're made out of *bricks*."

Oh, sweetie. "George, you see that thing like a big box?" He wouldn't know about Dumpsters. "People take houses apart and put the bricks in those big boxes. That's what they want to do to your house."

He walks toward the Dumpster, curious, through the fence;

he doesn't notice the fence. My stomach flips, seeing him do something that's so ghosty.

He turns back to me. "Take my house apart?"

"Is your grandfather here with you?" America's first millionaire might know what to do with Tom Menino.

"Grandpapa isn't here now."

"Will he be here later?" Great. Can I talk to *another* ghost?

This is hard for George to explain. "He isn't *here* now. Not *here*. He looks after me. But I live *here*."

"He doesn't live here the way you live here?"

George nods, satisfied.

"What do you want me to do?" I ask him. "George, why do I see you?"

George shakes his head. He doesn't know.

"Do other people see you?"

"Dogs see me. Sometimes."

"Would it be bad if your house was torn down?"

"I live *here*," George says.

Oh, shit *shit*. "Does your grandfather look after you?"

"Grandpapa looks after me from Heaven."

Great. Big help.

"Grandpapa went to Heaven," George says, "and then Uncle Eddie took care of me. Then Uncle Eddie went away too."

"You could go to Heaven and be with your grandpa." And the house wouldn't be haunted anymore. An unhaunted house, maybe it'd have a better feel and people wouldn't want to tear it down.

George shakes his head stubbornly, mouth tight, like a kid who's resisting temptation. "I have to stay *here*. I have to stay to watch, and I have to be home by dark."

Give Down syndrome kids rules and they'll follow them. Rules are a good way to keep a muzzy-headed kid focused. You can only go such-and-such places; you have to be home by dark. You can't go to Heaven, or wherever the next place is, even though you've been dead for a hundred and fifty years.

"It doesn't have to work like that now, George."

"Yes," says George firmly.

"Aren't you lonely?"

"Yes," he says in a smaller voice.

"Don't you want to see your grandpa?"

"I *do*."

I have to stay to watch, he said. "What are you watching? The house?" If the house comes down, can he go to live with Grandpa again?

"I'm watching the *box*," George says. "*In* the house."

"Oh, there's a box?"

"A box with *treasure* inside," he says.

This sounds exciting, boxes with treasure, but it's a trick Mom used to do with Down kids. You make them responsible for something. Something a kid will appreciate, something glittery or brightly colored, something with spangles or stripes or glass diamonds, *special toys, George, so you have to check on them every night,* and George would remember to come home and not stay out late throwing balls for dogs. It works with kids who have trouble remembering things.

Except it didn't work with George the night the house burned.

I don't have to ask why he went back into the house. I know what happened to George.

He went back for the box.

And he's had to take care of the box ever since.

"George," I say, "did you have to look after your treasure box?" He nods. "You don't have to anymore. The treasure box burned. You don't have to stay at Pinebank."

Maybe this is all I have to do for him. Tell him he can leave. *Go find your grandpa.*

George shakes his head vehemently. Just talking about it is getting him agitated, the way that kids get when they're not being listened to. "*No.* If anything happens to the house," George says, "*I* am to get the treasure out." He's quoting someone. "The treasure is *mine* to care for. It is *the most important thing* Grandpapa owns. If I move away, or if anything happens to the house, *I* must get it out. Nobody else thought about the treasure when the house burned. But I *remembered.*"

"But you couldn't get the treasure out, George, could you?"

"But it's *safe*. I'm *telling* you. I couldn't get it out so I put it in the *secret* place."

"The secret place?"

"Yes. It's *safe*," George insists. "In the *secret* place in the *cellar.*"

I'm getting such a bad feeling about this conversation.

George looks at me. In the dusk, I can only half see him; all I get is the impression of his eyes. He's a little boy. But being with him is like being with someone who's old and dying and leaving something he's responsible for, and he's not sure there'll be anyone responsible after he's gone.

What's it like to get burned alive because you're responsible? Grandpapa looks after him from Heaven, he says, but Grandpapa isn't here, and he's had to be home alone by dark, and to watch alone, for an awful long time.

For a box full of spangles and marbles and glass beads. In the cellar.

For what he died for.

"Please," George says, "if Grandpapa's house . . . If it gets torn down . . . will you help me get the treasure out, before?"

I ran from him before. I wish I could this time.

"Okay," I tell him. "Sure."

"Don't you do it, kid." Dad is sitting on the radiator, frowning. "Didn't you tell me the inside is burned?"

That's exactly the kind of answer I want. I can count on Dad.

"Don't you go doing something dangerous," Dad says.

Am I making Dad up? He's so convenient. But if he's a ghost— If I'm not making him up— That would be weird. Kind of scary. Kind of wonderful. If I'm not making him up, my dad wasn't such a lout after all. He loves me. That would be true.

I would see any number of ghosts for that.

I know it's not a real treasure. It's just toys or something. But Dad? I mean, he died for it. Somebody has to help him. Could you do it?

"Doesn't work that way."

You're a ghost. He's a ghost.

"I'm your ghost, not his. I'd do it if I could."

I wish the rules were the same for all ghosts.

"Yeah, for all people, too," Dad says. "What worries me, maybe he's one of them kind of ghosts that sucks you into some dark place, scares you to death."

Thanks, Dad.

"You said yourself, there ain't no treasure. Ignore him, kid."

That's not the point. The point is, he thinks there is and he's responsible for it and he wants to get it out.

"No concern of yours."

I sort of think it is.

LAW

"LAW'S GOT A GIRLFRIEND, LAW'S GOT A GIRLFRIEND!"

"Any bets on how long he keeps her?"

The Gang has got together to study for Chem midyears, and Shar starts giving a full report on Katie and me. "He was having coffee with her at Starbucks."

"She's not my girlfriend. She's got enough troubles without that."

My girlfriends generally last as long as it takes them to meet Dad and Mamma. After Katie left, Mamma asked me what her name was, and of course once she heard "Katie Mullens," she had the whole story at her fingertips. She hadn't forgotten a thing. Whiskey Point, divorce, and she knew about Katie's nervous breakdown. Count on Mamma.

And Dad— Racism is not a part of our household, oh nosuh not us, but Dad measures skin tone on a righteousness scale. Not to mention education, family background, church, connections, dedication to the Democratic Party, and a total lack of interest in landscape and architecture. In the eighth grade Andrea Johnson ran out of our house crying and wouldn't come back in, and she and I were only going to the movies.

My palms are going to be hairy forever.

"How's your Walker Prize speech?" I ask to change the subject.

"I don't know what I will write about. The Walker Prize is all about African Americans. Who cares about Brazil?"

"You care about Brazil. You shouldn't play politics."

"You talk about silly reparations, that isn't political?"

"I'm not going to talk about reparations."

Shar just looks at me. "I know your father, you know."

"Yeah, dude," Bobby Lee says, "we all know your dad."

"Maybe I'll talk about my great-great-grandfather."

My great-great-grandfather was named Walker, and he never had a house in his life. He started out named Scipio, but he kept running away, ran away from three owners one after another, kept getting caught too; he was unlucky. Or lazy, his owner said. *That boy a runner but he too lazy. He nothing but a walker.* So Walker he was.

When freedom came, someone asked what name would he take instead of his insulting slave name, and what first name did he want? "Don't need no nother name," he said. "Ask for Walker, people know who I am."

He never had a house. He had a store that he lived over. On Sundays he had a pulpit. Grandmam, who knew Walker when she was a kid in the neighborhood, told me how fine it was in that household, everyone welcome, sitting round the kitchen table. Walker's son had a pulpit and two stores until the Depression made hard times for everybody. Grandmam married Walker's grandson, a Tuskegee Airman who died over Italy. She had a job in the telephone office and a typewriter.

Dad is a professor at Harvard. He married a historical architect whose family lived on Brattle Street. We have a house. Dad and Mamma are millionaires, I guess. We have a house that looks like a plan-ta-thi-on.

People know who we are. But people really knew who Walker was. And everyone was welcome at his table.

I could write about Walker, but that's not a speech.

"How's your speech, Darryl?"

"It is beautiful," says Shar. "And I will write a good speech. But we won't win. You will."

"Is everything okay?" Katie asks me.

We've met at Starbucks again. Katie looks better. She's been handing out "Save Pinebank" pamphlets with a friend of our family, Dorothy Clark, a singer and playwright and preservationist and all-around nice person who can make anybody happy. I've promised Katie a draft of the website so she can draw me some more pictures.

"I'm stuck trying to write a speech for this thing, the Walker Prize."

"Named after your family?" she guesses.

I grin and shake my head, and think there's a big divide between Katie Mullens and me, that the Walker Prize means nothing to her. "Named after David Walker. David Walker was a famous radical in Boston in the 1820s, makes Malcolm X look like Booker T. *America is more our country, than it is the whites'. . . . The greatest riches in all America have arisen from our blood and tears.* He was the first man to say we should kill whites, sorry about that. Are you amazed Buttrucci doesn't mention him?"

"What happened to him?"

"What do you think, he got killed. 'Died suddenly of tuberculosis' right on his front step. So anyway, winning the Walker Prize for Rhetoric in History marks a man for life, so my dad says. Dad would give every tooth in his head to have won it. But it's a Boston prize, and he lived in Philadelphia when he was a kid. So he wants me to win."

Katie looks at me over the rim of her peppermint latte. Why do girls drink those things? But it's bringing a nice pink to her cheeks. I could just look at her.

"You don't want to win?" she asks.

"Sure. It would pretty much sew up getting into any college I want."

It would sew up getting into Harvard, under Dad's thumb forever.

"You don't sound like you want to win."

"I don't feel like I deserve to win."

I'm not going to explain to her about feeling race-deprived, or about Shar and Darryl competing against me, or about Dad looming over Harvard. "But you know what my dad does? He's sort of the David Walker of his time." Sort of. With Brooks Brothers suits. "Great orator. As far as Dad's concerned, if I don't win, I should move to another city and change my name to Shit. He's after me day in, day out, 'What have you been reading, Lawrence? What approach are you taking?'"

"What's that thing with Lawrence?"

"No son of Dad's going to be named after any landscape gardener. He wants me to write about reparations."

"What are reparations?" Katie asks.

This is less like not knowing the Walker Prize and more like not knowing the Earth goes round the sun. "Reparations are what your folks owe my folks. More history you won't get from Buttrucci."

"Isn't that what your dad does? Reparations?"

"Yeah, and it's not what I do." I do a stretch-piano-fingers gesture. "Okay. American History 101, Why We Are Owed. Before the Civil War, most of my folks are enslaved, right? We don't have the legal status of people at all; we're property. So how much are we worth?"

Katie looks uncertain.

"My great-great-grandfather was sold for fourteen hundred dollars, and he was a troublemaker. So how much are we all worth?" I've heard this around the dining room table, but it's new to Katie. "How much of all the business that Americans do before the Civil War is buying and selling people as if they were cotton and sugar and chairs? What percent?"

"Ten?"

"Higher."

"Fifteen?"

"Try sixty. Before the Civil War, over half of what America produced was people. I'm not talking about cotton, or sugar, or rice, any of the stuff that we produced. I'm talking about us. We were a cash crop. Plantations were baby farms and people were treated like animals. Kids got fed out of troughs like pigs." I can hear myself talking like Dad. I take a breath and slow down. "People were sold down South at ten or twelve years old. Not because they'd done anything wrong. Just because on the sugar and rice plantations, the death rate was always higher than the birth rate and the South was starved for workers. Planters in Virginia were breeding people, to sell them to places that weren't a heck of a lot better than Nazi labor camps."

"I am never, never, never going to visit a plantation," Katie says in a low voice. "I feel like I ought to say I'm sorry."

"My dad feels you ought to say you're sorry."

"You ought to write about *that*."

"Everybody knows about that, Katie. I mean everybody who's going to be judging the Walker Prize. It's—I'm not saying anything against you personally, I hope you know, but it's white people who don't know that."

She looks at me, stricken.

"Reparations means that white folks ought to pay black folks for all the work we did, back then. Not you paying me, but generic white folks paying generic black folks. I think it's stupid and confrontational, but that's what my dad says he believes in. I guess that's why he's against Thomas Handasyd Perkins. You know Perkins was in the trade, that's how he made his money."

Katie's mouth drops open. "Oh no."

"Oh yeah. Any black person in America," maybe not Shar, "any African American, when they hear about a rich white man before the Civil War, their first question is where did the money come from. Perkins made his first fortune in the slave trade. White people accept that the money's there, and the family silver, and the paintings, all the *stuff*. But the *stuff* came from dealing in flesh."

"Wait," says Katie.

She has her sketchbook by her chair; she dips down and swoops it up, digs a tin box out of her purse, and flips out a pencil. "Stay like that," she says, "don't move." Her eyes unfocus, staring at me, not blinking, through me, and her pencil whips around the paper, she smudges a line with her thumb. I hold still. Something is happening. Her hand is moving fiercely fast, but her eyes on me hold as still as I do. Between us the whole world is still.

Finally she sighs and pokes the pencil into the spiral binding of her sketchbook.

"What was that?"

"I don't know," she says as if she's coming out of anesthesia. "You just looked like, I don't know. I've been wanting to draw you."

"Let's see."

She looks first, as if she doesn't quite know what she's drawn, and frowns. "It doesn't look like you."

"Let me see."

She has drawn me African. Much darker than I am, really black-skinned, with a highlight gleaming across my forehead and cheekbones. My lips are wider. My hair is kinked. She's drawn me older by a few years too, and wearing a clumsy open-throat shirt.

A year or so ago I spent a month obsessed with Second Life. My avatar in SL is African. That's the feeling I get from this picture; this is my avatar, familiar and strange, not me, a deeper me.

"Maybe I was thinking of David Walker," she says, suddenly defensive.

Walker.

I know the face, though he was never photographed until he was old, the old man with the honorable glasses that meant he could read. (He couldn't. He memorized the Bible.) This is a man in his twenties, Walker the slave, who ran and ran, who wouldn't give up heading North to freedom.

Here is my ancestor.

My skin crawls, the way it did when I saw Katie's picture of Pinebank. How did she get this so right?

I look up, across at Katie, and she's not there, the way she wasn't there at Pinebank. She's looking right at me but not seeing me. "He had another name," she says in a sort of misty voice, like a ghost would sound if it could talk. "His real name.

Not Scipio. But where he comes from, if you speak a man's name after his death, his spirit is healed and can go to rest. And he wanted not to rest. To keep walking. Until freedom."

And then she's back. Back and looking at me like I caught her stealing.

I say, "How'd you know about Walker?" My lips are numb. "I didn't tell you about Walker."

"I just make those things up," she says desperately. "They're stories."

But this is more than a story. This is my family. Did she see the tintype of Walker in Dad's study? Did Dad ever write about that story? He must have. The way she must have Googled Pinebank and read about George Perkins. And found the second Pinebank. And—

Who am I kidding.

Because she's told me more of the story than I knew. Because if Dad knew this story about why Walker didn't want to tell his name, he would have been speechifying me about it from when I was two. *Your ancestor, Lawrence, would not tell his real name to anyone for fear his spirit would rest before his people were free!* I can hear the man. Dad would love this story.

But he doesn't know it.

"How do you know that, about his name?"

I know how.

I don't think she ever read *Merchant Prince of Boston*, either.

I've never believed in "the ancestors," it's one of those African spirituality things that were all made up in the 1960s.

My ancestors this, *my ancestors* that, *that bus woulda squashed me flat, flat I tell you, boy, if the ancestors hadn't looked out for me.* Ma Prentice at church says the ancestors told her to buy her condo.

Here is Walker. My ancestor. If I were back in Africa, he would be one of my gods.

Starbucks is full, too full. "Are you done with your coffee?" I ask her. She nods, speechless. "Come on, then. We need to talk."

Down the street from Starbucks there's a set of stairs up past the Pierce School toward Town Hall and the library. Halfway up the stairs we aren't visible from Starbucks or Harvard Street. Not from anywhere. We are alone. "Stop," I tell her.

She leans against the wall, shivering.

"You don't make those things up," I say. "Do you? You see things."

"I'm sorry," she says. "I'm really sorry. I didn't mean to see anything of yours."

She closes her eyes for a moment, as if that will help her.

"What did you see in the park? Did you *see* George Perkins? And the second Pinebank? And Walker? Did you *see* them?" I'm almost shouting. I can't believe I'm saying this, me, Law Walker, I'm shouting at a girl from my own high school and saying she sees haunts.

She looks up at me helplessly. It feels like she screams, though she's whispering.

"Yes."

We stare at each other, horrified, and she begins to sob, gut-sucking sobs, like she can't get her breath, like she's drowning, like whatever she sees is caught in her throat. I grab her by the shoulders like I'm trying to shake it loose. She fights back and twists away, rears back and glares at me, angry, terrified. "It's all right," I say. "Katie, it's all right." *It's all right,* I say, *it's all right,* I'm feeling a dizzy sense that I know myself better than I did, because it *is* all right. The first thing I think after *Katie sees ghosts* is *I wish I could point her like a camera.*

The landscape and the gardens, the— All of it. All of it together, the whole thing. Katie can see it.

There has to be a better way to say what I'm thinking, but what I end up saying isn't it.

"I envy you."

She stares at me. "You idiot."

"I'm sorry. I mean it must suck for you. I'm really sorry. But I'd do anything to talk to dead people, some of 'em anyway, and to see some of the things you see, and Katie, it's a gift." She twists away. I keep talking to the top of her hair. "The old ladies at my church would say, 'God gave you a gift, child, and God don't make mistakes.' I mean, seeing Walker, that picture of Walker. That story. He's important to me. And you drew him for me."

Turned away from me toward the wall, she's crying again. I put my arms around her and hold her while she shakes with wrenching sobs that make me half-sick too.

She cries, leaning against me inside my arms, warm against

my arms, shuddering. I've made Katie tell me something that she doesn't want to tell anyone and I'm not sure I want to hear, and still, still; Katie's not my girlfriend, I've had girlfriends, at least until I brought them home, I know what getting it on with girls is, more or less.

But in all my life, I figure, only one girl is going to tell me she sees ghosts. And this is it, right now; this is now.

And I can't blow it. For either of our sakes.

Finally she stops shaking and sighs against my arm. "You're kidding," she says to the wall. "A gift?"

"A gift."

Katie who I liked in seventh grade. Who I've liked since seventh grade. Sees ghosts. *Ghosts.* She turns around and looks up at me like I'm a hero. I don't feel like a hero. I feel like I'm in the middle of the ocean with no oars. Now I think of it, I'm actually pretty scared.

"Will you give me that picture of Walker?" I ask her.

"Really?" Her nose is running. "You want it?" She wipes her glove across her face without thinking and then looks horrified at the glove, which has a big snail-trail across it. "Dad says it's a gift too and I should do something about it, but I don't know what."

"I thought your dad was dead," I say without thinking.

"He is."

I jerk as if I've been poked by a live wire. I'm not handling this. Not at all.

"Welcome to Scaryland," she says.

"What's it like?" I make myself say.

She shakes her head. "Ghosts are all different. I mean, there are no rules about ghosts as far as I can tell. Dad's nice. There's a guy on the stairway of my building who really frightens me. Mostly they died violently and mostly I see them where they died. I wish I could control it more, is all."

"Mostly? How many ghosts do you see?"

"You're so comparatively not freaking. I mean—You believe me. That's so weird."

I thought I understood the drawings. I didn't. "You want some cocoa? Library cocoa, fifty percent sugar?" Not the cocoa experience I was aiming at. "I think we need a lot of sugar."

"What is it with you and sugar?"

"Mamma's Sugar Cure. She believes in it for troubled moments." Of which this is the biggest one in my life so far.

Katie half hiccups and half giggles.

"What?"

"You and your family."

There's a lame café in the library basement by the young adult section, supposedly so young adults can hang out in it. The actual café customers are two old Russian ladies with industrial-strength hair dye. They complain to each other in Russian. We sit at the other table and whisper about ghosts.

"I like libraries," Katie says. "Nobody ever died in a library."

"The guy you drew, my great-great-grandpa Walker, died in bed. Happy. With all his family around him."

"I love people who had long happy lives."

She holds her paper cup with both hands. Her hands are trembling. Mine too.

"How does it work?" I ask her. "Life after death and ghosts and all that?" I go to church and I guess I believe in God. But God and Jesus and Heaven are in one part of my head and ghosts are in another.

"I don't know," she says. "I just thought I was crazy and making it all up."

She thought she was making up all that?

"I guess I'm not. Weird." She takes a sip of her chocolate.

Yeah. Weird. We sit for a while in shaky silence.

"It's like history actually exists," I say finally.

"Well, doesn't it?"

"Not the way my dad plays it. It's politics." Katie nods. "I mean, the whole world is political with him. But history exists. History's not just his private thing. You could draw some amazing things."

"I just wonder why me," she says. "And why—I mean, I don't draw amazing things, I draw people dying."

"That's not all you draw. You drew Walker. Maybe there's a reason."

"Then I want there to stop being a reason," she says. "Or somebody to tell me. Because it's tough, let me tell you. It's tough."

I can't even imagine. And I want to ask her something, but I'm not sure if I should. It'll sound completely self-serving, and it isn't, not entirely.

"Can you find out specific things? I mean, could you ask Walker his real African name?" We don't know it.

She shakes her head. "George and Dad are the only ones who talk to me."

"George Perkins *talks* to you?"

It would be like Washington talking. Jefferson. History. The stones of Pinebank.

"What does he tell you?"

"Tell me?" She shrugs. "We just talk."

"About what?"

"Oh, dogs, his grandfather, stuff like that."

"He knew Thomas Handasyd Perkins." I've given her a ration about white people thinking only about money. But I have to ask this. "Did George say anything about the Perkins Bequest?"

"What's the Perkins Bequest?" she asks.

"Did he ever talk about it? It was a part of Perkins's will. A lot of money."

"George has a box with 'treasure' inside. That he has to look after," Katie says.

I can't even speak; my tongue goes numb.

"He hid it in the basement," she says. "That's why he died. He went back after it. He wants me to get it out."

"A box with *treasure*? There's a treasure *inside Pinebank*? Now? Still?"

"It can't be anything important. I figure it was marbles or something."

I hear myself making a dry-mouthed squeaky giggle, the

kind of noise that would ruin me with any girl but Katie, any time but now.

"Not marbles," I manage, pitching my voice very low in case the Russian women are listening. "And not toy treasure. Depending on what it is? The Perkins Bequest could be about fifty million dollars."

KATIE

PEOPLE IN BOOKS DON'T HAVE TO TAKE FINALS, but Law and I do. Fifty million dollars or no, things totally stop for a few days. It's the Friday before Christmas when we take our last exams, my algebra and Law's Latin. Law probably aces his, but if I can even add I don't notice. Afterward he and I meet each other at the grotty high school T stop. It's the middle of the day and not a lot of people are on the T, so even on the D line we can get seats in a corner away from everybody else. Law rummages in his backpack and comes up with the Seaburg book.

"I stole this from Dad's office, for the description of the Perkins Bequest. I want to tell you this right." He leafs through pages. "Okay, here it is. By the time Perkins is about to die, he's the richest man in America. He writes his will. Two-thirds of his estate is divided among his family. The other third of what he's worth, he sets aside. Five hundred thousand dollars in pre–Civil War money. Now worth about fifty million dollars. Conservatively. That's the Perkins Bequest."

"Holy Pete. Who was it for?"

"That's the thing, nobody knows who or what. He picks five trustees and gives them secret instructions. 'These five men were not to be accountable to anybody for their disposition of the money,'" he reads. "'To this day nothing is known of where this money went or how it was spent.'" He thumps the book closed.

"And George was supposed to guard it?" I say. "George knew about it?"

The two of us sit there for a moment. The T train slides past Fenway and goes into the tunnel.

"The guy who wrote that says 'spent,'" I say, pointing out the obvious. "Like they *spent* it. Not put it inside a box."

"Seaburg wrote that and he didn't know. Even the family didn't know, or told my dad they didn't. Dad was a graduate student for Seaburg and he interviewed these people."

A treasure? In a box? Which George wants me to save?

"Seaburg thought it was insurance," Law says. "Perkins is about to die. The next generation isn't up to his standard. You know how rich people are about money. They want to give it to their kids, but they're afraid the kids will spend it the wrong way. You know the Kennedys don't give any of their kids money? It's all in one place; the family keeps it and professional money managers look after it."

"I'm amazed you know this kind of stuff."

"Dad. Harvard."

He's totally out of my league.

"Seaburg thought the Perkins Bequest was some kind of investment. Something with long-term value."

"But, Law, would they have just put all that money in a box in the basement? That doesn't sound smart. I mean, can you even *fit* that much money inside a box that a kid like George could carry?"

This is the weirdest conversation I have ever had.

"It couldn't have been gold," Law thinks out loud. "Or not just gold."

We've reached our stop, Park Square. Outside it's pouring, and all around people are flocking and shoving, heading down to Downtown Crossing for last-minute Christmas shopping. For a moment I panic, thinking *I haven't got anything for Mom yet.* And then I remember. *Oh, Mom.*

Law and I head up toward the State House under his umbrella.

I'm under Law's umbrella, with Law, holding on to his arm. And last night Law put his arms around me and just hugged me for as long as I wanted. Mom and I used to hug all the time. People with parents and brothers and sisters probably don't think much about that, but before Mom died, Phil and I didn't know each other well enough to hug like father and daughter, and since then it could be a little bit creepy. Phil cooks for me, I do dishes for him, we like each other, but it's so nice to be hugged again.

Especially by Law.

"Gold, that was my first idea," Law says. "But raw gold, in 1850s dollars, that's about a ton of gold."

"A ton of gold."

"I worked it out."

He would.

"Maybe jewels. But jewels weren't much valued then. I read a story about a pirate who was given a big diamond, and he smashed it into little diamonds so he'd have more of them."

We're at the top of the Common. Above us the State House dome looms like a ton of gold.

"Law? You realize you're believing all this because a ghost said so? You shouldn't do that."

"Yeah," Law says. "Crazy. From hanging out with you."

He smiles as if it's a joke.

"But I've got an idea what it could have been," he says. "I'll show you."

We head down the tag end of Beacon Street, where it turns into a narrow little alley, sandwich shops on one side, old Boston buildings on the other. "Perkins was a big philanthropist, toward white people anyway." He stops in front of one of the old-fashioned buildings. "He helped found this. The Boston Athenaeum."

He holds open the heavy door for me and I go in.

And we're back in the century of Thomas Handasyd Perkins.

A clock ticks ancient seconds. On the pale green walls, dead Boston Brahmins smile in gilded frames. An old guy in uniform asks me to sign the guest book but recognizes Law. Law heads toward the reference desk, waving his copy of Seaburg at a librarian who's wearing a velvet hairband and clothes that were new when the Beatles toured.

"I called about looking at the Simón Bolívar," he says to her.

Who or what the Simón Bolívar is I do not know. I'm staring across the hall, through open glass doors, at an enormous painting.

The picture on the cover of his biography was black and purple and small. The painting is more than life-size. Thomas Handasyd Perkins, George's grandpa, is a red-cheeked old man lounging on a gold brocade sofa as if it's the Throne of Heaven. A Chinese vase, an art portfolio, papers are scattered around him; he's surrounded by stuff that slaves paid for. Behind him is a window, and out the window there's nothing but clouds, as if he's a thousand feet up. The king of the world on a golden sofa. On the Friday before Christmas, Thomas Handasyd Perkins and Law and I and the librarian and the old doorkeeper are the only people here, and Grandpa Perkins is the most alive of us all.

He looks a little like George. Not like a slave dealer. I guess he is what a slave dealer looks like. I turn away from him and back to the other important people of Boston, smiling spookily in their frames. I wonder how many of them were slave dealers too.

The librarian has sent a guard off to get the Simón Bolívar. We have to wait a few minutes. I look out the windows at an ancient burial ground, crooked rows of headstones and flat tombs like tabletops, dinner tables for ghosts. I don't see anybody in the graveyard except tourists. But sitting right across the room, on the glass of one of the library exhibit cases, a sly-eyed man in old-fashioned clothes points his finger at me and leers.

I ignore him.

A guard comes back carrying a little red leather box. "Come into my office," the librarian says.

Her office is a tiny place mounded with papers. She puts the leather box very carefully on her desk and turns to us. "Thomas Perkins was a collector. Of course he went *everywhere*, knew *everyone*. Do you know the story of his visiting George Washington? At the end of the evening, the President himself showed Perkins up to his room and held the candle for him. Perkins was *unutterably* honored. He kept the candle all his life. I believe one of the family has it still. Later in life he collected Lafayette's chair and the steps from John Hancock's house. Of course," the librarian breathes, "he was particularly interested in coins."

She picks up the little box very carefully, like an egg, between her two hands.

"Presented in 1846 by General John Devereux to Thomas Handasyd Perkins."

She opens the box.

On its square of crimson velvet, a gold coin glows. The Simón Bolívar.

I've never seen color like this, not red, brassy, silvery, but *gold*. It's like a portable sun. If you held it up in daylight, people would worship it.

"We don't touch it," the librarian warns.

She lets me lean forward to look at it. The color is what is perfect, but you can see every detail of the guy's profile, the little braid on his uniform, every hair on his head.

"It is one of only sixty of that coin ever made," the librarian says. "Thomas Handasyd Perkins was very generous to the Athenaeum."

"And he collected coins like this," Law says, looking out of the corner of his eyes at me.

I get it.

If he gave this one away, what did he keep?

When we leave the Athenaeum, we go back down Beacon Street.

"So George is guarding a real treasure?" My George? I like George, but I wouldn't choose him to guard gold and jewels.

"Katie, if Perkins put coins like that in the basement, they would more than keep their value. It would be unbelievable how much the Perkins Bequest could be worth." Law is grinning a strange, tight grin.

"What's the matter?"

"Come on," he says. "Come with me a moment."

After a moment I know where we're headed; I follow him toward the Robert Gould Shaw Memorial, and we stand for a moment looking at the horseman in the midst of his soldiers. Robert Gould Shaw was the white colonel of the first black regiment in Massachusetts. Most of them died in a battle together way down South somewhere. Nobody's haunting the monument. The mounted man is high above us, idealized like the angel floating on the bronze sky behind him, but the men on foot are real. The two drummers make the wood sticks boom against the drums. The bearded sergeant purses his lips, thinking about the battle. The guy to the left of him has flipped his cap bill up so he can see the fort he'll have to storm. His face is always in sunlight. The sad-faced man with the long, straight nose is thinking about his family, his kids who he'll never see anymore. I wonder if the sculptor saw ghosts.

"These are the people who earned that treasure," Law says to me. "Every time I think about the Perkins Bequest, I feel as if I should be thinking about them instead. But then, man! We could find Perkins's treasure. I could find out what happened and save Pinebank. And it's so cool. I feel like some dumb kid about it. I don't know what to think."

I know. "I know."

Across the bottom of the monument the men's booted feet march steadily. Men whose families were long free, marching for freedom for everyone. For once it isn't awful, seeing people who are about to die. I wonder if that's what art is for. Making things not so awful.

"I'll buy you coffee," I say finally.

This time I pay.

Reparations.

LAW

WHAT DO OTHER FAMILIES DO the weekend before Christmas
when they don't have history to yell about?

Mamma hears the news on the Friday before Christmas:
The word is that on the twenty-seventh, next Wednesday, the
historical engineer John Wathne is going to tell the Landmarks
Commission that Pinebank can't be saved. Wathne is tops in
the field, and Mamma is alternately crying and furious. "Boston
just wants to save money." By the time I get back from the
Athenaeum, Mamma is out at a strategy session with Hugh
Mattison, head of the Friends of Pinebank, and I'm left alone
with Dad.

Who's made his plans for me. Have I finished my Christmas
shopping? Yes, Dad. Have I wrapped my presents? Yes, Dad.

Then I can be working on my Walker essay, can't I? Have
I finished my Walker essay already? Do I at least have a draft?
Don't I realize it's due the last day of December? Do I realize
how soon that is? When can he see the draft?

I don't tell him I haven't finished my Walker essay because

I haven't started my Walker essay. I've put together the website for Pinebank. I have Katie's pictures of George at the fire. Bobby Lee has pulled together some video for the site. Dorothy Clark has trolled the *Globe* site for articles about the house, and I've anonymously bought the domain.

The site is shaped like Pinebank. Not that I have much of an idea what Pinebank looked like inside unless Katie can draw me something, but I figure public downstairs, private upstairs, and I know Perkins had an office in one of the downstairs rooms. A house, with every room linked to something in the history. Olmsted's idea of Pinebank as a meeting place. The Perkins family. Perkins's philanthropy. Perkins's business. This is an old idea: People used to use the idea of a building to pull ideas together; they called it a memory palace.

Will it be enough to stand against John Wathne and his reputation?

It's just another site, but what can I do without going up against Dad?

Dad, without Mamma to argue with, works on his own new book or works on me; he finds plenty of time for both. So Saturday and Sunday, we're talking Christmas Eve, after church and before church and between church, I sit in my room staring at the screen and keyboard and not daring to work on what I want to.

What am I writing about for the Walker Prize?

It ought to be Pinebank. That perfection in the landscape that even my friends are laughing at.

I sit in my room and play Spider Solitaire, and dip into Second Life, and look through the notes I've taken as though I have a plan. I look up at Katie's picture of Walker, stuck on the wall above my desk, and think about my website. I think about Thomas Handasyd Perkins and the Perkins Bequest and Katie.

I've texted Katie that I can't hang with her until the essay is finished. I wonder how she's spending Christmas. I wish it were with me.

Reparations. Reparations are *stuff*. Pirate treasure, pieces of eight, moidores, Brasher doubloons, escudos; rare coins of Simón Bolívar; Lafayette's chair, Hancock's steps. Scholarships, Brooks Brothers suits, agents and contracts and success. The Walker Prize. We want reparations, stuff, what we pile up around us and not who we are. Walker, who never had a house, gazes down at me from my wall. I Google the Shaw Memorial and look at those men walking toward death. *Don't need no other name, ask for Walker, people know who I am.* Men like that don't need reparations; they aren't broken, they don't need to be repaired.

I want Pinebank.

I want Pinebank, I want to study plantations even if I have to pretend to be Spanish, I want to write about architecture for the Walker Prize and forget about pleasing Dad.

Pinebank, I type, and the words just come.

What I want for Christmas is Pinebank. Olmsted's welcoming place, the restaurant where everyone would feel at home; the house at the end of the winding road, under the trees, where people have sat and watched Jamaica Pond for two hundred years. The house that should belong to all of us now. I'm sitting in Pinebank, which looks a little like Starbucks, with comfortable chairs and a smell of coffee. Katie and I are in the prize seats of honor. Dad and Mamma are at a table. Mamma is happy because Pinebank is safe. Dad blinks around at everyone else who's there, black people and white people, rich and poor, Chinese and Vietnamese and Irish and Brazilians. He says *This isn't so bad*. For once he agrees with Mamma. With us. We're gazing outside the windows, all of us, all Boston, peaceful as bright-eyed lambs in a manger, watching the snow fall and the stars smile in the sky.

I think I could be happy being who I am.

That's what I need to say about Pinebank.

What I want for Christmas is Pinebank. What I get is a Nintendo Wii, and both Dad and Mamma instruct me I can't even crack the box until after I finish my essay. We spend the afternoon with Mamma's Brahmin brother and his pearly white family, who treat Dad and me like interesting aliens.

Twenty-fifth, evening. Six days to go, Dad reminds me. I fall asleep staring at a blank screen and wake with my cheek on the desk, drooling. Sleep in heavenly peace.

Twenty-sixth. Resentful because no Wii. No life either. And no essay. Five days.

The evening of the twenty-sixth, I've finally had enough. I go and stand at Dad's office door until he looks up from what he's writing.

"Dad, I want to talk to you about my essay."

He's still writing in his head. I recognize the not-there look. "Lawrence, you know this essay must be entirely your own work."

"Okay, then, I want to talk to you about my life."

I come in and sit down in his whiteboy-colored leather chair.

"I don't want to write about reparations," I say. "I want to write about houses. Buildings."

"Houses," Dad says, and manages to make it mean *Is this any son of mine?*

"I'd like to study houses," I say, dry-mouthed. "That's what I want to do with my life. Study the history of houses. Maybe do architecture myself. And I want to write about houses for the Walker Prize."

"Do you mean," says Dad, "you want to work with your *hands?*"

The man would say he isn't prejudiced.

"I don't want to be a builder, Dad. I mean, I am a historian, like you, like Mamma. I'm interested in the history." Dad looks like he believes me as much as if I've said *I just arrived from Mars, proof, here's a Mars bar.*

"Dad. Let me explain this. You know that Renaissance idea, memory palaces?"

"*I* told *you* about memory palaces, Lawrence."

He did: Dad's idea of casual conversation in the car is advice about giving speeches. The man's never off. Other people relax: at the beach, playing golf, after church, sometime, with someone. Dad, never. He's always the teacher, the Voice of Our People, the Man. Even in pajamas, standing at the top of the stairs and saying, "Susan, I have lost my toothbrush," his voice quivers with the weight of four hundred years of injustice.

Never off.

At least not with Mamma or me.

Anyway. Memory palaces. People used them to give speeches. Picture a building you know. Fill it, room by room, with things you need to remember and tie together. Then walk through the building. Suppose your building is a Starbucks: too small, but you get it. Introduction, the front door. First point, the line. Second point, ordering. Third point, paying; fourth, waiting for your drink. Suppose you were going to give a speech about reparations, the front door would have one gold handle and one handle of human bone: "Today I'm going to talk about gold and the price of lives." The line would be a coffle of slaves, and so on. Like that.

"Dad, do you remember when we went down to Virginia? I went looking at the plantations. And it struck me, you know, real houses? They're the opposite of memory palaces."

"Don't say 'you know,' Lawrence."

I keep going. "The plantations were a kind of memory palace, but inside out. They were built to forget us. Our people were stuck away somewhere, at the side of the road or round the back. The slave lockup way at the end of the garden, the same place they'd store tools." One of the things that impressed me most about plantations? We were almost all the people living on the plantation, we did most of the work, but the houses were designed to make us invisible. "If the whites had thought differently about us, they would have built a different house with us really in it, and it would have told a different story." Dad purses his lips. "The way people think is the way they build; the way people build is the way they think."

"This is your mother's work."

I'm knotting my fingers. I pull my sweaty hands apart and plant them on my knees. "Every one of those plantations, Dad, they had porticoes, big rooms, libraries, rooms to show off in. If our folks built a big house, the center would be the kitchen, where the visiting happens and the work gets done. That's the kind of thinking I want to do about architecture. I want to think about people in houses."

Pinebank. The Perkinses. Olmsted. The people in the restaurant Olmsted wanted, the restaurant that welcomed everybody.

"People in houses? You come with me then," says Dad. "Get your coat."

We take the car. Dad thinks he can get a parking space anywhere, even in Christmas week in downtown Boston. He makes a phone call on the way—laws against using a cell phone in the car don't apply to Charles Randall Walker—and we slide around the Common with its cloud of lit Christmas lights and up Joy Street, up Beacon Hill, toward the African Meeting House.

If you're one of us in Boston, the Museum of African-American History is home. They have exhibits. They have openings. They have talks by famous historians. They have homemade cookies, none of those anemic little white cheese plates. Those cookies made a big impression on me when I was young and waiting around for Dad to finish talking.

And above all, they have one of the greatest treasures of American history, our memory palace: the African Meeting House.

The black Faneuil Hall. The black Independence Hall. The African Meeting House is the oldest African church building in the United States, and when it was built it was the largest building we owned anywhere. From the pulpit of the African Meeting House, David Walker shocked the congregation. Frederick Douglass and Maria Stewart spoke for us. From here our New England Anti-Slavery Society first admitted whites. The Underground Railroad, the road from the slave South to freedom, ran through the basement of the African Meeting House. Outside these doors men stood in lines to volunteer their lives in the 54th Massachusetts and to die with Robert Gould Shaw.

The African Meeting House needs six million dollars' worth of work. The restoration committee, which includes Dad, has raised two million so far.

By the time we park illegally in the yard, Dad's friend Alex, the Meeting House publicist, has arrived and turned on the construction lights in the Meeting House. The windows hang over us like dim angels. Dad takes a flashlight from the glove compartment and shines it up onto the brick above the doors, onto the simple little block of white granite.

A GIFT TO CATO GARDNER, FIRST PROMOTER OF THIS BUILDING, 1806.

"'A gift,'" Dad reads. "'To Cato Gardner.'" The brick walls and the cobblestones echo his big bass voice.

I grab a flashlight from the car too, and we follow Alex through the basement, which is piled with old flooring and new plywood, and up the plywood stairs. Upstairs it's so cold we can see our breaths and too dark to see much else. I can smell damp plaster and dust. We can hear, high up, the flustering feral pigeons that haunt the space under the roof. Dad unerringly heads for the pulpit-place on the bare floor, where his voice will echo best.

"A gift," he says. "To Cato Gardner. Who was Cato Gardner, and who gave him this gift? Do you know, Lawrence?" I don't need to answer; he's surely going to tell me. "Cato Gardner was an ordinary man. The community around him was an ordinary community. Sailors. Barbers. Servants. Dealers in used clothing. We had no money in our hands, but they were proud hands. They could give a gift."

Dad's flashlight stabs at the wall where plaster has fallen away. The bricks stagger in uneven rows. It was barbers and sailors and butlers who built this house, not bricklayers.

"We shaped these bricks with our working hands. We gave a gift out of common clay, that same common clay God shaped to make all mankind. My son wants to hear about buildings designed by famous architects, possessions of white millionaires, built on a shifting sea of stolen blood. Look at that house Pinebank now, ruined, burned out, ready to tear down. And look at this one, our Meeting House, look at this strong foundation. Out of our empty hands, we are giving America this gift again."

This is a prime slice of Charles Randall Walker rhetoric. Dad looks at me, expecting, I guess, that I'll jump up and say, *Yes! Yes! Why didn't I think of it before! I have to write about fundraising for the African Meeting House!*

Dad looks at me.

Alex looks at me.

I look at the bricks and the floor.

"A gift," Dad says softly. "What do we own? Not our possessions. Not our lives. Not this very day. This very day our lives may be demanded of us. There are no millionaires. There is no power. The only power we have is the power to give away."

Shit, Dad's good. I'm never going to be as good at anything as he is at talking. "If there are no millionaires, why do you want their money?" I ask to get his goat. I walk away from him, look at every inch of the African Meeting House, poke at bricks and wave my flashlight and pace out the measure of the meeting room as if I were the architect historian I want to be. I ignore poor Alex, who stands nervous and shivering in the cold while Dad and I have our silent fight.

Eventually we leave.

I stand by the car, expecting Dad to unlock it, but he starts off down Joy Street, shaking his head in sorrow, just looking back once to make sure I'm following him. Of course he's going to the Shaw Memorial. I hang back while he walks downhill, shaping phrases in his head, and delay catching up to him while he stands looking at it.

He's a thick man, and it's cold, and he outlasts me, until I can't feel my nose at all and have to shove my hands under my armpits to feel my fingers.

"Dad, it's my idea to write about houses. I believe in it."

"Lawrence, you believe in houses like Pinebank."

"And I believe in the African Meeting House. I believe in all sorts of buildings, Dad. I believe buildings are important." My teeth are chattering and it doesn't come out as well as I want.

Dad is shining his flashlight up onto the monument, on the faces of the soldiers. I think of Katie and me here. If only it were as easy to talk to Dad as to Katie.

"Lawrence," Dad says, "do you know the names of the soldiers on this monument?" He sweeps the light over the marching men and their mounted white colonel.

"Robert Gould Shaw," I say obediently. "The others I don't know. I guess they're models."

Dad focuses the light on a bearded soldier by Shaw's horse. "Sergeant William Harvey Carney," he says. "In the assault on Fort Wagner, when the color-bearer was shot down, Sergeant Carney rescued the Union flag. The flag of the Fifty-fourth Massachusetts. The flag of men who gave the gift of their lives.

For that he received the Congressional Medal of Honor, the first of our race to achieve it. The flag hangs in the State House today. And you do not know his name?"

I'm not too cold to feel myself flushing red.

"We are invisible men," Dad says. "Never forget that. Lawrence, do you think we will really get reparations for our years of service to them?"

"No," I mutter. "Sir."

"The white men own this country. Make no mistake. They are mighty. They call this the Shaw Memorial, not the Carney Memorial. And we believe them. We believe them, Lawrence, because we know no better. We believe them because they have taught us to bow down and not to look them in the eye. We think they define us because they taught us not to define ourselves. But every time a man stands up," Dad says. "Every time I stand up. Every time I say 'You are wrong. You do not own my soul. What I value is not yours.' Then I am a visible man. Then my soul is not a white-made soul. Then my soul and my hands are my own. Then I can give my gift. That is the gift I have given all my life. And I will give it to my last breath. To Cato Gardner, to Scipio Dalton, to Cyrus Vassall. To Sergeant William Harvey Carney. To David Walker, Maria Stewart, Frederick Douglass, Sojourner Truth, to every man and woman who has stood up for our race. What gift will you give, Lawrence? What do you have to give?"

Dad, why do you make me feel so small?

"You're cold," my perceptive father says. "We'll get coffee, and I'll tell you about Pinebank and that Perkins family. A story about a gift. A gift of evil.

"Have you ever heard of the Perkins Bequest?"

We don't go to the Harvard Club. We get coffee at a Dunkin' Donuts and drink it sitting in the car, in a parking lot in Allston. This is a measure of how seriously Dad takes what he is telling me. What he has to say is worth getting coffee stains on the car's upholstery.

All I can think is, *He knows about our treasure.* He probably is planning to claim the Perkins Bequest for reparations.

"This is from my new book. I know you will say nothing about it to anyone."

Dad is having me sign a nondisclosure.

"Just before the Civil War," Dad says, "I believe there was a movement to bring back the legal importation of slaves. That is what my new book is about."

"What?"

This is dynamite. If you listen to people like Petrucci, you probably don't know this, but you should. America didn't ban slavery itself until the Civil War, but one great thing America had done, fifty years before that: It had banned the importation of slaves. Jefferson might still own his own children. We were still owned. But there would be no more slave ships. People would still die on the sugar plantations, but not on the Middle Passage.

"America was going to bring the slave trade *back*?"

If Dad's right, he's going to set off a big fat bomb in the

middle of American history. He probably sees something like this on my face, and he smiles grimly. My father will enjoy throwing that bomb.

How could the South think that the United States government would allow slaves to be imported again legally? Most civilized countries, once they ban the trade, never go back to allowing importation. Never. Civilized countries don't do that.

Who said America is a civilized country?

Hope's eternal, man.

"Did anyone think they could do that? Who?"

"Who?" Dad says. "Think of the whole history of the 1850s. It is a single concerted attempt to strengthen slavery. 1850, the Fugitive Slave Act: Federal officials are required to assist slave catchers. A black man may be arrested on the mere word of a white man. 1854: Slavery is allowed into the new American territories. 1857: The Supreme Court asserts that we are property. Our people, slave or free, can never be citizens, can never sue in court even for our own freedom. Never.

"Think where it leads, Lawrence. Slavery has been allowed to enter the new territories. The expansion of slavery is allowed. And this leads to great prosperity! Not only for the South. Southern cotton comes through New York, to Northern cotton mills. That cotton must be picked. Those enormous new territories must be farmed. Where will the slaves come from? There are not enough of us. The white man needs more of us."

I think of those baby farms in Virginia. I think of the kids fed from pig troughs.

But raising kids took longer than buying grown men. There were plenty of people still in Africa.

"In 1858," Dad says, "a ship, the *Wanderer*, funded in part by Northern money, is sent to Africa to buy slaves and import them openly into the United States. Openly. The 'cargo' will be seized, yes. The 'owners' will be prosecuted, certainly. But the issue will be brought to the courts. A majority of Supreme Court justices are Southern. Will the Supreme Court rule that a man's possessions are not his own?

"The plan almost succeeds. The owner is declared innocent of all charges. He is encouraged to run for governor of Georgia. For governor, Lawrence."

"The Supreme Court?" Control the Supreme Court and you control the law. "The Supreme Court would do that?"

"In 1859 the schooner *Clotilde* imports a cargo of Africans. One hundred sixty men, women, and children are imported successfully and distributed successfully to 'owners.' The captain, William Foster, says that he bet some 'Northern gentlemen' that he could import us without getting caught."

Bet probably means the Northerners gave him the money to do it.

"Lawrence, what does this sound like to you?"

Like a push to restore the trade. Southern slavers, Northern money; money from Northern men dependent on Southern cotton.

I think of the Perkins cotton mills.

"Thomas Perkins was a slaver," Dad says. "I believe he continued to be."

"He'd *been* a slaver, Dad. But that was years before."

"Do not believe Seaburg. Seaburg whitewashed him. Perkins was a slaver until the very last moment before the trade was abolished. Until the very day, the very evening of the day. There is an evil that brands the soul." Dad puts his coffee in the cup holder. His hands rest on the steering wheel and tighten on it. "He had done deeds so morally reprehensible he would not dare to repent of them. Do you understand how a man's most evil actions can hold him to those actions? Do you understand, Lawrence, that if he thought of repenting he would be forced to confront himself first?"

"What did Perkins do?"

"I believe he went further into slaveholding. Before he died, he set up a trust. Five hundred thousand dollars. A major business venture. To go on after he died. The trustees were to be headed by his nephew, Edward Perkins. The proceedings, and everything about the Perkins Bequest, were to be handled in the utmost secrecy. To be invested in secret, managed in secret."

This is what I'm looking for? I swallow; my throat is dry. "The Perkins Bequest was to get the trade *back*? To send ships back to Africa to deal in slaves?"

"What legal business would he have done in secret? What other business would have paid him so well? Think of the enormous profits. Fifty dollars to buy a man on the Slave Coast. Hundreds to sell him here.

"And the chance, Lawrence. The chance to enslave us forever.

"Our blood bought Pinebank. Our blood built Pinebank." Dad's blunt finger stabs the steering wheel. "Thomas Handasyd Perkins was used to dealing in our flesh. I think he directed his associates to buy more of us, I think the Perkins family used the Perkins Bequest to deal in slaves. I mean to see that building destroyed stone by stone."

"But—"

But what? But, Dad, a ghost says the treasure is still there. Kill me now.

Dad drives us home, and I go upstairs and write my Walker Prize essay, all in a couple of hours. I write about the African Meeting House. I have nothing against the African Meeting House. It's a good speech. I get some of it from Dad. I use Sergeant Carney. I talk about gifts and heroes. I end with a fund-raising appeal. Give a gift to Cato Gardner, I ask my audience, and I can hear those checkbooks rustling. I read it over, copyedit it, save it as a PDF the way they want me to, and e-mail it off before I can change my mind.

At least it's done.

And then I sit on the edge of my bed just staring at the Wii Dad and Mamma will let me play with now. Playing with toys, I'm one fucking cool dude, that's about all I'm good for. I've done just what Dad wanted me to do. No, not even that: what he wanted to do himself. He wanted to win the Walker Prize.

Now he's going to. I'm not talking about reparations, that'll disappoint him, but come MLK Day, it'll be Charles Randall Walker's boy up there parroting Charles Randall Walker's ideas.

Whatever gift I have to give, it's not in that speech.

I want Pinebank.

I want the story behind it.

I want to know what Thomas Perkins really did.

I want to be my own man and not some faded Xerox of my father.

My phone rings. I dig in my pocket. "Katie?"

"Law? Can we get together somewhere? Right now? I really need to talk to you."

"What's happening?"

Katie almost sobs over the phone. "Ghosts."

KATIE

CHRISTMAS IS GOING TO BE A TOTAL LOAD. Law's disappeared to be with his family and write his essay. I picture them all together, at a table filled with his mom's cooking, with a lot of famous guests who fit in better than me.

Meanwhile Phil tells me we're going to have Christmas dinner with Lucy Rosen. Lucy Rosen, Ms. soul-sucking Understanding.

I point out the obvious. "She's Jewish, Phil."

"Holiday dinner, then," Phil says. "Lucy, um, she wants to cook for us."

Last year Mom had just died and we got Chinese takeout. I gave Phil a book and he gave me an iTunes card. All we wanted was her. We missed her so much we could barely move. It's not going to be fun this year either. But still, it's a family day. Lucy Rosen can cook for us some other time.

"Katie," Phil says.

La la la, I don't want to hear.

He sits down at the kitchen table and looks up at me. I

don't want to see him look like that, pleading for something, wanting something, regretful because Phil doesn't like to be stubborn. He's never been stubborn with me. Never asked me for anything.

"She wants to cook us a real family meal," he says.

"She's not part of our family."

"Sit down, Katie," Phil says.

I sit at the kitchen table. Before Mom and Phil got married, she painted the table yellow with a green edge. It was cheerful. It needs painting again. I run my finger along the edge, thinking I should paint it during Christmas.

"Katie," Phil says, "you know we're a family, the two of us, you and I. Nothing is ever going to change that."

"What do you mean, nothing?"

"I've been talking a lot with Lucy. I'll love your mother forever and miss her forever. And you're my daughter. But Lucy has been helping me to"—he swallows—"to learn to live with it."

Why does he want to learn to live with it? Mom's barely been dead a year.

"What is she, your shrink?"

"Katie," Phil says. "She's my friend."

"Are you guys dating or what?"

Phil doesn't say anything.

I can just see it, cups of coffee in the teachers' lounge. They always eat lunch together.

"I'd like you and Lucy to be . . ." Phil doesn't know what to say. "To like each other."

"She's not my type." I have her whole story, just as if she were dead. "I bet she's been taking care of her paralyzed mother or whatever, and now she's like thirty-five and by the time her mother dies she's never going to get married. So she has instant coffee with you in the lounge, and the two of you eat your sandwiches together, and that's as close as she has to a relationship,"—I swallow *as close as you have because you're taking care of your dead wife's kid*—"and she worries over me like I'm the daughter she never had and never will, Phil, you're so clueless, but I've got a mother, and I don't want to get over her. So screw you both. I bet she made you a mug for your coffee with your name on it," which is the height of pathetic.

No. The height of pathetic is Phil taking care of me when I'm not even his kid. Maybe Phil doesn't want to be as pathetic as I hope he does.

"It wasn't her mother," Phil says, and his voice is harder than I've ever heard it, leathery, dry and hoarse. "It was her husband. Karl had been dying ever since I've known her. Ever since your mom and I knew them. He died last spring. Lucy and I have always been friends. Heaven knows, Katie, I loved your mother. And I won't get over losing her. But I need you to be understanding about this."

I don't listen anymore; I slam back into my room. I grab my pillow and press it against my mouth and nose, not like I'm going to smother myself with my pillow, but because I want to scream or begin crying or I don't know what.

After a few minutes, Phil knocks on my door. "Katie," he

says through the door. "Please do this. Be nice to her."

I'm not his kid. Since Mom died, it's just been weird, our pretending to be a family. And sap-sucking Lucy Rosen has decided Phil will make a good second husband.

That's what she's after.

In a couple of minutes I hear Phil shuffle away.

"You could give him that," Dad says. "Cut him a little slack, huh?"

I hold the pillow over my ears, but ghost voices can get through pillows.

"A man's got needs. Even Phil."

That's disgusting. *He's going to marry her, Dad. And she sits by me and looks at me and says, "Tell me how you feel," and I just feel like there's no place to hide.*

"She wants to be friendly."

I get to say who my friends are. Like I have friends. Except for Law, maybe.

"Just be nice to her, like he says. You can do that, kid."

I can be nice to her. I can stick a pencil in my eye. I'll be eighteen in three years and then I can move out.

"You remember," Dad says softly, "I told you maybe you needed to do something for that ghost, George? But hon, nothing you can do's gonna make much difference to him. Doing things for live people, you got more chance there."

Go away, I tell Dad, and roll over and stare at the wall until I'm sure I'm alone.

The morning of Christmas Eve, Phil goes out to do grocery shopping with Lucy Rosen. He's looking forward to it like a kid. He has this sappy grin all over his face because he's going to buy potatoes with his girl.

So here I am, alone with the laundry and cleanup. The washing machine and dryer we share with Mrs. Beal are in the basement, which means I have to take the laundry downstairs. When I look out the front door, there's the end of rope that means the man is hanging from the stairs again.

Crud.

Nobody is going to save me from my life. Nobody's going to be my mother. Phil's going to get married again. My life is my own, and I hate it.

I look out the front door to the sunlit hall and that twist of rope, ordinary white cotton rope, wound twice round the thick stairpost on the landing, and I wonder what would happen if I cut it and put that ghost out of his misery.

Would it really make a difference? Would it change something, like if Law and I got that treasure box out of Pinebank for George?

I'm going to give myself a Christmas present. Before I can think better of it, I'm out there in the hall with the big carving knife from the kitchen, sawing away.

The ghost rope isn't there and isn't not there. It's like when I was a little kid and made an imaginary cake and cut it into slices for my imaginary friends. There's only the slightest resistance, maybe just the slightest shiver of the knife handle as I cut deliberately, stroke by stroke. But it's important to cut it just as if it were real.

And then it's gone. Dissolved. Whipped away as if a body took it when it fell.

I stand up and put my hand on the railing. "Okay," I say out loud, hoping Mrs. Beal downstairs is extra deaf today. "Whoever you are, you've got to go now. I don't know why you want to scare me, but it's not right. You don't want to be remembered for having hung yourself. There must have been more to you than that." I look down. The hall downstairs is empty; nobody's lying on the floor. I think about the woman who threw herself off the roof, and all the people I've drawn. "All of you. Out. Because I don't want to deal with this. I'm only in high school and I never invited you and you can't just move into my head as if I don't count. From now on, I have a say."

It's quiet all through the house. Quiet in the hall, in the sunlight. Quiet in my head.

"I don't want to see *any* ghosts." I think about that. "Only if you're going to help me." Or if I love you. Mom. Dad. "Or if I have to help you." I need to see George if I'm going to help him. "But that's it. Understood?"

Quiet. Really quiet. No rustles in the dark corners of the hall. No purple faces or dangling legs. Nothing awful scratching on the other side of the cellar door.

It feels as though I've done something.

I go downstairs. Still nobody's sprawled on the hall floor.

I go up and down the stairs all morning, doing laundry, and there's nobody on the stairs but me. I sweep the stairs and dust the banister.

If Mom were here, the two of us would have spiraled paper chains up and down the banister.

After a while I go downstairs to our storage in the cellar and find the box of Christmas ornaments. I get out the old faded paper chains and weave them in and out of the banister rails. The colors have gone brown and it looks like Christmas in a haunted house. Still it feels like Mom is here a little.

And nobody else is.

I don't feel haunted.

Is this normal?

I like it.

I want to make sure I'm not completely unhaunted, so when Phil and Lucy come back and Phil grins and tells me how clean and nice everything is, meaning *Thanks for making Lucy welcome*, I just mutter something neutral and head out the door toward Pinebank.

George is down by the trail around Jamaica Pond, in among the Canada geese that are pulling at the dead grass. They don't see him. Note to self: Geese don't see ghosts. Smart geese. They honk at me and waddle away.

"Hello!" George says.

"Hey, George." On the freezing Saturday afternoon before Christmas, there's nobody here but us. I can ask him about the treasure without anybody overhearing or thinking I'm weird.

"George, that box— Do you know what was inside it?"

"Papers," George says. "And things."

"What kind of things?"

"I don't know." George shakes his head like a puppy shaking off water. "It's locked."

"And you never opened it?"

No. George has been taking care of it all this time without knowing what's inside.

"Aren't you curious?"

A guilty nod.

"You could probably look inside. I mean, you're a ghost."

George thinks about that. "Dark," he decides.

Couldn't he glow spectrally or—? Never mind.

"Is the box heavy?"

"Oh, yes."

"But you could carry it by yourself?"

George nods his head. "When the fire happened, I was going to carry it outside. I was big then."

"Big," I say blankly.

"I was almost *all* grown up," George explains patiently. "I was this old," and he holds up the fingers of his right hand, five and five again and five and five, and then his left hand, four fat little-boy fingers and the thumb folded over his palm. "Next year I would have been this hand again. That's all the numbers there are. Then you start over."

George was twenty-four when he died. A full-grown man.

Another thing I can add to my list of how ghosts work. Ghosts don't always stay the age they were when they died.

But that answers one question. If one twenty-four-year-old can carry the box, Law and I together can.

"You're good with numbers, George." He's really good, for a Down kid.

"Grandpapa taught me to count all by myself."

I wonder what Thomas Handasyd Perkins was like. Slaver, pirate, philanthropist. He taught George things. I like that. Not long ago, people usually just gave up on Down kids.

"George, did your grandfather ever tell you what the treasure was for?"

"It's for *them*," George says.

"Them who?"

"The other people." George drops his voice to a stage whisper. "The ones we don't talk about."

"Which other people?"

George gives me a don't-be-dumb look. "We don't *talk* about them."

George has rules, and I'm not going to get round them.

"But— Are these people, I mean, do these people get what's inside the box? Are these, like, living people?"

George shakes his head. "It's *for* them," he says.

I'm completely confused.

"*You* can look inside the box," George says. "I can show you where it is, right now."

It's beginning to get dark and no one else is around. All I can hear is the rustle of trees: not a voice, not a car. Even the geese are silent.

It's in the basement. . . . I know what happens to the girl in the horror movie when she goes into the basement.

Still, wow, to find where the treasure is, and what it is? Right now?

"Give me a moment on this." I pull out my phone and text Law, GOING INTO PINEB WITH G 4 TREZ. BASEMENT.

At least he'll know where to find the body.

"Is that a lantern?" George asks, looking at the phone glowing in my hand.

"I guess it is." I put my phone in one pocket and unclip my bike light and put it in the other. I have one of those flashlights that glow when you shake them; I shake it and show it to George and bring that too.

George leads the way up a set of overgrown, tilting granite stairs. He drifts up as if they were nothing; I slip and scramble. Back at the pond the sky is full of the pinks and blues of sunset, but up at the field the lights are already on. The trees wrap the house in dark. A really good time to go into a haunted house. I'm so stupid.

George is already on the other side of the fence. I chunk the toe of my sneaker into one of the too-little meshes of swaying yellow plastic fence and start pulling myself up. I feel like I'm climbing a curtain. Even my own weight starts pulling my sneaks out of the mesh. I grab a clump of grater-sharp plastic between my knees, haul myself upward, throw myself forward so I'm looking down at the ground through the mesh. I'm so high I'd better not fall.

I'm going to start paying attention in gym.

I lean forward over the top, flop like a fish, bump and bounce down the other side, thud onto the ground, and hope that someone left a big knife inside the house. A knife that cuts plastic fence.

George is leaning over me, concerned. "Katie?"

"Fine." My arms feel like I've spent the weekend with the Spanish Inquisition.

The door's boarded up. I hate this. Underneath the roofless brick portico, the old double door is a big sheet of plywood covered with a tangle of graffiti. That plywood has been here for years and it's not going anywhere tonight, not with what I've got in my pockets, which is not, for instance, a crowbar.

"George, is there any other way in?"

George looks from the door, to me, to the door. I wonder what he sees.

I shine my bike light up the brick face of Pinebank. Up on the second floor, the windows have completely fallen away. They're wide open, a dark gap. On the second floor. Terrific.

I wish Law were here. Guys are good at this stuff. Guys can climb up the side of a building. Look at Spider-Man. Look at George, he can just drift.

There's a tree.

It's a big old oak, close to the side of the house. Theoretically, people can climb trees. What I need is a rope, though; the trunk is too wide for me to do more than tree-hug and the first side branch is way above my head.

What I need is about five years' training as an extreme ninja.

Or a smaller tree, something I can get my legs around . . .

Like the porch pillar.

Granite and brick base; brick pillars up above, holding up the remains of the porch roof. Brick is good. Brick has lots of pieces to cling to. If I climb up the pillar, I can scooch my way across the edge of the porch. There's a brick arch. Brick is solid.

Sure.

I pick my pillar, grab on, and begin to climb like a caterpillar, hump-and-slide-and-grab, holding on with the soles of my sneaks. Twelve feet to the roof. Then eight, then—I grab hold of the edge of the roof and don't quite eviscerate myself pulling myself up. Something on my jacket snags and I hear tearing.

I'm sitting on the edge of the roof. Fourteen feet below me is the granite base of the porch. Inch by slow inch, with my butt cheeks balanced on something sharp, I slide myself toward the wall. I will not teeter. I will not fall and die.

And I'm there, leaning against the side of Pinebank. I made it.

It's freezing and there's a little wind, but the bulk of Pinebank is still warm like the side of a big brick animal. The moon is beginning to rise. I can see the pointed roofs towering over me. The white bricks, the famous terra-cotta, are crumbling away around the window. I cautiously stand up, balancing on the beam, and grab the windowsill. The remains of sharp little stone flowers jab into my palm. I can feel the brick weight of the house. It isn't a ruin at all. Cautiously I stand on one foot, bring up the other, and ease it around to swing it inside the house—

"What you doing?"

A leering white face bursts into flame inside the room, and I smell charred wood and something rotten.

I break the record for the screaming backward broad jump. *Ghost, yeek,* I'm halfway back along the porch, holding on with arms and legs and my palms full of brick splinters, until I realize that the glow coming out of the window is a Coleman lantern and the face is a man's.

George, you could have told me. Of course George is nowhere. Nada. Zip. Gone.

"It's people living here! You want to be careful!" The man holds up his lantern. He's an old guy in a ratty wool cap and a grease-slick jacket that probably hasn't been washed since Reagan was president. "Yah! No smoking, this is Massachusetts! There are bad people in here, you don't want to know! No trespassing! Take the Red Line! No, sir! Yah!" He leans out and says with a leer, "You want to come in, kid? I got something to show you."

"Oh, gee, thanks," I mutter, easing back along the beam. My scraped palms pricker and pinch, ow ow ow. All this for nothing.

"Gimme seventy-five cents!" the old guy yells after me. "I got to get to Malden!"

At least bumping back down the porch pillar is easier than climbing up. And Crazy Old Guy has to have figured out the fence; I find where he slid under it and slide under too, trying not to think about his jacket. It was so dirty it looked like it hunted its own food.

I bike home with my bike light fading and wobbling and spend an hour before dinner picking brick bits out of my hands with a pin. Clueless Phil is so busy looking up turkey recipes he doesn't notice. I volunteer to make a pumpkin pie, which means Phil has to go to the grocery store again to pick up supplies. I don't think about him getting hit by a car in the parking lot, leaving me all alone except for Ms. Understanding. While he's gone, I put my filthy clothes in to wash. My pink Chucks will never be the same.

And I make a phone call.

"Hello, Boston Police? I was over at Jamaica Pond this afternoon, and this crazy guy came up to me. . . . He didn't do anything, but I was *really, really scared*, you know? I think he lives in that abandoned house."

Every year the police arrest homeless people just before Christmas so they'll be warm and get a good meal.

Tom Menino's Boston has to be good for something.

Why did I say I was making a pie?

When I'm queen of the world, pumpkins are going to be illegal. My original plan was I was going to make a pumpkin pie from scratch, and Phil would be so impressed he wouldn't notice I loathe Lucy.

Have you ever tried to make a pie out of a pumpkin?

There's this enormous pumpkin that you'd think is full of

food, but it's all seeds and orange string. Phil and I cut it in half, and we take big kitchen spoons and we scrape and we scrape and we scrape, and eventually the whole kitchen is full of slimy seeds and orange macramé and maybe a cup of actual pumpkin. You're supposed to bake the pumpkin and then mash it up and make a custard with eggs and milk and stuff, and then bake it in a pie crust.

Don't even ask about pie crust.

About seven in the evening on Christmas Eve, I end up with this gray thing in a black shell that looks like something Tim Burton made in kindergarten. Phil and I run out to the one grocery that hasn't closed and get pumpkin in a can and one of those frozen pie crusts and more milk and eggs and cinnamon, and about nine thirty at night, there we have my creation. Whatever. It's pumpkin pie. Happy Christmas Eve, Merry Christmas.

After that, Christmas itself isn't so bad. Lucy can't cook either. We have frozen string beans and frozen squash and microwaved instant potatoes, but by some miracle the turkey comes out tasting like turkey. I have sort of wrapped up a pretty drawing for Lucy, at least rolled it with a glitter ribbon, and she gives Phil a manly scarf, and me she gives a scarf too. It's so not me, it's silky and wifty, vintage sixties-ish, but I sort of like it because the pattern is branchy and it reminds me of Pinebank. She painted it. Of course she painted it. But it's not totally gross, and I almost feel bad having been all snidely about handmade stuff. She gives me a sketchbook, too, which

I hope I'm going to fill with normal pretty pictures. Me, the unhaunted normal girl.

The pie's a total hit, and we sit around watching old movies and everything's great until the end of the evening, when Phil suggests that tomorrow he's going to go to Bloomingdale's because our Christmas ornaments are a little sad (no kidding), and maybe we'd both like to go too.

I can't tell you how unlike Phil this is. His attitude toward shopping is once every year he'd like to have a box delivered with flannel shirts and corduroys and cotton socks, marked WEAR THIS, and he would.

This is a strategy to get Lucy and me together, just us girls.

But . . . ornaments at Bloomie's.

Back in elementary school, my friend Pat and I went to the Bloomie's sale. They had lots of beautiful stuff, and really weird things like glass pickles with GOOD LUCK painted on them and glass peaches and silver sushi. I bought a glass pickle for Mom. Mom was never really about Christmas glitter; she was all popcorn balls and paper chains and hippie stuff. But she loved the glass pickle. It wasn't haunted for me and I could keep it. It hangs over my desk now.

Good luck. Sure.

But I know what Dad would say, *give Phil a break*, so the next day, bright and early, we're up on the second floor of Bloomie's. Phil wanders off, like I figured he would, and the two of us are left alone.

"Do you have a Christmas tree?" I ask. "Being Jewish?"

"My husband was Jewish," Lucy Rosen says. "Nonobservant. I'm just nonobservant everything."

I don't really want to hear about her husband. I've worn her scarf today, the one she gave me. That's as close as we need to get.

Lucy Rosen holds up a Santa in camouflage like a soldier.

"That's so wrong," I have to agree.

"Karl was in the army," she says. "Like your father. He hated it." She's going to talk about him whether or not I want to hear. "He learned Arabic, to be fair, he said." She smiles as if she's sharing a joke. Not with me. "He believed in fairness. He got cancer from whatever they sprayed on the battlefield, and he still believed in fairness."

She puts the soldier Santa down and her mouth tightens a little. I know that grimace, and I move away and look at nutcrackers.

I know something about Lucy Rosen. She may like Phil but she loved this Karl.

"What did your father think about the war?" she asks me.

"It killed him so I guess he was pissed about it." We don't talk about the war, Dad and me.

"I suppose it did kill him," Lucy Rosen says.

"He got blown up in a tank, I think. Mom never told me much about it." Lucy Rosen gives me an odd look. I guess I sound too calm about it; her husband died just this year. "It was a way long time ago."

In front of me is a shelf of hanging ornaments and one of them catches my eye. In among the glitter and gold, it's perfectly simple: a clear glass ball, and inside it, floating, is a single feather. A little white feather like off an angel. I pick it up and turn it this way and that way, and I can't see how that feather is hanging there.

That's the one I would give Mom.

"That's the best one," Lucy Rosen says, coming up beside me.

"Yeah, it is, isn't it? I wonder how the feather stays there?"

She looks at it; she's still a little teary-eyed. "Our lives are feathers in the wind," she says like she's quoting. "When Karl was dying, I kept saying to myself, what can I *do*, how can I help to make it easier for him? He was in so much pain. One day I was washing dishes. I broke a cup, and there it was in pieces on the floor, there was nothing I could do about it, and it came to me I had no control, not the slightest control over anything. Nothing is fair, Katie. Not what happened to your mom and dad and Karl. Nothing we can do about it." She shrugs. "What holds the feather up? I wish I knew."

I do not need sermons.

"Tell me what you do to make things better," she says.

Draw people dying horribly. "I don't."

Around us the pillars are mirrors and they reflect us. A middle-aged woman and a girl in black, holding a feather in a globe, with a scarf around her neck that isn't like anything her mom would have given her. Lucy Rosen's eyes have wrinkles around them, her long hair is graying. Still she doesn't know how to live her life. Lucy Rosen, you so don't want advice from me.

"Painting," she says, answering her own question. "Going

out for coffee. Little things. Christmas ornaments. Pie. The secret Super Glue of holding on." She turns over ornaments in the bin, carefully. "This," she says, holding up a blown-glass smiling moon. "Not fair I spotted it when someone else might have. Oh, Katie, I know that Phil and I being happy isn't fair to you or Annie. It might be good. It won't ever be fair."

She's not looking at me. I'm only looking at her in the mirror. I could talk with her, I think. She thinks the world sucks too. We'd have things to say.

I don't want to talk with her. Never.

"Or this one," she says. "What do you think? No; I think the moon."

I'm going to give the feather ornament to George. Next day I pack it carefully in an old shoebox and wrap the shoebox and take it out to Pinebank.

I want Law with me, and his car, or better yet his mom's car or his dad's car and a big ladder, and I want him to go inside while I stand outside and hold the ladder. But Law's not answering his phone. At least it's bright morning this time. I climbed that porch once and I can do it again.

I leave the shoebox down on the ground, in a mesh shopping bag with a string tied to the handles and the other end of the string tied to my wrist. I shinny up the pillar and stand on the porch beam and yell *hello hello* inside the house. No reply; the homeless guy must still be having turkey in jail. The coast is clear. I pull the shoebox up.

Inside the house the floorboards look gray and cardboardy and rotten. I swing my leg over the crumbling brick sill and put the shoebox down on the floor, and flop around and put one foot down on the floorboards, and then the other, still with my stomach over the windowsill in case the whole floor gives way. But the boards bear my weight, and I cautiously ease down until I'm just holding on to the sill.

I'm in Pinebank.

I turn around, and I'm in a big dusky ruined room, a tall-ceilinged room smelling of dust and plaster and old homeless man. In one corner there's his pile of stuff: a sleeping bag, a couple of milk crates holding cans, and a box of cereal. In the fireplace are the remains of his fire. Over the fireplace is a mirror eaten away with black. That's it for furnishing. The door is ajar. Through it I see the burned-out roof.

"George?" I whisper into the stillness.

"Here I am," he says behind me, just like in a horror movie.

"Will you not *do* that?"

"You *came*," he says.

I remember, too late, that I should have texted Law and told him where I was. I feel in my pocket but I haven't even brought my phone; it's on my desk, charging.

I'm here. I'm not going to leave.

"I brought you something. For Christmas."

"Is it Christmas? Merry Christmas!" George says. "Thank you, Katie!"

How do ghosts celebrate Christmas? I hold the box out to him and realize we have a problem.

"I can open it for you."

George watches while I tear open the paper. Another thing you never get to do again once you're dead: tear the wrapping off your presents. I hold the globe with the feather up in the light by the windowsill.

"Oh," says George. "*Geese* feather, Katie! A feather! From geese!"

He holds out his hands for it eagerly. I put it into his hands and it drops right through his palms, not even disturbing the feather. Just in time I catch it.

"Never mind," says George, with a look on his face like when the dog went away at the park. "Never mind, Katie."

"No. Wait. We can do this."

I hold the globe in the cup of my hands. "Now put your hands the same way, the other side. Can you do that?"

He holds out his hands too, and cups my hands with his little cold ones, and like fog his hands slide into mine.

Sunlight dazzles me. There is more light in the room, and it's warm. The windowpanes paint blocks of sunlight across the carpet, and the new mirror blooms with light. Logs pop and hiss in the fireplace. In the hall I hear voices.

George snatches his hands away. In the cold, ruined house, he and I stare at each other.

"Does my house look like *that*?" he says. "It's *dirty*."

George, did your house look like *that*? It was beautiful.

He looks at me solemnly and reaches out his hands. Cupped around the glass ball, our hands meet.

We are in a comfortable room in spring. It's the sunlight that astonishes me first, coming through windowpanes that have bubbles in them. The bubbles make sparks of light on the floor like little magnifying glasses. The room is an old man's bedroom, not George's; it smells like old person and tobacco. The walls are papered with striped wallpaper and silhouettes of people in gilded frames.

This is before photographs.

This is *then*.

"This is your grandpa's room?"

George nods.

I just stare around for a moment. The man who sleeps in that bed, under that blue woven bedspread, remembers the American Revolution.

And he dealt in slaves. Those glasses on the little table beside the four-poster bed, they're a slave dealer's glasses.

Standing against the wall there's a big glass-fronted cabinet.

A collector's cabinet.

"Let's go see what's in there."

I keep hold of his hand, and George and I stare through the glass at Thomas Handasyd Perkins's treasures. Ivory figures, old medals, a little jewel-covered box that looks expensive. There is a stub of white candle on top of an engraving of George Washington. That has to be the candle that Washington gave him. It still looks almost new.

And there it is, by the candle: the Simón Bolívar, the gold coin.

What did Grandpa put in his treasure chest if he gave the Simón Bolívar away?

I hope not the candle.

The door to the hall is half-open.

"George, let's go find your grandpa's box."

We open the door into the bright sunlit hall of Pinebank.

So many pictures, that's the first thing I see. Pictures three high on the wall. A little table. A clock enameled in a hundred fascinating colors. The ceiling stretches above us, all the way to the roof, white, strong, unburned plaster.

Law wants pictures of Pinebank. Law, can I draw stuff for you.

At the bend of the stairs, a white and blue vase is bursting with peonies. I can smell them. My hand touches smooth new honey-colored paneling. Down in the front hall, top hats glisten on a stand and canes grow like cattails from a Chinese jar. In the kitchen someone is baking bread. I can smell fresh grass. Someone baked bread, someone came visiting, grass grew a hundred and fifty years ago; but for me it's now.

Not quite now. I can see every twist and turn of the stair rails, every painted animal on the clock. But the numbers on the clock face don't have any shape. The pictures inside the frame are smoke.

This is George's Pinebank. Pinebank the way George felt it. Grandpa's house, where George was loved. The house Law described to me, the place that Frederick Law Olmsted wanted to keep part of his park.

"Show me where the box is, George."

It's hard to keep contact with him. We touch hands, lose hold. I walk across a flowered carpet, across a rotting jouncing floor strewn with leaves. I slide through a warped and swollen door, fling it open. The inside of Pinebank is a cold dark barn open to the sky. In a sunny hall, George and I see dust-flies dancing in the light.

"That's the cellar door," George says.

A low, dark door under the stairs: I feel scared for the first time since I told myself I wasn't going to see ghosts. I don't want to go down in the cellar. It feels bad.

I lay my hand on the brass knob, though, and doing it, I slip away from George. The dark green door fades and twists: it warps, swells, sprouts graffiti tags. I grope for George and see the door again. He turns the knob and tugs.

"It's locked."

In his time it's locked. In my time somebody came here and nailed it shut. It wasn't long ago. The nailheads are still bright.

Did someone find the treasure? "Is the box still down there?"

"Yes, Katie. I'm taking *good* care of it."

"George, I can't open this door. I have to come back with tools and stuff."

And Law. And a lot of bright lights. And an exorcist and a submachine gun.

George is looking past me, at the hall table with the top

hats. "I *bet* I can show you what went in the box," he says.

"What? How?"

"When Grandpapa told me to keep the box safe, I saw what went in the box."

But that was a long time ago—

A long time ago is now, for George and me.

"Show me." I put my hand on his little cold shoulder and walk with him like a blind person guided by someone seeing.

Around us walls shift, light shifts from warm to cold. I smell bitter new paint. *When Perkins was old,* Law told me, *he rebuilt his house.*

Gentlemen, says a man's voice.

George and I are in an office. It's night. The room looks like an old-fashioned parlor or a library, but the painters' brushes and paints are still on a drop cloth by a wall where a new door has been cut. In the middle of the room is a huge dark desk with a green leather top. A man is standing at the desk, an old man with long white hair. He looks over his shoulder, peering into the corners of the room as if he has sensed us. I choke back a scream. One side of his face, the side that didn't show in his picture at the Athenaeum, is covered with a red shadow.

I am looking at Thomas Handasyd Perkins.

Thomas Handasyd Perkins turns his birthmark-stained face toward his guests. Four old men and one younger one with a black beard are helping themselves to liquor from a cabinet in the corner. They are looking at each other the unsure way people do when they see each other in an unexpected place. A young man wearing a cap is sitting by the fire; his cap is pulled down over his face. George and I crouch by the fireplace behind a green leather chair. I can feel the fire hot on my cheeks. I can smell whiskey.

The shelves on three sides of the room are crowded with books. The green walls, all but the one by the door, are hung with picture upon picture all the way up to the ceiling. Over the fireplace is a picture I know, the king of the world on a golden sofa, a thousand feet in the air. Thomas Handasyd Perkins, rich and flawless, hiding his birthmark on the side the picture doesn't show.

And on the desk, all by itself, is a box. A wooden box, the size of a child's coffin, painted black and covered with iron straps.

I look at George. George nods.

Thomas Handasyd Perkins reaches out his hand. The younger man brings him a wineglass and stands behind him.

"Gentlemen." Thomas Handasyd Perkins lifts his glass, and the red wine throws red shadows on his red cheek. "I give you America and the liberty of our forefathers." This is the sort of thing politicians say before they cut school budgets. I wait to hear what he means. The ghosts seem to know, though. They raise their glasses.

"That's Uncle Eddie," George says, pointing to the man standing by Thomas Handasyd Perkins. Edward Perkins has a big dark mustache and crooked teeth behind his beard.

"Sit you, sirs." Thomas Handasyd Perkins puts down his glass on the desk. There are chairs for all the old men, matching formal gilded chairs. You can see how important they are in the way they sit, spread-legged, taking up room. The fattest and grayest man looks at his chair as if he wants to get his weight off his feet, but he doesn't sit down; he licks his lips nervously. The youngest man with the cap stays at his place near the fire, hiding his face. Edward Perkins, George's Uncle Eddie, stands behind his father's chair.

"Sirs, you do me honor to meet here. To each of you," Thomas Perkins says, "I have opened my mind severally. You each did not know the purpose behind our speaking. You do not know it still. Your principles are known to me. We are now gathered together. Look at your fellows, gentlemen, and decide whether you are ready to risk your fortunes, your hope of honor, and your very lives in each other's company. For I assure you it will come to that."

The fat man shakes his head nervously.

"To each of you I am extending an invitation. Should you decide that principles or prudence restrain you from accepting it, assume your fellows' invitations were merely to a dinner, such as any man might accept without consequence. Simply decline, and, sirs, I shall happily continue to meet you at my table and yours, with no further word said; and so shall my nephew Edward after I am gone. For I am the coward of you all; I am an old man, and this that we put in train today must continue past my lifetime."

What is he afraid of? What is he doing? Not just putting gold in a box. What is the Perkins Bequest?

Thomas Perkins takes a key out of his pocket and unlocks the center drawer of the desk. Out of it he takes four long, white, folded pieces of paper, each sealed with red wax. Edward Perkins takes them and goes round the desk to hand one to each old man. "Sir," Edward Perkins says to each. Each of them nods and takes one. Two have knives in their pockets to lift the wax away. Two use their fingers and thumbs. Each turns a little away from the others to read.

I've got to see what's on those papers. I hope they're not hazy like the numbers on the clock. "George." I nod at the letters.

"That's nosy," George whispers.

"Yes, it is," I hiss back. "Come on, George, please."

I don't dare move without him or I won't see.

"George," says Edward Perkins, "is that you behind the chair? Come out, child."

The four old men and the young one look right at us. At George and me.

"Come here, Georgie boy," says Thomas Handasyd Perkins. "Don't be afraid."

They look at us, but they only see George. I'm just a shadow, something to see out of the corner of your eye. A ghost. George moves forward, and I keep hold of his elbow.

The men surround us. Thomas Handasyd Perkins, Edward Perkins, and the four old men. The young man is still hiding his face by the fire. I smell their wool suits and cigars, and smoke from the fireplace. And very faintly behind it, I smell the men's fear and the dirt and decay of Pinebank.

"George," says Grandpa Perkins, a little too cheerfully and a little too loud, "I shall share a secret with you. In this box is a treasure. Your Uncle Eddie will be in charge of it, and I shall put you in charge of it too. You and he together will care for this treasure, and use it wisely, and make of it more than ever it was. But we must do it in secret. Do you understand, George?"

"The boy is an idiot," the nervous man says.

"He is biddable and does not fail in his duty; and who will think him a keeper of secrets? George," says Thomas Handasyd Perkins. He stands and comes limping out from behind the desk. Slowly, breathing heavily, he kneels down to George's level and mine. "You will be in charge of this box. You will watch over it, and if any man ever comes in search of it, you will tell me or your Uncle Eddie. You must keep it safe."

"You mean if mobs come to burn you out," says the fat man. "Perkins, this is no time for such ventures. We are breaking the law, and worse."

"The law must be broken," Thomas Handasyd Perkins says.

The oldest of the men nods. "So say I. Tom, I accept your invitation."

"I shall not," says the fat man. "Gentlemen, I give you good day. And sir," he adds to the man in the cap, "you must not make yourself a spy for this mad notion."

To me, the fat man just fades out. The others look after him. In the silence I hear a car honking its horn on Perkins Street.

The tallest of the men steps over to the desk and scrawls a few lines at the bottom of his letter, then signs it with a flourish. He hands it to Thomas Perkins—through me. Briefly, he shivers. "A goose on my grave," he says. "Tom, put that in your safe-box." Edward Perkins takes the letter, opens the lid of the box, and puts the letter carefully inside.

Law and I are going to read that letter.

"George, child, if people come to burn this house, hold this paper safe. I would have my sons know why I indulged such madness."

"I will swear on the *Bible*," says George. "*I* will be in charge of the box. *I* will keep it safe."

The second man signs without a word, sits down, and folds his arms as if he's cold.

"On the Bible it is," says the third man. "We are committing treason, gentlemen, and courting war, and I for one am glad of it. We must swear it on the Bible, as the boy says; all of us and the boy. Tom?"

George reaches out his hand, away from me. They flicker out. I'm alone in a ruined room.

"George!" Committing *treason*? What are they talking about?

I grope forward, trying to connect with George again. The desk was right over here; where has he gone? For a minute I think I find him. The room, which is freezing now, is briefly warm again, heated by a ghost fire; then I lose it, as if I walked through a warm current at the beach, then through it into cold.

Then into a terrible cold, a heat and cold at once, a burning.

I can see the men and George. Thomas Handasyd Perkins is holding a big leather-bound book. George and all the men, including the young man with the cap, have their hands on it. They are swearing the oath that killed George. For the first time I see the face of the young man with the cap. His face is familiar, but I don't know from where.

The other men have all sworn. Thomas Handasyd Perkins's lips are still moving and he is clutching the Bible like a life preserver. Light from the fire moves like red crabs over his face. Edward Perkins is reaching into the desk and bringing out chinking leather bags and putting them in the box, one after another. "Some moneys we have to begin the work. We shall ask you for more, and for your guidance." He brings out boxes, closed leather boxes holding something precious, and lays them carefully on the coins.

I am looking at the Perkins Bequest.

But the old men and the money are ghosts to me. The old men are speaking now and I can't understand them. They're in a dimness now, surrounded, in a darkness they don't notice; in an intensity. I can see only the old men and Edward Perkins and George, but I feel as though I am in the midst of a crowd of people, and the crowd, the intensity, is their longing and terror and hatred. They hate, hate, hate like I hate the man who killed my mother.

And Thomas Handasyd Perkins sees them too, clutching his Bible, staring at them out of his bloodstained face. The Other People. The ones who will never forgive him.

And then the Other People turn their eyes on me.

Law

"I saw them, Law," Katie says. "And they saw me. They know I can see them."

I pick her up, shivering, at the bottom of the stairs by Perkins Street. We sit in my car in the dark, in the parking lot below Pinebank. Katie stares through the windshield, a thousand yards through the windshield.

"Who are *they*?"

She puts her hands over her eyes. I put my arm around her, turn the heat up as far as it will go, hold her tight. But I'm scared of this. I'm scared of her.

"I can't really see them," she says. "You know, like seeing something out of the corner of your eye? Even when I try to look at them, I can't— Just something— I'm afraid of looking." Her voice shakes. "I'm really afraid. But they want me to look."

She saw the Perkins Bequest and Thomas Handasyd Perkins. The Perkins Bequest exists. Guarded by ghosts.

"George said there were other people," she says, "and he

wasn't supposed to talk about them. I don't think he sees them. But I do."

She turns toward me, her face a white glimmer and black shadows in the darkness.

"Help," she whispers.

What am I supposed to do?

"Who are—?" I swallow. "Who are these ghosts?"

"They're *dark*. Maybe black, but *dark*. Like out there, darkness." There are no lights in the parking lot. Our breaths are making the car windows opaque, frosted. Outside the windows of the car there could be anything. "I look in the dark, and something comes out of the darkness . . . They smell. Bad. Law, take me where it's lighted. I can't look. I don't want to look. I'm going to have to draw them."

Mamma and Dad are both out. We have the house to ourselves. Mamma's Victorian fireplace has a gas fire; I take Katie into Mamma's office and turn the fire up high and turn on all the lights. Katie's eyes are a thin ring of green around black pupils.

"They can't actually hurt you," I say. "They don't hurt you, right?"

"They don't have to hurt me," she manages, "if they scare me this bad."

Yeah. Okay.

"They want the box. They want something in the box. Not gold or jewels, or not just gold or jewels. Something *else*." She turns and looks at me. "I know this."

"What else?"

"Maybe . . . the explanation. The men in charge of the Perkins Bequest, why they did it, what they did. Thomas Handasyd Perkins had each of his friends sign a paper and the papers went in the box. They were talking about liberty and treason and spying and risking their fortunes, but I don't know what they meant. It might be in the letters. And *they* were there. The Other People. Watching. Law," she says, "will you close the curtains?"

She's looking past me, into the dark outside the windows. I get up and twitch Mamma's heavy curtains closed past the taped-up sign that says *Save Pinebank.*

"I don't know who they are," she says.

I turn to see her looking up at me, past me, with the look she had when she drew Walker. In another universe. Standing at the crossroads in the light of the moon.

Dark people. Black people, people who smell. Like they've been crammed into the hold of a ship.

I know who they are. Oh my G–d, I know.

"I think," I start. "No. I *know* what the Perkins Bequest was for."

I sit on Mamma's sofa with her, in front of the fire, and hold her to keep her warm, and me too, and tell her Dad's theory. The *Wanderer,* the *Clotilde,* a conspiracy between Northern industrialists and Southerners to bring back the trade in slaves.

"Slaves? They were planning to buy *slaves?*" she says.

It was all history when Dad said it. Now it's right here in my life. Katie can see slaves outside my windows. "Not only buying and selling, Katie. They were planning to import slaves from Africa. To start the trade again."

She shakes her head. "Did George's grandfather swear him to secrecy for *that*?" she says. "Did George die for *that*?"

I wanted Katie to see old houses for me. *Point her like a camera*, sure, but I wanted to control what the camera saw.

I wanted to know what Thomas Perkins really did.

I didn't want this.

"Dad would still be a slave," I tell her. "If they'd got what they wanted. A slave instead of a professor at Harvard."

And I probably wouldn't exist.

"Thomas Perkins knelt by George and said *a treasure*," Katie says. "He called it *a treasure*. And he killed my George. I tell you one thing," she says. "Thomas Perkins stood there with the Bible, it was a big one, and he held it against his chest like he hoped it would save him, and he knew they were there too, or he felt them, and he knew nothing would save him. I know this. Law, we have to get the box out and tell what he did."

I don't want to be an angry black man like Dad. I don't want to spend my life yelling about slavery and reparations. But—

"Yes," I say. "Yes. We do."

Mamma has John Wathne's plans and pictures of the inside of the house. He gave her a copy to convince her that the house couldn't be saved. She has it all: Wathne's survey of Pinebank, his photographs and elevations. I go hunting on Mamma's office computer, hoping we can figure out where the box is in the basement.

What Katie did in Pinebank scares the shit out of me. She points to a window on the second floor. "That's how I got in," she says, and I barely see how she could have without killing herself.

"You went across that roof? Did George tell you it was a good idea? Katie, did you go down those stairs?"

Katie looks at the picture of Pinebank's ruined porte cochere—through it, as if she's seeing another house. "I wasn't looking. It was dark the first time. The stairs had a banister," she says, puzzled. She points. "Right there."

"They don't now." The stairs look ready to rip out from the wall. What house was she in?

What Katie says was Thomas Handasyd Perkins's office is on the ground floor. It has a big elaborate chimney, two stacks that enclose a window. In Wathne's photos, the floor is ankle-deep in plaster from the ceiling and the rest of the plaster sags away from the laths.

"It didn't look like that at all," she says. Her sneakers are covered in plaster dust, but Katie has been in another house.

"I'm not crazy," she says, maybe seeing something in my face.

The office is the safest of the rooms. All over the first floor, plaster has ripped from walls and ceiling. Entire walls are gone. The floors are humped with little dunes of dirt and leaves, or powdery with rot. Smoke and char stain everything.

"That was the door I saw," Katie says. "The one to the cellar." In Wathne's pictures it sags open. "But it has plywood over it now. He nailed the cellar door shut, or somebody did."

"Oh, shit, Katie."

We've reached the pictures of the cellar.

I'm not scared of old buildings. But there's a difference between "not scared" and "stupid if you're not scared." The cellar of Pinebank is your classic death trap. Wathne's pictures of the cellar aren't going to help us find the treasure's hiding place, because he took only three pictures, all from the bottom of the cellar steps, then he probably beat feet and ran upstairs as fast as he could. The good news is that the steps to the basement were sheltered by the old granite foundation and look pretty much intact. The foundation is good, big granite blocks. But the rest of the house? From below you can see what the hills of plaster dust hide from above. The entire first floor, beams, flooring, everything, has sagged downward and is being held up by one rusty Victorian lally column. There's a brick pillar by the wall that I'd guess is the bottom of that big chimney in the office. The bottom of the pillar has an arched recess, I'd guess for storing firewood, and the strength of the arch is probably the only thing keeping the chimney up. The bricks at the bottom of the pillar are half chewed away by water damage. One wrong move and Chimney Surprise. Near the chimney the floor beams, oak ten-by-tens, are charred and balancing on crossbeams. If a dog walked over them, they'd crash into the cellar.

Oak beams weigh hundreds of pounds each.

The only safe way to find something in this cellar is going to be to break through the roof, gut the entire innards from above with an excavator, and pick out those beams like pickup sticks. That or send in a gang of ten-buck-an-hour guys who are willing to take the risk.

"Katie. We can't do this."

Katie just looks at me, pleading. Someone can do it, obviously; she did, she can. What am I supposed to tell her? Sorry, Katie, you're crazy after all, only a crazy person would take a risk like that?

"I know. But this place is death waiting to happen. Katie, my mamma's an architect. I'd like to be a big man and try this, and I know we have to find what's in that box, but no kidding, if I went in there she'd ground me till my hundredth birthday."

"Are we going to leave the box there?"

Her eyes are huge, betrayed.

"No. We're not. We'll figure something out. Tell me more about the box. Tell me everything you know."

She doesn't know where the box is, only that it's in the cellar. Katie describes it. A sea chest, I figure. Not black paint but tar, and iron bands around it.

"How big?"

Katie holds her hands apart. Maybe two feet by three by two high.

This is a clue. "It could be buried in the floor, inside a granite coffin liner or something." I scroll back to Wathne's pictures. The basement floor is covered with debris too, but underneath the debris it looks like flat square paving stones. Just made to be pried up. "Probably not in the walls." Pinebank has always had that same foundation, big granite blocks. But unless one of them is hollow, which you wouldn't want to do with a foundation stone—

"What did Perkins say about the box?" I ask her.

"Nothing about where he was putting it. George said he put it in the basement, the 'safe place,' during the fire."

"So he could get it into the safe place fast. What else did he say?"

She thinks. "Those people, you know, the—them—George said what was in the box was *for* them."

"To give to them?"

"He said *for* them."

"*For* them."

Like some white man paid fourteen hundred dollars *for* my great-great-grandfather Walker.

Yes. Those white men were going to buy slaves. Buy people. Like me.

"Perkins and his friends looked so ordinary," she says. "They were just afraid of getting caught. They were saying things like 'It has to be done.'"

"Would you draw them? Would you draw their faces?" I want to see their faces as they said that. "I just want to see their damn faces."

Katie nods.

She doesn't have her sketchbook. I find paper and pencils in Mamma's supplies and sit her down at Mamma's desk.

I go in the kitchen and turn on the coffeemaker for us, go hunting in the pantry for something to eat. I come back and watch the coffeemaker perk and face up to what Thomas Perkins did.

Thomas Perkins, the owner of Pinebank. He invested in the slave trade. Right here in Boston, after the trade had been outlawed for fifty years.

Outlawed maybe only in name, but it was still the law. Americans could not buy human beings in Africa and sail them three months across the sea, "wasting" maybe a quarter of us on the way. They couldn't starve us on a ship. They couldn't chain us on a ship. But they could chain us. They could starve us, brand us, whip us, buy us, sell us. All the white law allowed us was we couldn't be bought overseas for fifty bucks a head and flood the South like cut-rate electronics, to give the South an advantage in the census. That was how the North abolished slavery. We had to be farm-raised in Virginia. We weren't allowed to be free. Just not cheap.

That was the protection we'd had. Not for us, for them; for the North.

And Perkins and those white men wanted to take that little bit away.

For money.

For *stuff*.

The coffeepot's still perking. I have time to look something up.

In our front hall there's a marble mantelpiece, and over it Mamma has hung a nineteenth-century painting of a ship under full sail, a two-masted snow. A fast little ship, the kind used as slave ships. I want to take my penknife out and zorro the painting.

Instead I go across the hall to Dad's office and look up the names of the Perkins Bequest trustees in Seaburg. Edward Perkins, a Cabot, a Gardiner, a Winthrop. Their great-grandsons are probably in the Somerset Club. With Dad.

They wanted to bring the Middle Passage back?

"Law?"

Katie's calling from Mamma's office.

She's sitting at Mamma's desk, drawing. She's not looking at the paper. She's not looking at anything. Her hand is drawing. She comes out of it, looks up at me, "Law?" she says, but her hand doesn't stop carving thick black lines into the paper. She rubs her forefinger against the lines as though she could smear them like charcoal. She rips off one of the Band-Aids on her fingers and picks at the scab, then smears the paper with her own blood.

I asked her to draw—

I reach over Mamma's desk and grab her bloody hands in mine. It's like holding wild animals. "Katie? Stop. Stop, Katie. C'mon, stop." I go around the desk and hold her, peel the pencil out of her blood-smeared fingers, hold her arms and half pick her up out of the chair.

Out of the corner of my eye I see what she's drawn. Five

white men swearing on a Bible. And around them—

I see them. Now I see them too.

"C'mon, Katie, let's go in the kitchen. There's coffee. You don't have to look at that. Don't draw them anymore. It's okay. It's going to be fine. We'll just go in the kitchen."

"That's how it *is*," Katie says. "That's what they *are*."

My hands are bloody too. I pull her into our warm bright kitchen, push her down in a chair. Coffee. Cream. Things she likes, cinnamon, sugar. "Mamma made cinnamon rolls. Here, these are good." Cinnamon rolls, as if I could fix this with sugar. Bloody thumbprints on the icing. Katie stares at the dark outside the kitchen windows. I go over and pull the drapes closed, and when I come back I sit in the same chair with Katie, crowded up against cold shivering Katie.

That's all it takes.

She's so cold; I'm shivering too. She drew them and now I see them too. I'm so scared I'm panting, I can't breathe. I wrap my arms around her like we're drowning, and our lips are an inch from each other. I can feel her breath stutter against my skin. "It's all right, Katie, all right, don't be afraid." It's not all right. It's never going to be all right. Talking to her, my lips touch hers. We grab on to each other, trying to drive the dark away. Band-Aids scratch my back like skeleton fingers. There's a smear of blood on her nose, blood on my shirt. I can taste tears when I kiss her. They're all around us, black skull-thin faces, eyes like starving mouths. Branded faces. Burned faces. Crushed skulls. She's crying. Maybe I'm crying.

And I'm kissing her, and her lips are the only good place in this world.

"Don't be afraid." But they are all around us, what Katie sees, the slaves, nameless, on a journey to some unknown country, ripped away from their lives and their land and their own children, never able to own or have or be anything again, never entitled least of all to what I'm doing, kissing white lips, white breasts, white skin. Katie's kissing me, untucking my shirt. Katie's white hands are on my brown hips and my brown hand on her white stomach. And it's good, it's so good, my whole body is waking up and knowing what it's for, our bodies are telling us we're alive, we're not like the people she drew, we're—

I am afraid.

I am afraid of what happened in the Middle Passage between human and slave, in the land at the end of the passage where there was nothing but slavery.

I'm afraid of the white men who thought they could buy and sell us.

I am afraid of liking this white girl.

I'm afraid of never being an ordinary human man, of being like Walker, who lived for nearly a hundred years but wouldn't trust his family with his name. I'm afraid of thinking that being free is always just a little out of reach, that freedom will never come, that for eternity I will have to walk toward it.

I'm afraid of the anger I feel. Of measuring myself against a white yardstick or a black one; about always having to pay for freedom with another march, another protest, another explanation. Of hating all whites. Of hating us.

Kissing white Katie, I know: Kissing a white girl is freedom. But it isn't enough freedom. Not in front of the ghosts. If I'm going to be a free man with a white girlfriend, what's between me and Katie can't be black and white or slave or free or showing off for the ghosts, it has to be just her and me. And how do we do that when everything that's between blacks and whites is haunted?

At the worst possible wrong moment in my life, I think of Dad and reparations.

Is that what reparations are, showing off for the ghosts? Collecting stuff for the ghosts? I rear back from Katie and take a deep, horrified breath. Does it make the ghosts go away to marry a rich white girl from Brattle Street, the kind of trophy white girl any Harvard professor would dream of having? That no slave could have?

If Dad meant Mamma to be his freedom, his reparations, the least he deserved for what the white folks had done—

Making people into stuff, there's a name for that.

I can't do this now. "We shouldn't do this," I tell Katie and disentangle us like a good Christian boy and pull up her jeans over those sweet hips, *oh fuck that hurts*. But Jesus has nothing to do with it, and Dad and Mamma way too much.

The phone rings on the counter. We listen while the voice mail takes a long message from Hugh Mattison about Pinebank. Katie looks up at me. "I'm sorry," she says.

"No, I'm sorry." I can't look at her. Almost going to have

sex, maybe, and I think of *my parents*? Why was I thinking? I am a fucking wuss. I take off my sweater and help her put it on to stop her chills.

"Can you get that drawing out of your mom's office?" she asks. "Burn it or something? Before she comes back."

Yeah. That I can do. "Then I'll drive you home if you want."

"Yeah, that would be good," she says. "I don't want to go home alone."

I can't tell her about Dad and Mamma taking over my brain. "Your hair's all messed up. You can use my comb." I get it out of my back pocket and give it to her.

"Law," she says, barely a whisper, looking at my comb and not me. *"They want what's in the box."*

"I know. And we're going to get it for them. We have to. I know. Drink your coffee."

Yeah. How exactly are we going to get them what they want?

Back in the office, I grab Katie's picture and take it out to the hall, where a fire is going in the fireplace. It feels like when I had to get a drowned raccoon out of our swimming pool. I just have to toss the picture in the fire, like I had to turn the net and dump the raccoon into the garbage can, while dripping bits of it sloughed off.

I make the mistake of looking at the picture again.

Eyes.

What do they want? They want everything. They want the shackles off their wrists; they want food to eat and a place to wash themselves clean. They want to see their shoreline and their village. To go back to their burned houses, their dead friends and family, their son who died of dysentery, their slaughtered elders. They want their own names. Reparations? I look up from their eyes to Mamma's pretty picture of the ship, the sweet-smelling crisp-sailed slave ship.

Reparations?

Fucking reparations?

I don't burn the picture; I roll it up, feeling sick to my stomach. Mamma has a set of nineteenth-century cubbyholes where she keeps blueprints. There's an empty cubby near the floor; I push it in down there until I can retrieve it.

Mamma's office. Our house. Books and pictures, antique furniture, Chinese porcelain, a designer stove. Computers and houseplants and a Wii. Awards. Stuff.

I fish the drawing out again and unroll it to look at the white men in the middle, the men who were going to start up the trade again. Five men. Three older, two younger, swearing on the Bible with George.

I look at the fifth man, the fifth secret-keeper of the Perkins Bequest. The man with the cap. Not Perkins, whom I recognize from the Seaburg biography. Not a Cabot or a Gardiner; Katie has drawn their faces plain, and I've seen enough Cabots and Gardiners to recognize one.

Thin face, long nose, drooping mustache. Almond-shaped eyes, almost Chinese-looking.

No. Oh, shit, it can't be him.

On the wall of Mamma's office, here he is. Young, with long

hair, wearing a Greek fisherman's cap, while he was writing *The Cotton Kingdom* for the *New York Times*. Standing king-of-the-hill on a mountain of dirt in Central Park. A long-bearded old man in a garden.

The man who created Central Park. Who built Prospect Park and the Emerald Necklace. Who designed the grounds of the U.S. Capitol. Who moved rivers and built hills. America's greatest landscape architect. The man who saved Pinebank once.

The traitor. Conspirator. Supporter of slavery.

The man I'm named after.

Frederick Law Olmsted.

I'm beginning to know what haunted is.

"You look guilty," Bobby Lee tells me. "You score?"

"Shut up, Bobby Lee."

"The man look happier than that if he got some," Darryl says.

"*Looks* happier," Shar corrects Darryl automatically.

We're all sitting in Bobby Lee's media room, having a fight. Bobby Lee's dad works for Bose and has every media gadget there is and some he invented. Usually I like being here, but today I'm in a mood to be pissy with everything and everyone, and Shar is fighting right back.

"Darryl turned in his Walker Prize essay." Shar looks at him as proud as if she invented him—they are so simple together—and then turns to me. "Me too. Yours is done, Law? Of course?"

"Yeah."

"So did you write on reparations?"

"I fucking did not."

Everybody gives me the half-smile, like *Law's stopped being daddy-whipped at last*. But Shar says, "What did you write on?"

I don't want to say what I wrote on. I'd like to talk to them about almost having sex and being haunted. I don't want to say a thing.

"How long till you all find out who's in the Walker finals?" Bobby Lee asks, trying to lighten things up. "What happens if you all get in? Can I take bets?"

"I wrote on the African Meeting House," I say.

"Oh *man*," Bobby Lee says. They all know my dad is on the fund-raising committee.

"Shut up, Bobby Lee."

Shar is just staring at me. "And so you are going to win," she says flatly. "And no chance for us."

"I don't care about winning. And at least I didn't write about reparations."

"Next thing to it, dude," Bobby Lee says.

Shar stands up and turns around, facing away from all of us. Unflappable Shar, the princess: Shar is almost crying. "We *try*," Shar says. "We try so hard and you don't care. You write on what your dad wants. '*At least* I didn't write about reparations.' You are such a jerk."

"Shar," Darryl says, "hey, come on, cut the man some slack—"

She turns on him in a fury—"*Slack?*"—and back to me. "Law, you are so full of privilege and you try to pretend you are not. For years your dad has been a judge, so you will win. It's the way things are. Why do you pretend it's not?"

"Would you shut up about my father?" I shout at her.

"Privilege is to have, okay," Shar says. "But not to ignore." She grabs her coat and stomps up the stairs. Darryl looks at the two of us, spreads his hands, *I don't know*, follows her.

Bobby Lee and I look at each other helplessly.

"Forget it, she's just standing up for Darryl," Bobby Lee says.

"Sure. Yeah."

"You know, though, dude?" Bobby Lee says. "She's right about the Walker Prize. It's not what you know, it's who you know, and this time it's going to be who your dad knows. They're not going to give your dad's son the Walker Prize? Fuck that. And here are Shar and Darryl working their asses off and they don't have a chance."

"Yeah. Fuck that." I shake my head. "Maybe I can vomit on stage or something."

"No way, man. The mayor's wife is always pretty, the mayor's daughter always gets a date, and you probably even wrote a good speech. You're doomed."

I call up Katie and tell her what I think about Olmsted. We're both feeling pretty awkward. I ask her if she wants to go to Olmsted's house.

"You really want to try talking to him? Like a medium?" she guesses. "I'm no medium."

"I know. You want to try anyway?"

Frederick Law Olmsted started his landscaping firm in Brookline in 1883, the first professional office for landscape design in the United States. Frank Lloyd Wright apprenticed here. Olmsted Brothers lasted until 1980, and when it closed down, the entire site—house, landscape, offices, and archives, about a million records—was bought by the National Park Service. It's still right here in town.

Katie and I talk ourselves into the main office and sit there, a little ways apart from each other, awkward, pretending to do research for a paper, trying to contact the dead.

The old office of Olmsted's firm looks as though the designers have just stepped out for lunch. Wooden paneling, wooden drafting tables, an old-fashioned typewriter. An old clock ticks on a wall. Framed on the walls hang original plans for almost every great park in the United States. Mamma comes here to worship.

Katie has shadows under her eyes like she's been up all night too. I wonder what she thinks about last night. She has her sketchbook out on her lap and a pencil in her fingers. It doesn't move.

I try to tell myself I want her to be drawing ghosts.

Wind rattles the windowpanes. Outside I can see Olmsted's front yard, which is a pocket-size version of the Ramble in Central Park: shadows, a shiver of sleety ice on the grass, light hitting a big tree.

Katie sits with the blank sketchbook in front of her, and I

try to call up Olmsted in my own way. Mamma is an expert on him, Olmsted has been a fourth at a lot of our meals. I should know him.

Why would he get involved with Perkins's schemes? He was supposed to be against slavery. He didn't think it worked. Not for moral reasons; he wrote that it cost four times more to produce anything with slave labor than with free workers.

But if believing in slavery meant being in with the Perkinses—in with the family of the first American millionaire, who could get him rich commissions—would Olmsted have been tempted?

Like Dad was tempted by Mamma's Brattle Street connections?

Katie's fingers are tight around the pencil. She shrugs and smiles apologetically at me. She doesn't want to draw anything. I'm the one who's pushing her.

From what Katie said, Olmsted got involved with the Perkins conspiracy around 1852. That would be just after he'd finished his book on English farming, just before the *New York Times* sent him South to write about plantations and slavery. If what Katie says is right, the reporting would have been a cover. Olmsted was really going south as a spy for Perkins, or to contact fellow slavers like the ones who would later finance the *Wanderer* and the *Clotilde*.

But nothing he wrote about plantations supported slavery.

Except the way he described us.

"What are you thinking?" Katie whispers to me.

"Olmsted said slavery was inefficient. Us simple happy darkies didn't have a reason to work, so we just sang and lazed around and strum' de banjo all de day long."

Katie focuses on me. "Is that tough?" she says. "To have the guy you're named after say things like that?"

Yeah, Katie. Mamma ignores that part of Olmsted's thinking.

"Yeah. But Olmsted wasn't easier on white Southerners. He thought the only pure human way to live was exactly the white Northern way." Like Mamma's family. "That was the point of Pinebank. Everyone was going to meet in the café and get to know each other. But the black folks would learn from the white folks, not them from us. There was no jazz in Olmsted's restaurant."

"I bet the Irish were going to learn too," Katie says.

"Yeah."

Why would Olmsted have got involved in something he didn't think would work?

Why did Dad marry Mamma?

Olmsted developed his ideas about slavery after he'd been to the South. After he was already implicated in the Perkins Bequest.

Katie looks out the window at the front yard, the area Olmsted called the Hollow: the gray lumps of Roxbury puddingstone, the vines, the looping path. She stands up and walks around the room, looking at the plans of his parks framed on the wall.

"His landscape is all like this." She clasps her fingers together and then swivels her wrists. "Twisty."

"Yeah." All Olmsted's paths curve. All his spaces, even the littlest ones, unfold to release a bigger space, wider inside and more complex. He had a mind like an origami master.

I wonder if she's getting something from him.

"Want to go outside?" She'll get more from the landscape.

A little wind whirls outside the front door, but down in the Hollow it's sheltered and the air is still. Dark vines smother the rocks. Katie walks along the winding paths, quivering and alert like a dowsing rod.

There are prettier girls at Brookline High, and saner girls, and girls I ought to like more, and girls who are a comfortable color, but not a one so alive. Not a one who makes me think so hard.

She deserves a better man than me.

"He's not *here* here," she says finally. "But the shapes? It's like we're walking in someone's head. It's funny. Weird. I mean . . . Making landscape like that. It's beautiful, but it's sort of like—" She looks around her at the famous little park. "Like advertising? For something?"

"Propaganda?"

"That's what I mean."

Maybe Katie doesn't see ghosts at all. Maybe she just knows people. The Hollow, Central Park, all those rambles and English gardens, are exactly like the inside of Olmsted's brain. His first book was about English gardens and he never got over them.

I like English gardens.

I like a white girl.

I remember what Dad said: We're influenced by whiteness without knowing it. Yeah. Like a fish is influenced by rivers.

I feel as though, if I stood still a moment, if I only allowed myself to stand still, the slaves would get to me. I would begin to know what it's like to be black. If I let those burning coals of slavery alight on my soul, if I let them burn me, I would know my soul through those scars.

I would be like Dad. Always angry.

I wouldn't like a white girl.

But I might marry one.

What is Dad's story with Mamma? Did he marry her for herself, once upon a time? Which self? The history-and-lit graduate student, before she discovered hard hats and shovels? The Brattle Street girl with a father who could get Dad into clubs?

Does Dad know about Olmsted? Does he suspect? That has to be part of it. Olmsted never concealed how he felt about us.

"Olmsted reminds me of the father of a girl I used to know?" Katie says. "A dentist? He hated Halloween, and he didn't want Emily to go trick-or-treating. But she always would find a way. So then it comes the year she gets her braces on, and he's home the day before Halloween with a *two-pound* bag of Skittles, which she loves, she's always sneaking them, and he says she can go out if she eats them all. Two pounds. It's like Olmsted saying look, here's a restaurant, here's a park, come on and enjoy them and let me show you how to think like I want."

"She ate the Skittles." I know about being the child of parents.

"She barfed so much she had to go to the hospital."

"But she went trick-or-treating."

Katie nods. "And ended up having a big problem with bulimia."

The fault isn't Katie's that I can't simply like her and not think about white and black. The fault is mine.

Nothing I do is entirely honest. Nothing I do is simple. I am not free.

"Yeah, maybe that's what Olmsted did," I say. "Maybe he was tricky. Maybe all the Perkins Bequest people were being tricky."

"How do you mean?"

"Suppose Perkins and Olmsted want to give the South its bag of Skittles and teach it a lesson. If slaves are bad for the South, the more slaves the South has, the worse off the South is, right? So Southerners want to import slaves again? Fine. Southerners want to send the *Wanderer* and the *Clotilde* to Africa? Fine. Perkins and Olmsted will help 'em, give 'em more slaves, give 'em all the sugar-candy slaves they can stuff in their mouths. If the South figures out slavery is bad for them, that's fine too. If not, the South's teeth will rot every year the slave trade lasts. And the Perkins gang will be patriots."

Katie nods. "And Perkins gets a ton of money *and* makes himself look good."

Is Katie my sugar candy, my bad-for-me white girl, who'll teach me I ought to love some good-for-me trophy sister? Am I doing that to myself? What am I doing to her? "They aren't even being conscious hypocrites. That kind of political thinking?

Even to itself it looks so smart and kind and helpful. Perkins must have thought he had a great idea. All the major Southern politicians' money comes from the near South, Virginia, where the plantations raise slaves for the Deep South." Kids. Fed like pigs. "Suppose slave imports are legal again? That money dries up. Less political money for the South, less Southern influence. Who gets the money instead? The people who import the cheap slaves. Perkins and Olmsted and their friends. They're rich and they're patriots and *they feel good about themselves.*"

Import. It's such a clean word.

"But they weren't importing candy. I can't let them feel good, Katie. People like that go to Hell and they think they're bound for Paradise. I will not *let* them feel good."

I can't let myself feel good.

I saw a bad boat accident once when I was a kid. A speedboat hit a sailboat, and both of them just flew apart, scattered all over the water. I was a kid, and it looked so much like a movie or a computer game. *This is so cool,* I remember thinking, *this is terrific.* I wouldn't have been surprised if a *Spider-Man* villain had shown up in a black yacht. It was all CGI and candy, and I could ignore that three people had just died, and I wanted to stuff my mouth with ignorance, because if I didn't, I would be very, very scared.

Import. The trade. Feel-better words. Some feeling good is just wrong.

Such a clean word, *girlfriend.* Use it and you know what you're doing. You're not a coward. You like her and you take her out for coffee and feed her sugar, and you stuff your head with ignorance and don't think she had a nervous breakdown last year and now she's seeing ghosts because of something you asked her to do. And you think you're up to being her boyfriend. If it weren't for the ghosts.

"What happened to Olmsted?" Katie asks.

He lost his mind.

We go and sit in the car with the engine running, in case Katie picks up anything. But she doesn't. Eventually, warm in the car and the sunlight, she falls asleep and I stare at her.

After I take her home, I drive over and look at Pinebank again, the landscape of the water and the house, the mindscape of Olmsted's brain. Olmsted wanted to keep this building, right here, this memory palace, an object to remind him. Of what? How white culture was naturally better than anything else? How he and his friends weakened the South with poisoned sugar, and made gold?

How the treasure is still there, ready to be used again?

Or was Pinebank his palace of ghosts? His reminder of the slaves he'd seen in the South? His reassurance that as long as he knew slavery was wrong, he wasn't really wrong to keep helping the slavers?

As I'm trudging back toward the parking lot, I stop and turn back. It's just dusk, and in among the trees I can see the peaked roofs that echo the pine trees, the perfectly placed windows in a house that belongs here.

And fuck it, I still think it's beautiful.

KATIE

LAW DOESN'T LIKE ME ANYMORE. He doesn't know it yet, I think, but we can both feel it. It's not because we kissed. That was so good.

It's because of the Other People.

Other ghosts pretty much stick to where they died. But the Other People know I see them, and they stick to me.

Law must feel them. Why shouldn't he get chills, and be afraid of them, and look at me like I'm something he doesn't recognize? That's how I feel.

I wanted to be normal. For a little while, I almost was.

On New Year's Eve, Phil and Lucy go to First Night and Law has to do something for Kwanzaa. If I were black like him, if I were an ordinary girl, would I be going with him to whatever it is? Phil and Lucy ask me if I mind staying home alone and I say no problem, it's all right. I make myself some popcorn and cocoa and put *Little Miss Sunshine* on the DVD.

It's no use. It's like being inside the apartment when I know the guy is hanging from the stairs outside. Like watching a horror movie and knowing that the monsters are just about to do something horrible to the girl. I'm just waiting, scared, waiting to be more scared.

I can't see them. But I can feel *I want, I want* like you hear that little hum from lightbulbs. You don't notice it until you do and then it drives you crazy.

What would they be like for Law? Like a bad smell. Like I'm a dog and I've rolled in something dead.

What do they want?

I go into my room. "Hey, Dad, come on, I need to talk to you."

Nothing.

It strikes me that I haven't seen him since Christmas. No. Since the day before Christmas, when I thought I'd sent the ghosts away.

"Dad!" I yell in a panic.

Nothing.

"Come on, Dad, you know I didn't mean you."

This isn't like him. Generally I only need to call him and he's right there.

"Dad. Please."

The faintest fog in a corner.

"Don't get all ghosty, I've got all the weird shit I need. I have to talk with you right now."

I can see right through him, but he's there.

He's there, but he's faint, worn. "You were right," he says. "Seeing me ain't good for you. You got to grow out of this and send me away for good."

"Dad, first I would never send you away, and second, I need a parent right now and you're it."

I tell him about the ghosts. He was always a good listener. With him there I have the guts to get out Lucy Rosen's sketchbook and show him what I saw. The pictures just flow out onto the page. George's little-boy hand on the Bible; the older men; and flowing and spreading out from them in all directions, pieces of faces in the dark like reflections in a pool of blood.

Broken faces. A bloody collapsed eye—

"I'm really scared of them, Dad."

What I mean to say is *Help me.*

"Honey," Dad says, "I'm no good at this."

"You think I am?" I want him to tell me what I need to do and how, and I want him to tell me how to make them go away.

I want to tell him about kissing Law. I want to kiss Law again, more than anything. But who would kiss something like me that smells of ghosts?

"I'm sorry, Katie."

And he fades away. He leaves me.

"Okay, Dad, I believe in ghosts. If you weren't real you wouldn't leave me right now, because I need you. Dad? Dad? Come on!"

But he's just not here.

On New Year's Day I text Law HAPPY NEW YEAR. ("Happy" is sort of dubious.) He texts back he's busy with his family again. He wishes me Happy New Year as an afterthought.

Dr. Petrucci gave us homework over the holidays. I sit down and start it to give myself something else to think about.

But what do you know, it's halfway through the year and halfway through American history, and we're starting on the causes of the Civil War.

Fugitive Slave Law, Kansas-Nebraska Act, blah blah blah. It's nothing real, not human real. I flip ahead in the book and see a picture in the text showing a slave auction. Everything looks so pretty, the lighting is worked out right and everything. I can't stand it. I get out the sketchbook Lucy Rosen gave me and begin to draw.

A shadowy dark room, a warehouse. Stifling. People are slumped on the floor all round the walls, panting. Some of them are wounded. I draw feet, sore and cracked and bleeding. The smell is awful: A guard leans out the doorway trying to get a breath. In the shadows, eyes turn up, mouths slump open. Outside the warehouse, in the sun, hunched silhouettes: women and children and old men crouching in a scrap of shade. I draw a hand begging water. It belongs to a woman who doesn't have anywhere else to go. The raiders burned her village. She's going to let herself and her children be enslaved so they'll be fed.

I draw a fat white man writing a list.

I draw a man pointing at the shadows, this one, that one.

The shadows stare at the man with the paper and pen.

Slavery: People are captured and taken away and never come back. It is happening to these people right now. The man who is writing is changing people to slaves.

A fat black man is pointing into the shadows. I write numbers on the page he holds, 1, 2, 3. Then I write a scribbled something next to the numbers, their names that they will never be called by again, that nobody knows but this fat man and the paper he writes on, their illegible real selves. The man's foot kicks ribs covered in shadowy skin. He pushes backs and shoulders into line. 1, 2, 3, 4, 5 . . .

A skeletal shadow reaches toward the paper. The fat black man hits a huddle of legs and arms. No. I have your names now. You don't have a name. You are a slave. You have a number.

A white hand drops a paper into a black iron-banded box.

A black hand reaches out for the paper as if it were a drink of water.

I have to text Law, even though I don't think he wants to hear from me, because I think I know what the ghosts want.

WERE SLAVES GIVEN NUMBERS INSTEAD OF NAMES?

They lost something when their real names were taken away. They want it back.

Law's not answering, so I Google "slave name" and get Afro-American name stuff and some ultracreepy bondage-and-discipline sites. "You don't even have the right to determine what you call yourself," one of the sites says. "You have to adapt to whatever your Master chooses to call you."

YES, Law texts me.

I know what the Other People want. I know it like I know their story.

They want to be who they were.

They want their names back.

January second, with *We want* humming in my head, I have to go back to school.

Brookline High is modern, with bright fluorescent lights. But there are dark places in the gym locker room, and it's really dark in the corners of the cafeteria where the lights don't reach.

And the lights hum.

We want . . .

I skip lunch and tell the gym teacher I have my period.

I skip history class too. I don't need to hear Dr. Petrucci talking about the causes of the Civil War.

I go home while it's still light. At least there's nobody on the stairs.

But in my e-mail there's an announcement, sent from Law's mom to all the volunteers who are distributing leaflets about Pinebank. An announcement from the Department of Parks and Recreation of the City of Boston.

Warrant Hearing on the Final Disposition of Pinebank.

They're ready to tear it down.

The Friends of Pinebank meet that night at the Mattisons' house. Law asks me to go and picks me up in his car. I sit close to him for protection against the darkness, not sure how welcome I am next to him. Law's mom comes in just as the meeting is starting. She projects John Wathne's pictures on the Mattisons' white walls. Mr. Mattison's face sags into tired lines. Dorothy Clark winces. Mrs. Mattison can't take the pictures of the collapsing floor; she goes into the kitchen to get cookies and cheese and grapes.

"We have one last chance to save Pinebank," Law's mom says when the lights come up. "How are we going to do it?"

Law piles up a plate with cookies and cheese and gives it to me. I feel like I do when Phil takes me out for ice cream because he can't think of anything better to do.

The National Association for Olmsted Parks has written to Mayor Menino, who's ignoring them. The Emerald Necklace Conservancy won't intervene. Pinebank is already on the National Register of Historic Places, the whole Emerald Necklace park area is, but it isn't helping. Dorothy Clark reads a list of neighbors who want it saved.

"We have one last meeting with the board," Law's mom says. "We must come up with something new."

I say the only thing I can think of.

"Mrs. Walker?" I say. "There's something in that house."

Everybody looks at me.

"I went inside. It's not as dangerous as it looks."

"You *went inside*?" Law's mother says. She looks past me, at Law. She's worried about him, not me.

"I was up on the second floor and down in the basement."

"You mustn't do that," Law's mom says. "You must stay out of that house. It truly is dangerous."

"In the basement I saw a really old-looking chest, like a little trunk? Is there any chance that the trunk could have something valuable in it?"

I know what it is, I want to say. It's their names. They want their names.

"We don't want something from Pinebank; we want the whole house," an old lady preservationist says.

"And we don't want people going in there and getting hurt," says Hugh Mattison.

"If anyone died in Pinebank it would be years before Boston would listen to us about the Carlton Street Footbridge," one of the men says.

"Don't you go anywhere near Pinebank," Mrs. Mattison says to me.

Mrs. Walker is still just staring at her son. She cares about the house, but that's nothing to how she cares about him. I know that look. When Mom was alive, she looked at me that way sometimes. Mrs. Walker would fight for Law the way Mom fought for her kids or for me.

She knows about Law and me. I'm a danger to him.

"Mrs. Walker, I didn't want to go into that house, but I want to save Pinebank as much as you do." I don't want to have Law go into Pinebank. I'm not nuts. I'm not stupid.

But I see things. The Mattisons' living room has big windows, and I see myself mirrored against the dark. Behind me, darkness on darkness, I see dead people's eyes.

"I don't want anybody to get hurt," I say to her. "But doesn't somebody have to do something?"

I used to have an uncle, Dad's uncle Norry. He was a mean old drunk, and eventually his liver just rusted out, but when he was alive he had one answer for everything. Mom complained that one of her clients' parents wasn't taking care of her kid? "Sue 'em," Norry said. The landlord didn't fix the heat? "Sue the bastard." Drunkle Norry had spent some time in prison, another thing that would thrill Law's parents, and he'd read every law book in the prison library. According to him, he would have passed the bar if he hadn't spent so much time leaning against the bar.

"How about," I say, "how about somebody sues Boston and keeps them from tearing Pinebank down?"

"Who could do that?" Mrs. Walker asks.

"I don't know, maybe Boston was supposed to keep it repaired or something. Anyone can sue anybody about anything." I'm glad Norry never visits me, but he's coming in handy right now.

"Boston had money to maintain it," Mr. Mattison mutters.

"Are there still Perkinses alive?" I ask. "Could they sue Boston or something?"

"Does anyone know them?" Mr. Mattison says. "I tried to contact them, but—"

"Dorothy Perkins Perkins," says Law's mom. "The family historian. She married her cousin. They live on the North Shore. My husband interviewed her when Seaburg was writing the biography. But I'm afraid she's just not interested. I tried to contact her through the Athenaeum."

"Worth trying again," Mr. Mattison says. "Anything's worth trying."

Somebody suggests Law's dad should call her; Law and his mom both shake their heads at once.

"That was a good idea," Law says when we're in his car again. "It won't work, though."

"Law, the chest, I think I know what's in it. I know what the Other People want."

I tell him about the story I saw. "When the slaves were sold in Africa, I saw a man writing down their names on a list. And then they got numbers instead. Not even different names like Walker, but numbers. They want their real names back. Law, we should skip school tomorrow and go see Dorothy Perkins."

"That's not the way these things work," Law says. "You find out someone who knows her, and you get an introduction and write her. And 'you' is someone official and adult. Not us."

I just look at him. "How much time do we have? How much good is your website doing?"

"It's getting hits," he says defensively.

"Sure, but what's it doing, what are the Friends doing? Do you want to go into Pinebank and get that chest? You don't, and your mom doesn't want you to, and I sure don't. So we've got to talk to this Mrs. Perkins."

He thinks it over and nods.

Law

Mamma calls me into her office that evening. "Your friend seems like a pleasant enough girl," she says. With Dad that would be a prelude to *but*.

"But," she says. "She seems impetuous, Law. I appreciate her collecting signatures for Pinebank. I don't appreciate her going inside. Did you know she was going to do it?" She looks at my face. "I take that as a yes."

"Not when she did it. Afterward."

"It was tremendously reckless, Law. I want you to promise me that you will never do anything of the kind."

I look for a way I can promise this without meaning it, and take too long.

"Don't you be reckless," she says sharply. "You're the only child we have." She looks at me hard over her reading glasses. "What, Law?"

"There really is something in Pinebank."

"There's a story about every abandoned house," Mamma says. "Treasure chests. Bodies. Ghosts and murders. You know better."

"I think the box she saw has something to do with the Perkins Bequest. I think the money's still there."

"Oh, Law, I would love to think Thomas Handasyd Perkins put an enormous amount of money in a chest in the cellar of Pinebank. But I don't believe he did. Certainly not on this Katie Mullens's word."

On a ghost's word.

"It's an empty trunk, Law. Or an old wooden crate. You will *not* go in there. Law, you haven't promised me yet."

"I promise," I mutter. "But, Mamma? There's more than a treasure in Pinebank. It's about Olmsted."

For a moment Mamma just stares at me bleakly.

"Of course it is," she says gently. "But nobody cares about Olmsted. Not enough to save Pinebank."

KATIE

Someday I'm going to learn to drive, and then I'll just go away. Where I drive to, there'll be sunlight and beaches and I'll be normal again.

"And there won't be any ghosts at all," I say to Law.

"Sounds good," he says.

In the car, it's almost like before the Other People. Heading north from Boston, we crack the windows and I sing. "Going for a ride, going for a ride, going for a ride in the car car." Then I feel stupid because Law doesn't like me anymore, and I shut up. Law plugs his iPod into the radio and some guy with a voice like hard times sings a car song too.

> *Who been driving my Terraplane*
> *For you since I've been gone . . .*

"Have you got a plan?" Law says. "I don't have a plan. We've got to have a plan. We can't blow this."

"What did you tell Mrs. Perkins?"

"I'm writing a paper about Perkins as a collector."

"Okay," I say, "and then we ask her about the Perkins Bequest."

"And then what?" Law says.

"Then we work toward telling her about saving Pinebank."

And if Pinebank is saved, somebody's going to find the treasure chest for George, but it won't have to be me.

"It's that 'work toward' part I'm not seeing, Katie."

Off 95 the road gets small and winds through old towns, past big houses with one or two miserly lights on. Dorothy Perkins Perkins's house is set back from the road and guarded by giant old bushes. Their leaves are cracked and curled stiff against the cold. When Law cuts the engine, the silence makes a hiss and rattle in my ears.

The paint is peeling off the shutters. A piece of the wiggly roof trim is falling off.

"You see the size of those rhododendrons?" Law says. It strikes me as funny because I'm so nervous, and I giggle.

The door is opened by a tall old black woman in a maid's uniform. "You are expected," she says, as if she's telling our fortunes and we're going to die. "May I take your coats?"

I keep my sweater and I'm glad, because it's freezing inside Mrs. Perkins's house. We follow the maid through room after room. I look around to see what sort of woman Mrs. Perkins is.

Her house reminds me of what Pinebank looked like inside. Oil paintings hang three high in the hall, surrounding two big paintings, a man with a white wig and an old woman in a dark dress. A staircase with a massive oak baluster winds up toward the second floor. In the dining room a long table is set with twelve place settings. The sideboard is full of old silver. Painted blue and white and yellow plates hang on the walls.

But everything is dusty and shabby. The carpet under the dining room table has a hole in it. The china doesn't all match; two of the bowls are white plastic.

Mrs. Perkins might be interested in gold.

The old black woman swings open a massive door. "Miss Katherine Mullens, Mr. Law Walker," she announces.

"Florence, you may bring tea."

Mrs. Perkins is tall. Her hair is pinned up stiffly over her square, sad face, a hairstyle like in pictures of antique ladies. She's wearing lipstick and a gold Christmas mistletoe pin with pearls for the berries, real gold and real pearls, you can tell, but her red velvet skirt and twin set and even her shoes are fifty years out of date. She doesn't act poor, but it's as if she wears those clothes and those shoes and that pin because she always has worn them. I think the pin must have been her mother's. For a moment I see her as if she were a ghost.

She's sitting at Thomas Handasyd Perkins's desk.

When it was his, it was neater. Now it's covered with papers and magazines, *Genealogy* and *Antiques*. The walls of her room are the same dusty green as his office, and there are even more paintings than there used to be, all of dead people. It's not the same room, of course; that room was burned. But it really is the same desk with the same green leather top, except now the green is faded to dusty gray. Sometime between the time I saw it and the fire, the furniture must have got moved to some other Perkins house, and, wow, here it is.

"Do sit down," Mrs. Perkins says. "How can I help you with your research?" I sit down in the same leather chair George and I hid behind a hundred and fifty years ago. Mrs. Perkins gets up from the desk (she is straight-backed but slow, I think she has arthritis) and sits carefully down on a sofa facing us. A yellow sofa, pale faded parchment-yellow brocade. When Law and I saw it in the portrait of Thomas Handasyd Perkins, it was brilliant as gold coins. But maybe it was George's evil grandpa sitting on it that made it shine so. With Mrs. Perkins it's only doing its pale best, like the reflected light of the moon.

"You're Charlie Walker's son, aren't you?" Mrs. Perkins asks Law, and pats the fragile sofa gently, like an old dog's head. "Ted and I have met your father at the Athenaeum often. You may sit here if you wish. I trust you recognize it. Someday the Athenaeum must have this, I suppose. It is all such a worry, making sure that everything goes to the proper place. Historic old things are a great responsibility. Ted and I feel completely unequal."

Law has already whipped out his notes, giving no sign of any thoughts he might have about stuff and who earned it.

They talk about collecting. "Thomas Perkins was a great collector." Mrs. Perkins gets up to show us the room. On one wall is an old-fashioned plate with a scene of a man giving flowers to a girl, with gilding and painted flowers all round them. It's been broken and mended and put in a wood frame. "You know Thomas collected Revolutionary memorabilia. Thomas Jefferson ate from this plate. The steps of John Hancock's house are still at Pinebank." On a shelf is a little broken white clay pipe. "Benjamin Franklin's." There are jeweled gold earrings that Thomas Handasyd Perkins brought his wife home from Paris, and a clock carved all over in ivory dragons that he brought from China, with one of the dragons' horns missing and some pieces glued back on. Mrs. Perkins touches everything with her knobby fingers. A little color comes into her cheeks, as if having this stuff makes her a pirate and explorer and millionaire too.

They are really pretty cool. I wonder whether she thinks about slaves. But the stuff is cool.

On the wall, among the family paintings, I see a little faded picture, not a photograph but a ghost-thing, a negative of a photograph of a ghost in a mirror. Surrounding it, like a cloud under the glass, is a pressed spray of faded brown flowers. Mrs. Perkins sees me looking at it. "Oh," she says, "that is my great-great-grand uncle, Thomas Perkins's grandson. The flowers are from his funeral. Poor young man. He was mentally challenged."

She tilts the picture so I can see better.

George.

In the picture he's in his twenties, as old as he was ever going to be, but he looks just the same, friendly and eager and responsible. "He never had a proper funeral," Mrs. Perkins says, as if she has said it every time she sees George's face and those flowers. "He was burned alive, there wasn't a body."

"He died in Pinebank," I say.

"Yes, in Pinebank. Poor boy."

Right then the tea comes in. The old black lady serves us pale tea in little flowered teacups with funny handles. The tea comes with a plate of pink cookies so old they've lost most of their color. Law and I each bite into one and look at each other and hide the rest under the saucer.

"Mrs. Perkins," Law says, "I'd like to ask you about Pinebank," and he goes off talking about it, how Olmsted wanted it, how it fits into the landscape, and he talks about its history and the history of the Perkins family. Every time he talks about her family history, Mrs. Perkins nods a little.

"Do you know," he says, "the City of Boston wants to tear it down?"

"Yes. A great shame. There has been a Pinebank for two hundred years," Mrs. Perkins murmurs, right at home with two hundred years. I'm not over her still having the flowers from George's funeral in 1868.

"When your family gave Pinebank to Boston, didn't they mean to preserve it for Olmsted's landscape?"

"I do believe so. I would have to look it up."

"There might have been a proviso for ensuring that," Law says. He has found the right word, "proviso," which is so Law.

Mrs. Perkins looks down at her hands.

"Have you ever thought of requiring them not to tear it down?" he asks.

"Requiring it?" she says. "You mean, by asserting some sort of *ownership* over Pinebank?"

Law nods and sits silent, letting her work it out. We don't either of us dare to breathe.

"That would be rather *rude*," she murmurs. She is tempted; I can see it. Her cheeks go pink again. There is a little pirate in her.

But not enough. She gets up slowly and goes over to the desk, the hundred-and-fifty-year-old desk that is too big for her and that is crowded with all the things she is doing because of all the stuff she has, all the *Genealogy* and *Antiques* and the events calendar for the Boston Athenaeum.

"My dear Mr. Walker," she says. "When I was younger, it was much more exciting to have responsibilities. The responsibilities go on and the fun slips away. I am seventy-two and Ted is nearly eighty. What would we do with Pinebank if Boston gave it back to us? There would be enormous taxes to pay, and no doubt it needs renovations." She has no idea. "I would be like a dog that has chased a truck and caught it. I am too set in my ways, I am afraid. No. It would be too much."

Come on, George, tell me what to say to her.

"There's a Friends group," Law says. "They'd fund-raise."

She sits silent, pursing her lips.

"Mrs. Perkins," I break in, "there's a chest in the house. A box. I've seen it."

On your desk, I want to say. I want to tell her this, make her part of all this.

"It's this big, it's black with iron bands around it. It belongs to your family. To you."

This is Stuff. She understands Stuff. "How could there be anything of ours there still?"

Law is glaring at me, but I improvise. "It had Thomas Handasyd Perkins's name painted on it. It belonged to him. It could be full of gold and jewels, or plates like the one Thomas Jefferson ate from, or the candle that George Washington gave him."

"No," Mrs. Perkins says, "that is in this room. Would you like to see it?"

"Yes," Law says. *Shut up,* he mouths at me.

"Mrs. Perkins, I think I know what's in that chest, I think it's valuable. It might be enough to save Pinebank and restore it. I think it's the Perkins Bequest."

I know the exact moment when I lose her. She smiles. She would be laughing at me, except that she's way too well brought up. She smiles and there's a silence and I don't know what to say. "Oh no," Mrs. Perkins says softly. "It is certainly not the Perkins Bequest."

She knows what the Perkins Bequest is.

I have to keep going. "It has *something* important in it. It was what George went back for. He was given it to take care of, because it was part of a secret. He looked after it. He *died* for it."

And I have no idea what it might be. Except a list of names. A story. A story about slavery, which Mrs. Perkins probably doesn't want told.

Mrs. Perkins stands up and looks at me, and now she is not smiling.

"Miss Mullens, you appear to know my great-great-grand uncle's name, though I do not recall telling it to you. I am old but not stupid. Apart from that, you know a great deal that is not true. George Perkins was much loved, but no one would have put him in charge of anything of value. He would certainly not have been involved with the Perkins Bequest, which was a simple charitable trust, wound up long ago. I was one of the last trustees. I can assure you there is nothing important left in Pinebank. I wonder if we might finish now? I have further things to do this afternoon."

And, quick as she can say "Florence, please show them out," we're back in the hall, with the thick doors firmly closed between Mrs. Perkins and us. The old black lady, Florence, gets us our coats and helps us on with them and even takes my gloves out of my pocket and gives them to me, and we're outside in the dusk and cold.

"Shit," says Law.

"I'm sorry."

"She wasn't going to help Pinebank anyway." He opens the car door for me and goes round and slides into the driver's seat.

Whether she was or not, I've lost our chance. Ghosts buzz like flies in my ears. *We want.*

Yeah, well, I want too and so does Law. Law wants Pinebank. And I've just blown it for him. And I want a normal life and I've just lost that.

And I've lost Law.

He drives for a while and we don't say anything. The heater

fan buzzes like a ghost and stops. Law hits the glove compartment with the flat of his hand and swears.

"Now we have to deal with cutting school," he says.

"It's okay. I've done it before."

"I haven't."

He pulls into the parking lot of a little strip mall and phones his house. I watch him in the red neon light from a package store. He leaves a message (for his mom, not his dad), saying that he and I have gone off to do some work for Pinebank and telling her pretty much to the minute when he'll get home. He reminds me of someone, his handsome, serious face and wide mouth, and it comes to me suddenly that he's like George. Law is smart and George is dead, but being responsible matters. He's a little like George too because he's got more responsibility than he knows what to do with.

Oh, I like him so much.

He kissed me once, but I lost him.

"I'm sorry," I say. "I made her think about the box and not Pinebank. You were doing fine. I was the one who screwed up."

"Mamma will figure we went off and screwed up everyone's chance with Mrs. Perkins just out of being irresponsible."

Which is what I did.

He starts the car again, and I watch for the entrance to 95.

"Mrs. Perkins knows what the Perkins Bequest was," I say.

"And she doesn't think it's important, and it's all spent anyway."

"Maybe she doesn't really know what it was. Maybe she'll

be curious. Maybe she'll try to get the box."

Not her. She has arthritis. She'll think about it, but it'll be too far outside her habits, too far to drive, too much to ask her old husband to do, and who else would she ask? Somebody from the Daughters of the American Revolution?

"Never mind. What happens if the house gets torn down?" Law says. "What happens to you?"

I huddle down into my coat. I don't want to think about it. I feel a wordless undertow from them: *Turn back. Turn back. Make her do something. Go to Pinebank, do something. . . .*

"If Boston tears down the house, as far as I can tell, Law, they might as well tear down me."

"Don't say that."

"Yeah, well, what am I going to do? I could take a shovel and try to dig out the basement of Pinebank once they fill it in. I could be homeless and live in the park."

I could go crazy full-time, Law. You know that. I jam my hands in my pockets, because they're shaking and I don't want him to see. I'm not going to get much more time with him. I want what I have.

In the left pocket I feel something stiff. A card. I don't remember putting anything in my pocket.

I pull it out and turn it over, and I can see writing.

"What's that?" Law asks.

He swings the car over into the parking lot of a fast-food place, punches the reading light over the windshield, and looks over my shoulder.

It's a small, thick piece of notepaper, slightly browned at the edges, with one line of neat handwriting:

Please be careful. Stay away from that house. It is dangerous.

And then, on a line by itself, as if she thought about not signing it, but then decided she was better than that:

Florence Wilson

Mrs. Perkins's maid.

And she's written her phone number.

I have an appointment with Mrs. Morris, my shrink, the next afternoon, but I tell her I have a family party and blow her off, and Law drives me to Dorchester to see Mrs. Wilson.

Mrs. Wilson lives in a third-floor walkup off Blue Hill Ave. with her daughter and her daughter's two children. Mrs. Wilson introduces them and then nods at them, and the daughter and the two boys disappear into the bedrooms like mice. I get the feeling they do this a lot; Mrs. Wilson may be a maid in Manchester-by-the-Sea, but here she's queen. She sits us at the kitchen table and offers us hot chocolate and cookies. Hers are lots better than Mrs. Perkins's. She knows they're better. She's not trying to show off, but she knows.

"Now." She sits down on the other side of the table from Law and me. "You will tell me how you know about that chest."

I nibble round the edges of my chocolate chip cookie while I think what to say.

"For true," she says. "No stories."

"Why's that chest important," I ask her, "if it's just some

piece of junk that doesn't belong to the Perkinses?"

She just sits with her hands folded on the kitchen table and waits for us to say something. I look at Law. Law looks at me.

"Perhaps this will help," Mrs. Wilson says. She gets up and gets a box down from the cabinet over the stove. She sets it in front of me.

It's a Ouija board. For talking to ghosts.

I nearly giggle.

"You have been playing around with one of these," Mrs. Wilson says. "Or something similar. I think so. You have been trying to contact spirits. With something like this."

I shake my head. As if I needed some piece of cardboard. But how does she know about the ghosts? "What makes you think that, Mrs. Wilson?"

"If you don't say what you've been doing, I can't help you," Mrs. Wilson says. She sits back and folds her hands and looks at us.

I stare at the Ouija board. The board is covered with fake occult symbols, a crescent of letters, and the two words "Yes" and "No." There's a little plastic table that's supposed to move around the board and point to letters and spell out a message.

I try to decide how much I want to tell her.

That's easy. Excuse me but yeah, I am seeing horrible ghosts all the time? And they aren't just at Pinebank?

I remind myself I need help.

Law looks at his shoes.

Time goes by.

"What did you mean, Katie's in danger?" Law says, and at the same time I say, "What sort of help?"

They both look at me.

"If I were trying to contact spirits," I say. "Through a Ouija board. Or anything like that. What help could I get?"

"You need to keep away from things like that, miss."

Sure. How? I wait for her. The Ouija board sits on the table between us.

What sort of person keeps a Ouija board in her kitchen?

Someone who uses it.

I put my hand on the board. It's warm from being above the stove.

"I see hurt," Mrs. Wilson says. "Hurt is following you. Hurt, danger, and death."

"I sort of know that."

"In that house."

"I still have to get the box out."

Mrs. Wilson shakes her head.

"I promised. Look, the house, Pinebank? You're right. It's probably going to get torn down unless your Mrs. Perkins does something. There's one more meeting and one more chance to save it, next week, but that's it. And I promised."

"Who'd you promise?" she asks.

Um.

"Who'd you promise? Not Mrs. Perkins, not this boy here, not me. Who'd you promise, it's so important you risk your precious life?"

I touch the Ouija board table with my forefinger, and it slides a little.

I know about Ouija boards. They aren't real. Everybody's hands shake a little, and the table (I remember, *planchette*) is light and the board is slippery, so the planchette goes skating around the board. Once you decide it's saying something, what you expect pushes it in the direction you expect.

"You want to talk to the person I promised?" I ask her.

The slave ghosts probably don't speak English, and George isn't here. But I can push a little plastic table as well as anyone.

"You don't play around with the spirits," warns Mrs. Wilson.

"I'm not playing." I dare you.

I look right in her eyes. She does believe. She wrote me that note, and she's the one talking about spirits.

She looks normal enough. Apart from getting right to the point about ghosts. But maybe she sees things too.

"Uh-huh," Mrs. Wilson says, "uh-huh," as if she were saying *uh-oh*, but she shoves the Ouija board until it's between us on the kitchen table. She gets up and turns down the lights with a dimmer switch and sits down. She puts her hands on one edge of the planchette, lightly, like a pianist. I put mine on the other side.

"No sort of work for a Christian woman," Mrs. Wilson mutters, and then the planchette begins to move.

"You're not trying to push now?" she asks me.

I give it a little push toward *G*. "No, ma'am."

E.

O.

There's a push from the other side, and it swoops and hovers around NO, NO, NO.

"Is somebody there?" I ask, just like a psychic in a horror movie. My whole experience of psychics is from horror movies. I push the planchette back toward *R*, but Mrs. Wilson is shoving it too.

NO.

I give it a big push back toward *R* but the planchette is stuck like gum on NO. Mrs. Wilson has stronger fingers than me.

"We are asking you," she says now, chiming in. "This foolish girl wants to find a chest in that house."

NO, says the Ouija board.

"No what? Who's talking?" I say.

NO, NO, NO, then YES.

"Yes I should go?" I say.

"No, you shouldn't," Law mutters.

"Who is it wanting her to go?" Mrs. Wilson asks. "Anyone with her good in mind?"

Now I can actually feel Mrs. Wilson pushing it back toward NO. Her fingers are flexing, just a little.

"There's no one good wanting you to go."

"No fair, Mrs. Wilson, you're cheating."

"Doing no such thing. It wants to say no of its own nature."

I take my hands away for a moment, and it bucks and slides back toward NO, she's pushing it so hard.

She takes her fingers off, caught, and I lay mine back on.

She lays hers back on. Neither of us pushing now, or so gently that—

It's beginning to move.

It circles, as if it's looking around. It moves, slowly, slowly, toward a letter. Not *R. K.* Around the circle, sniffing a moment at every letter. *A.* Back down the crescent. *T.* I'm expecting *I* next, but it glides to *E.*

K A T E Y. K A T E Y. K A T E Y K A T E Y K A T E Y faster and faster—

Mrs. Wilson looks at it triumphantly and takes her hands away. I do too. I swear, for a moment the planchette moves by itself before it slides to a stop.

"You're wanting you to go," Mrs. Wilson says. "Only you. Nobody but you."

"That's not how I even spell my name."

"It doesn't matter if there are spirits or not or they can spell or not," Law says, "that house isn't safe."

I put my hands flat on my lap, away from that planchette. "I don't believe in this, okay?" I say. "But there is a box, and there is a secret, and something that some people need, and there's somebody who's been looking after it an awful long time, and he can't stop. Unless I help, or your Mrs. Perkins, or *somebody* helps, he's going to be stuck forever looking after something that'll never be found. And he won't be the only one stuck. I will too, and so will all those people. Come on, Mrs. Wilson. If you believe in stuff like this at all, if you believe in spirits, come on, if you even want to help me, you have to *do* something. Now."

Mrs. Wilson stands up. "Nothing I can do."

"Will you talk to Mrs. Perkins? At least? Please?"

"Miss Mullens? Let the dead rest. I can't help them. You can't. What I can do," she says, "is help you. Warn you. You," she says to Law. "If she don't have enough sense to keep out of that place, you keep her out. You hear?"

In the lights, in the puddles on the streets, in the ice and the reflections on the windshield, I see darkness, I hear cries and muttering. A gleam off a pair of eyes. The palm of a reaching hand. Glimpses out of the corner of my eye. I can smell that awful smell again, dirt and sweat and infected wounds.

You don't want to see us. But you will, more and more, you will. . . .

LAW

ON THE WAY BACK WE STOP AT SIMCO'S ON THE BRIDGE. I park the car on the inbound side and stand in line to pick up three of their foot-long hot dogs, one for Katie and two for me. Through the window she stares at me. She's about the only white face on Blue Hill Ave.

"With sauerkraut or without?" I slide into the seat next to her. "Eat." She shakes her head. "Yeah. Really. Eat. They're good, best dogs in Boston."

I can't do anything about this whole thing but give out food.

I start the car and drive down Blue Hill Ave., center of Dorchester. On a Saturday night, even in the cold hangover of January, the homefolk are out in force. At a red light, a car full of hood rats and hip-hop pulls up next to us. I see fingers stabbing from the backseat toward us, the paleboy and his white trophy girl. They turn the radio up to ramming speed and roll down the window. From the other side a drunk maneuvers toward my car, pushing his hand forward for a dollar bill. The light changes and I slide out from between them, turn left onto Morton Street, take a deep breath.

"What was going on at Mrs. Wilson's?"

Katie, oblivious to the Blue Hill scene, wipes her eyes and nose with her knuckles. "Mrs. Wilson was trying to push the planchette, and so was I, and then—" She swallows. "The KATEY, KATEY, KATEY, it was them. Couldn't you smell them?"

"They were there? In her kitchen?"

"They're everywhere, Law. What happens if Pinebank goes and I didn't get the box out? *What happens?* Do I see them all my life? I think I do. *What do I do?*"

I'm driving by the cheap gas on Casey Highway and my tank's low. I pull into the station. A black man filling a junker car looks at my Geo Storm, peers through the window, sees Katie, opens his mouth to say something. I drive through and keep going.

"You think that seeing ghosts makes you different?" I say.

"Well, yeah," Katie says.

I drive on for a few blocks without saying anything until we reach one of those magic zones between neighborhoods where nobody would pay attention to you if you were driving a neon pink Bradley tank and your girlfriend had tentacles. I pull over by the side of a dark road.

In the dark, on a strange street in a different town, it's easier to talk to her.

"This is between you and me. Ghosts? When I was a kid, I was—don't take this wrong—I was afraid of black people."

I still am. "Not all of us, not Dad's kind"—this is a lie—"but people like the Wilsons, the folks on Blue Hill Ave. Superfly. Badass. Homies with the wide pants and the do-rags. I felt like if I spent too much time around them, I'd end up talking street and playing pickup basketball while my grades went south. I'm afraid of all the bad things that happen in our heads because of our history in America." All the slave thoughts. All the trophy-gathering. All the awards in our front hall and the pictures of famous people in Dad's office. "And this was not just me, this was a message I was being given by Mamma and Dad."

Will Katie understand?

"Katie, it was pretty depressing in that apartment. Grandma's a housekeeper, daughter works at Wal-Mart or someplace. Not a man in sight is more than twelve years old. Look at a black man and most white Americans see lack of education, lack of respect, lack of pride. I am proud of being black, but let me tell you, I see those ghosts, I feel those ghosts, and I am not proud of them and I don't want them."

I'm trying to give her something to hold on to. But I hear Dad in me. Dad, my successful dad, who is so priggish about my doing anything that doesn't automatically spell success. Mamma, who wants a trophy girlfriend for me.

"You know what?" Katie says, angry. "Those persons you're afraid of? They're me." She turns toward me. "'Lack of education?' You should have seen my dad, he was lucky he got through high school. Mom went to college but it was no Harvard. We live in Whiskey Point. Just about in the projects.

Your Walker was sold for a lot of money but not to my folks, my folks couldn't have bought a potato. Don't think your dad doesn't know that about me."

"You're not black. White people look at people my color and they think I'm in reform school. When Dad was first at Harvard, the first class he taught? Some student thought he was the custodian."

"America's prejudiced," Katie says, "I know that. Against black people and poor people. Big surprise. But you're talking about history and, Law? I'm talking about seeing things in every dark corner for the rest of my life."

"Listen. I haven't got to what I meant to say. *You can live with it if you have to.* I'm not being hard. Not harder than I have to be. We live with it. I'm telling you. You can live with it. You have to, Katie. Everybody lives with it."

I look in my rearview mirror and see nothing: perhaps the ghost of the police car that stopped me the first day I had my license.

Reparations, I think. The reparations African Americans have to make, we have to make to ourselves. We have to emancipate ourselves; white people can't do it. Dad's looking for reparations to change himself. Not Katie.

So why does she have to see slaves? Why does she have to live with it?

Why do I?

Where's my emancipation? How do I get it?

Where's hers?

"I don't want to live with them. This is not some metaphor out of English class. I want someone to go inside the house and get the chest out," Katie says. "That's what they want and George and I want, too. But if nobody else does it, I have to do something and get it over with and not have to see them anymore."

"I want it too." Katie, you don't know how much. "I don't know how to say this any way except the old-fashioned way. I want to lay their spirits."

Katie nods, yes.

"But there has to be some other way than killing us both in that house."

"Thursday night, that's the last meeting," she objects. "And after that you know Boston is going to tear down Pinebank as fast as they can."

This is all I've got, so it'll have to work.

"I'm going to talk at that meeting," I tell her.

She looks at me and doesn't say anything, but her expression might as well say *What good will that do?*

I shake my head and laugh, not happily. "Dad's been showing me for years how to pitch a speech. I can give the speech I should have written for the Walker Prize. Dad beat me down and I sent in the speech he wanted. I should have written what I wanted. Thursday night I'm going to give my speech."

Yeah. Dad is going to speak at that meeting too. He said he would if Mamma did. He sure will if I do. And I'll have to speak against Dad. The Voice of His People.

For a slaver's house.

"I care about that house. Maybe I shouldn't, but I can talk about Pinebank because I do care. Katie? Let me do what I can before either of us tries anything else."

She looks at me, assessing me.

"Okay," she says. "I promise not to go back into Pinebank until after the meeting. But, Law? Make it good, because after that, I have to."

I have one more thing to give, something I don't want to give, but I have to, or be a coward all my life.

"After that," I say, "we go in together."

KATIE

THAT NIGHT LUCY AND PHIL GO OUT on a date and leave me home alone. I almost cry like a kid, *Don't leave me.* They trust me. I've been nice, I'm in good shape. They're in love and they don't care.

That evening I finish filling my new sketchbook full of pictures of the Other People.

I can't see them as whole people, but I'm beginning to see them more clearly. A closeup of a burned-off ear. The earhole is still there, clotted and oozing pus. A little baby's hand reaching for his mother. Feet chopped half off to keep people from running. I can see the splintered bones—

They smell of sweat and dirt, blood and cooking meat.

I can almost hear them. The memory of a scream.

After a while I put fresh batteries in my bike lamp and take off for Pinebank. I am not happy going out into the dark, but I'd rather do anything than draw them and think about them.

It's freezing cold, the kind of cold where your eyes hurt. I park the bike in the bushes, in among the branches and the fallen leaves. "George?"

No reply.

"George!"

I walk up to the fence and put my face up against the mesh. What is he, asleep? Ghosts don't sleep, do they? I can see Thomas Perkins's office. For a moment I think something is looking out the window, something that smells like burned flesh and blood.

Then I hear footsteps behind me.

But they're human, two shadows, crunching and mashing their way through the frozen grass. I drop down into the underbrush, flat on the ground, and swallow my heart.

"Gold in that house?" says the taller shadow.

"I tell you, Leroy. Ma Wilson told me to go fetch it. Her old white lady wants it. Ma Wilson says gold coins maybe. Treasure maybe."

"Tyler, man, you know the meaning of probation? That's what I'm on."

"It belongs to Ma Wilson's white lady," Tyler says. "Not like stealing."

"Gold coins, my ass."

"You want *me* to go in?" Tyler mutters. "I'm too fat, man."

Mrs. Wilson sent them? Because Mrs. Perkins asked? There are two of them, both about my age. Tyler is one of those big, sweaty, cushiony kids. He's wearing a baseball cap and a hoodie and a Red Sox jacket. Leroy is maybe a foot taller than he is, draped in an old man's wool coat, wearing it open like he's warm.

In the yellow lights around Pinebank, their skin is blacker than black.

"You go in," Leroy scoffs. "Sure you go in."

"You know about finding stuff," Tyler says, looking up at Leroy. "If a house got stuff in it, you find it. You do, man. You got a reputation."

"Yeah, me, my reputation. You gonna serve my time for me?" Leroy says, but at the same time he's backing away from the fence. He looks up at it, narrows his eyes, and then jumps at it; he's up and over like a squirrel before gravity can catch up with him.

He's going in? He's going to take the box out? For Mrs. Perkins?

"Give me the crowbar, man." Tyler hands it to him through the mesh. Leroy goes around the corner of the house where I can't see him.

The roof could fall in on him like Law is threatening it's going to.

That's all right. I actually think this. Leroy is just some black guy, and Mrs. Wilson sent him, and Mrs. Perkins isn't going to help, she just wants the gold back. I'm not responsible for Leroy. So the roof falls in on him. Worst case, they have to dig him out and they find the treasure and Menino spends it to restore Pinebank and the ghosts go away and I'm safe and normal and maybe Law will like me again.

Worst case, Leroy's dead.

I actually think that. That actually goes through my brain.

I hear a screech from inside. Nails being pried out of plywood, over the cellar door.

Just some black guy. He's a thief. He's on probation.

And I sit there, crouched in the underbrush, waiting for the rumble of the burned beams giving way. If I got up and warned him and Tyler, they'd be desperate and they'd do something to me. Rape. Murder probably.

If somebody's going to get hurt, better them than me.

Thomas Perkins must have thought something like that. *They don't count as much as we do.*

I'm not like that. I don't think like that when I look at a black kid.

So I have to stand up and call to them.

I half get up, but not all the way, because I'm scared.

"He's *close*," George says behind me.

"George!"

"He put his hand right next to the secret place," George says. "He could *lean* on it and it would *open*."

Tyler turns toward us; he's heard me. I hunch down, watching through the stalks and dead leaves. Tyler pulls something out of his jacket pocket, *oh shit, a gun*, but it's a flashlight. Light slices down the side of Pinebank: red brick, white terra-cotta trim, a window frame scrawled with graffiti. Tyler pokes the light beam into the bushes, toward us. George fades like smoke in sunlight.

"What you doing, fool?" says Leroy to Tyler from the window in the office. "You're getting the police here? Is that your plan?"

He's safe.

No thanks to me.

Tyler clicks off the light.

"What you find, Leroy?"

"Nothing."

"White girl said she saw a treasure chest."

"You been smoking it, man. Don't I find what's in a house if it's in the house? Ain't that my reputation?"

I'm getting my night eyes back. The fence *spangs* like a metal coil pulled and snapped, and Leroy drops down next to Tyler.

"Coulda been," Tyler mutters.

"Coulda been coulda been. Always coulda been with you, my man. Buy me a beer."

They saunter off, down toward the pond, scuffing their sneakers in the dead leaves and the grass. They're human again, and my age. They aren't going to hurt me, and I'm not hurting them.

And I know how to find the secret place.

George says Leroy put his hand against something—a wall? A piece of the staircase?—and almost pushed a secret door open.

The cellar isn't that big. I can find a secret door hand-high in it.

So there, Mrs. Wilson and Mrs. Perkins. You wanted Tyler and Leroy to find the chest and the treasure, but it's going to be me.

My stomach sinks.

It's going to be me.

Leroy went in the cellar and he's fine.

So if I have to go in the cellar, I will.

I promise.

I will be fine. I will be sane. I will save the list of names, and let George go home to Grandpa, and save myself.

I'd better.

Or I will be dead.

LAW

I WROTE ABOUT PINEBANK BEFORE. I pull the file up from my hard drive and stare at it, trying to turn it into a speech.

Olmsted's vision.

A restaurant overlooking Jamaica Pond. This time, though, what I see is the white people sitting down eating. We are the waiters and cooks and busboys.

I stare at the screen; I stare, trying to see the missing secret of Pinebank, the treasure, the Perkins Bequest, until I can't see anything but my reflected face.

After a while I go downstairs and retrieve Katie's picture of the ghosts from Mamma's plans bin.

I unroll the picture. Five men and a boy swearing on a Bible, and fragments of black people circling them. I don't want to look at them, any more than I wanted to look at those hood rats at Simco's.

Close to midnight, when it's obvious I'm not getting anywhere with the speech, I start Googling images of slaves. There's the famous one of a man whose back is a mountain of scars. He's stripped to the waist, facing away from the camera. His face is in shadow. I keep looking for a version that will show his face, but it's only a dark profile looking away. I find his name and some words out of his mouth. "'Overseer Artayou Carrier whipped me. I was two months in bed sore from the whipping' . . . The very words of poor Peter, taken as he sat for his picture." But in another version of the image, his name is Gordon.

So what did Gordon, or Peter, really say? What did he want? What would he say to me? I print him out and tape him over my desk.

When I fall asleep, just before morning, I dream of him turning toward me the same flat, dark, hungry eyes that Katie drew.

I want those people to leave us alone.

Tuesday the shit hits the fan for Katie and me. In Dr. Petrucci's class.

Buttrucci is droning on about the causes of the Civil War. Economic and social differences between North and South. The invention of the cotton gin. States' rights versus federal rights. When we get to World War II, Buttrucci won't have any trouble saying "Holocaust" or "death camps" or "Jewish," but he can't say those pesky words "slaveowner" or "slave."

Nullification, he says. The Panic of 1857. I have tuned out and I'm working on the first-floor plan of Pinebank when suddenly the whole classroom goes quiet.

I turn around. Katie is drawing on the blackboard.

She's not here—I can see her face from where I'm sitting. She looks like she did when she was drawing Walker's portrait. And all across the blackboard, in white chalk on the green blackboard—

A whip slashes across a back, so deep you can see bone.

A brand sizzles in the flesh of a shoulder.

"Is this supposed to be funny?" says the Buttman.

Katie doesn't even turn around. She drives the chalk squeaking down the board, and the long chalk line turns into flailing legs, a chained shadow falling from a ship.

"Is this some kind of a *commentary*, Katie?"

And I lose it too. I stand up. "Yeah, Buttrucci, this is a commentary. When do we talk about slavery? When do we talk about *those* economic and social differences?"

"Law, if you could once get beyond being the son of your father—"

"Fuck my father and fuck you too, you're leaving millions of people out of the story. Talk about the 1850s? Let's hear how it was for the slaves in the 1850s, there were five million of them and they weren't even treated like humans. Why can't we say what happened here?"

His voice hasn't brought Katie out of it, but mine does, and she stares at what's on the board and turns around and stares at all of us. Somebody goes, "All right, Katie!" as if Katie meant to draw these things.

Her stepfather has to come get her and take her home.

⌢

Mamma's waiting for me when I get home. She doesn't know what to say first. "You were sent to the principal? For swearing at Dr. Petrucci?"

Yeah, Mamma. Sorry, Mamma. Sorry for being a black man, Mamma. To the tiny extent I am.

But it's really Mrs. Perkins she cares about.

"Law, how could you?" She stands up and gestures to me to sit down. I don't. "You know there's only one chance at people like that. Dorothy Perkins refused to see Hugh today because she said someone from the Friends had already been there."

"Mamma. Do you remember I told you this was about Olmsted? I mean it was *really* about Olmsted. Katie and I believe that the Perkins Bequest involved Olmsted, that he was a secret trustee. We believe there's still something relating to the Perkins Bequest at Pinebank. In a chest. In the cellar. Katie says that Mrs. Perkins sent somebody there for it after we told her it was in the house.

"But this is about slavery too. I stood up to Bu—to Dr. Petrucci today, and I'm not ashamed of that."

"Your friend Katie. The same girl who drew those pictures today?"

Yeah, Mamma.

"Law, your friend is creative, everyone admires that, but she's also very disturbed. I spoke with her art teacher today, with Dr. Petrucci, with all her teachers. They're concerned. Some of them," Mamma lowers her voice, "some of them think she's on drugs."

"Mamma. For G—Pete's sake. Katie's not on drugs."

"She is also under a psychiatrist's care. Look at what happened today. I blame myself. I become too passionate about causes, I bring people in who *should not be*—" She shakes her head. "I might as well blame Tom Menino. Things are the way they are. But, Law, I think we're not a good family for her to know."

I don't get it for a moment. "Are you telling me not to see her?"

"Your father's work can stir up some very deep feelings. It's difficult for him even to write what he does, to study what happened, to face those terribly broken lives, and Charlie is a strong man.

"Your friend's mother was killed suddenly. She's never been the same since. I understand from one of her teachers, Ms. Rosen, that it has been terrible for her. Post-traumatic stress disorder, I don't know, it's not my place to diagnose her."

"You're doing it, though."

"You're old enough to make responsible decisions, Law. You haven't been making them since you've known her. That concerns me. I am concerned, not only about you; about her stability, the possibility that she is feeling too deeply about issues she cannot handle." Mamma reaches behind her desk. "I'm concerned because of this."

I recognize the picture before she unrolls it, Olmsted among the white men and the slaves, but there's a second picture rolled inside. Walker. Katie's picture of my great-great-grandfather.

Mamma makes a face at the first picture and spreads the second picture out.

"This is you," Mamma says.

"He looks like me, some. But he's Walker."

"Why does she draw Walker?" She lets the picture roll up again, presses her palms together. "She is focusing on slavery, Law, on suffering. And on you. I almost feel as though you're being stalked. I don't like to say this, but her interest in you is not healthy. And why is she bringing Olmsted in, *Olmsted* of all people? Olmsted is me."

"Mamma, you've got it completely wrong."

"Law, I want you to be responsible to us and to her. Don't say anything for a minute: I want you not to see her *for a while*. Until her mental status is clear."

"Her mental state is none of your business."

"What she could do to my son is my business," Mamma snaps, standing up. "Law, think. Is she still fixated on her mother's death? Is she just mourning, or is she angry? Does she talk about her mother's death? Death in general? Does she have fantasies or fixations about death? Hallucinations? You know where those things lead."

I think about Katie's portfolio. Katie sitting in Starbucks talking about the guy who killed her mother. *I hope he dies really, really painfully.* Katie describing the house she went into, not any house that can be photographed.

"She's not crazy."

She's not crazy like that.

"Your father and I have agreed. You will not see her."

"You may have agreed. But I haven't. Don't try to do this, Mamma."

I get up and leave before she can say anything more.

"She is getting frightening," Shar says. "I'm hoping you know."

We're all down in Bobby Lee's media room. "Nobody can decide whether it was cool crazy or scary crazy, what she did," Bobby Lee says. "But I wish I'd had a camera on Petrucci when *you* went postal. Son of famous Harvard history professor telling villainous asshole he's full of shit. And he was the one who brought up who your father is. That was perfect."

"Can we just leave my parents out of this?"

Shar takes a speculative look at me. "Did your dad call her stepfather?"

"J—sus G—d, I hope not."

"Five bucks he did," Bobby Lee says.

"Your father, I apologize, I know you and your father, but it is what my parents would do. When someone is crazy like that."

"Shut up, both of you. Mamma told me I shouldn't see Katie, but I'm going to."

"Man," says Darryl, "both your parents agreeing about something?"

"You will be too busy to go sneaking past your parents," Shar says. "Practicing for your Walker Prize victory speech."

"You folks heard already?" Bobby Lee asks. "So?"

Shar points at Darryl and at herself.

They all look at me.

"I haven't heard anything, and I don't care about the fucking speech."

"We all have got the whole list of finalists." Shar unfolds her letter and taps my name with a polished fingernail. She gives me a sharp, sad smile. "Congratulations."

Be a good little Lawrence and practice for the Walker Prize. Forget Katie, forget Pinebank, forget the way the house fits into its landscape like a note into music. Forget ghosts. Forget slavery. Forget Katie's white skin. Forget her saying that she's like what I'm afraid of. What Dad and Mamma are afraid of. What we never say.

Win the Walker Prize if I can. Beat my friends. Sure, go ahead, take the obvious reparations. Because that's easy, that's so fucking simple, to think of privilege as reparations, rather than part of my life that I've got to deal with.

What's my other choice? Give that speech Thursday, do no good, go into Pinebank with Katie to find blood-money gold and a list of dead people's names?

And have the first floor fall on us?

If I were smart, I'd figure out a way to get the chest out of Pinebank without hurting anybody.

If I were really smart, I'd figure it out before Thursday.

Which means I should lace up my hero sneakers and get going.

On my way back from Bobby Lee's I stop at Pinebank. I

leave the car in the parking lot, take my flashlight, go up the path, and stand by the fence. I stand there for a long time, thinking about those half-burned balanced beams.

I'm not a hero.

Instead I call Mrs. Wilson.

Off Blue Hill Ave., the rows of triple-deckers are featureless ugly boxes, stripped of everything: dented aluminum siding and no trim. No trees on the street, not even saplings. Cars line the street, rusted-out Bondomobiles painted radiator-paint gold. I find a space for my Geo two down from Mrs. Wilson's building.

"Mrs. Wilson, you and Mrs. Perkins sent somebody into Pinebank to find the box that supposedly isn't there. What's in it?"

"I have no notion what you're talking about."

"Katie saw Tyler and Leroy." I reach up above her stove and thump the Ouija board down on her kitchen table. "She's being driven crazy by whatever's in there. She can help you find the chest."

Mrs. Wilson purses her lips and shakes her head.

"She is haunted."

Something flickers in Mrs. Wilson's eyes.

"She wouldn't be the only one," Mrs. Wilson says. "Not the only one haunted."

Yeah, we all live in haunted houses. "Mrs. Perkins knows what's in the box," I say.

"Maybe," Mrs. Wilson says. "Maybe Mrs. Perkins knows, maybe she suspects something she wouldn't care to know. She got to protect her family."

"We know already Thomas Perkins was a slaver. That's in the record."

"You don't know anything about that," Mrs. Wilson says sharply.

"Ask Mrs. Perkins to help. Get her to look up how the house was given to Boston. Get her to file a nuisance suit. Anything." I scribble my number. "Katie and I have to get the box out ourselves if there isn't any other way. We have two days. Please."

Outside Mrs. Wilson's apartment I sit down on the stairs in sheer panic. Unless something happens, unless seventy-two-year-old Mrs. Perkins comes up with something or I speak with the tongues of men and of angels on Thursday . . .

When I get outside again, my little Geo is still there but the lock is popped and the radio's gone. Maybe I'm going to be dead in two days, so why should it matter, but I lose it. I have had it with black. I stand in the street and yell.

"You bastards stole my radio."

Everyone in Dorchester. Everyone in the world.

All of them.

All of us.

I don't even consider I might have been ripped off by a white man.

KATIE

PHIL'S PALE, I'VE NEVER SEEN ANYONE SO PALE; his nose is white, his eyes are all black. I haven't seen him look like this since Mom died.

Lucy Rosen has my sketchbook. She and Phil are sitting at the table, looking through the sketchbook she gave me for Christmas.

"A whole notebook, Katie?" Lucy Rosen asks.

"They're pictures of slaves," I say. "Law and I have been talking about slavery, and I've been drawing slaves."

"Katie," Phil says.

He has the book open to a picture I don't even remember drawing.

It's a woman holding a baby in her arms. Mother and daughter. The woman is curled up around her daughter, trying to protect her. Their heads are bald and bony; their lips are eaten away from their teeth. The skin is peeling off them.

Scrawled over them, yes, it's my printing, is KATEY KATEY KATEY KATEY.

"Katie, that's your name," Phil says. "Katie. I don't even know what to think."

"I don't spell my name like that. I know how to spell my *name*."

Phil and Lucy Rosen look at each other.

"Mrs. Walker called us. Me," Phil says. "You told me last Friday you were sick, but you skipped school with her son. Mrs. Morris called too. You told me you could go alone to your appointment last Saturday, but you told her you were going to a family party, and apparently you and Mrs. Walker's son were together again. Now this thing at school—"

"Mrs. Morris isn't doing me any good. I'm not even sure I need a shrink." Maybe an exorcist.

This isn't the right thing to say. They look at each other. They're sure I should be sitting and staring at Mrs. Morris's fat ankles.

"These are horrible," Lucy Rosen says. "Katie, this is out of control."

"Look," I point at the picture. "Things like that happened. Why shouldn't I draw pictures of them?"

"It's not healthy, Katie."

"People sold people once. Sold them and starved them and everything. People from *Boston* were even involved. Why shouldn't I feel *that's* unhealthy? Tell me slavery is healthy?"

I ought to be winning this argument but it doesn't feel like I am. Phil and Lucy Rosen look at each other, like *how to explain it to the girl*. The girl just hopes they haven't found some of the other pictures.

"Mrs. Walker feels that you shouldn't be involved in Pinebank anymore," Phil says. "So do I."

"No. Phil, this Thursday is the last chance before the city tears Pinebank down. Law is going to give a speech. I *have* to be there."

He has no idea how much I have to be there.

"Mrs. Walker also hopes you and her son don't see each other for now," Lucy Rosen says.

Not see Law?

"Katie," Phil says, "you should take a few days off from school."

"Why?"

"The school administration isn't sure you should be at Brookline High," Phil says.

"*No.*" I wouldn't mind not going to school, I mean, any excuse, always, but getting thrown out? That would mean I'm officially crazy.

And not see Law?

"I'll apologize. Phil, I just drew on the blackboard. That was all I did."

But when it happens the next time? What do I do then?

Lucy puts her hand over Phil's. The sort of gesture that people who love each other do without thinking. "Phil, I have a suggestion," she says. "Katie has been involved in the attempt to preserve Pinebank. It would be unfair to keep her from the meeting. Perhaps we should all go."

I scowl so I don't have to thank her. I excuse myself and go into my room, where I hide all my ghost roadkill pictures under the mattress. Nothing in my portfolio but lambs and kitties.

Throw me out of school?

On the other side of the door, I hear Phil and Lucy talking in low voices about "her father" and shock and abandonment.

Do they know about my talking to Dad?

Wednesday, the day before Pinebank's fate is decided: Pinebank's and the Other People's and George's and mine. I can smell them. Heavy and sharp in the air, dank, spoiled. Burned meat, and something secret and hidden. Sweat and fear.

I stay home from school after all. I'm supposed to be "resting," but once Phil and Lucy have left, I go to Pinebank.

The demolition machines are already moving in. The house is hemmed in on three sides. A big yellow backhoe, an earthmover, a scarred blue tractor-wheeled giant like a huge snowplow. My heart hurts.

On one side of the house, a man in a hard hat is in the seat of a smaller machine, scraping at the white patterned bricks on the side of the house.

"What are you doing?"

He idles the machinery and gets down to speak to me.

"Taking samples of the terra-cotta, miss. Going to save them for the historical society." He picks a broken white brick off the ground. "This stuff is no good. Frost gets into it."

He pushes the white brick through the net of the fence to me. It's like chalk. On the outside face is a carved pattern. A petal. Four of them would make a flower.

"The frost cracks it," the demolition man says, "and the facing comes off. Then the ice gets into the bricks behind it. The mortar goes, the bricks decay. You want a whole brick?"

He sorts through the debris at the bottom of the wall until he finds one with a whole pattern of flowers. It takes him a while. The outside of the brick is burned brown and gray from the fires of Pinebank.

I watch him while he scrapes the skin off George's house.

George isn't here. He's almost never here while other people are. But I can see flashes of dark at the corner of the house.

And then they come. They are as much like people as surf is like still water. A grimace, a bended back, a furious stare. Purple light off crusted skin. That smell again. I can hear their voices and their words, I know they want something, but the words make no sense, like voices in dreams or a foreign language, forgotten as soon as they're heard. Like the voices of adults when you're a child. *Bumbummey. Ogun ogun. Himook. He was hanging,* says a voice in English. I can't draw them, only pieces, they are too much a part of each other; they have had only each other for too long, they've sunk into each other, they're too old. Their smell is like dirty feet, like toilets and vomit and rats. *Voku. Ai ai. Ojoo. Emgiboo. Afa. Hikuja. Hey.*

I watch them while they boil around the man working. He doesn't see them. They are frightening, nauseating, the wounds I see and the scars, I don't want to see, I don't want to be haunted by them, but in the light, in the daytime, while they try to stop the man with the backhoe and they can't, what I feel for them isn't just that I don't want to see them but that nobody does, that nobody could want to listen to them or hear or understand them. Their secrets, like George's treasure, are just going to be buried. Nobody will notice they're there except me, and it's not because I want to. That's the worst part, that nobody will care except me, that they have to resort to being gross and frightening and still nobody will know what they're saying or care or find the story of them. Except me, and no one's going to listen to me.

Death's going to happen to me sometime too. Death happened to Mom, and all I can think about is the gross stuff, the blood in the gutter, but what really hurts is that she isn't here to talk with. Whatever she wanted to say to me and never said, I'll never know. I mean she isn't *here*.

I sit and watch the man with the backhoe and the ghosts, and I cry, for Mom, for Pinebank that was and isn't going to be, for the slaves. For what dead people can't tell living people. The man with the backhoe looks at me like I'm acting strange. I don't care.

I call and leave a message for Law, saying as best I can how sad it is when secrets will never be found out, and how ghosts are sad, and history is sad, and death pretty much sucks. It's a stupid message. I hope he'll call back, even though his mom and dad don't approve of me and I'm scary and he doesn't like me.

But he doesn't call.

LAW

TONIGHT I SPEAK OR DIE.

"You know I'm testifying for Pinebank, Charlie," Mamma says.

"I know, Susan. And I'm speaking against it."

Dad drives. Mamma sits as far away from him on the front seat as she can. I haven't told either of them I'm speaking too.

Meetings about the demolition of an old building happen in odd places, whatever isn't being used for something else. This meeting is in a basement room in Boston City Hall. Boston City Hallucination, Mamma's friends call it, a massive brick mothership floating above City Hall Plaza. Menino wants to tear it down too. Mamma doesn't care for it. I love the place. It would look great if there were trees in City Hall Plaza, and I hope it'll last long enough to be appreciated.

Menino isn't there tonight; the meeting is being chaired by a plump little white woman from Boston Parks and Recreation. The room is crowded beyond the capacity of the folding chairs; there are preservationists standing against the walls, white people in winter galoshes and flop-eared hats. The front row is reserved for suits giving invited testimony. Mamma and Hugh Mattison murmur identifications to each other. John Wathne, the famous preservationist engineer. Someone from the Friends of Jamaica Pond. Nobody from the National Trust for Historic Preservation or the National Association for Olmsted Parks. "Not good," Mamma murmurs. "*Not* good."

I'm looking for Katie. Whatever Dad or Mamma told her stepfather, she'll be here tonight.

Way in the back, standing against the wall, there's Mrs. Wilson. Surprised, I move over toward her. "Mrs. Perkins will come," Mrs. Wilson says.

"Will she speak for the house?"

"That I don't know."

"Then it won't do any good."

I don't see Katie.

Dad will say the Perkinses were slavers. I have to counter that. I look at my notes, making sure I've memorized them. This time I've used my own house for a memory palace. Thomas Perkins stands by the front door: introduction, Perkins's place in Boston history. Center hall, Pinebank, center for all Bostonians. Mamma's office, Olmsted's vision. Kitchen: Pinebank could be a restaurant again.

Dad's office is not on the tour. Nothing about slavery.

I'll have to speak after Dad, to counter whatever he's saying.

All I can think of is Olmsted, with his mind like a twisting path, swearing an oath to poison the South with slaves, and wanting to preserve Pinebank to teach us civilization.

The little white woman, Margaret Dyson, brings the meeting apologetically to order. She's so sorry, she says, it's hard when an old building has to go. Mamma hisses through her teeth. John Wathne gets up, shows his slides, says Pinebank is too badly deteriorated to save. The Friends of Pinebank bring on a woman historical engineer from Harvard, but the planning board has Wathne show all his pictures again: the bushes in the gutters, the missing windows, the charred beams. I can see those beams with my eyes closed. Someone from Parks and Rec gets up to testify: Pinebank is a magnet for vagrants and kids with matches, someday somebody's going to get killed, Boston will be liable for millions in damages unless they remove this public menace. A man from the Friends of Jamaica Pond says how disturbed the neighborhood is by this eyesore and how much better it will be to have the "completely natural" landscape. Mamma snorts; this is the Emerald Necklace we're talking about. Someone else from Parks and Rec gets up to talk about plans for "memorializing" Pinebank.

Have we got any chance against these people?

"We'll open the floor to public comment."

Hugh Mattison goes first: dogged, patient. Funds have been allocated to restore Pinebank, he says; where are the funds? Boston "funds" repairs but never does them. Without the Friends groups, nothing would ever be maintained but the tulips in the Public Garden.

"The Friends of Pinebank are willing to raise funds for restoration," Hugh finishes.

"Let's not focus on the past," says Margaret Dyson for lack of a better answer.

I still don't see Katie.

Mamma goes next.

"My name is Susan Walker. I am a landscape historian and founder and president of A House in Its Landscape." Mamma talks about the history of Pinebank and Olmsted's vision for the park. She's using some of the material I wanted. "The Emerald Necklace is not a 'natural landscape.' Olmsted changed the course of the Muddy River. The Emerald Necklace is a city park, for people. If you destroy Pinebank, you will destroy a significant part of Olmsted's plan for Jamaica Pond. You will destroy it, Margaret, and it cannot be replaced."

She sits down and runs her hands through her hair, Mamma the frazzled dandelion about to blow away. "How did I do, Hugh?" she whispers.

Still no Katie.

Two Walkers can't talk one after the other. Anne Lusk from Harvard talks about the importance of the Perkins family. Dorothy Clark says she writes music on the Pinebank lawn; it's a creative and meditative place for her. Still Dad waits to speak. A man from Jamaica Plain, whom we don't know, describes doing tai chi every day in the garden area. Two dog-walking women say they'd like to have a coffee shop there.

Margaret Dyson is beginning to get restless; she'd like to call the vote. I raise my hand.

But beside me, Dad is standing.

"My name is Charles Randall Walker. I am a historian at Harvard, and I would like to talk about Pinebank from another perspective."

Margaret Dyson starts to object, but she doesn't have a chance; Dad is rolling on like the mighty Mississippi.

"My colleague at the Harvard Design School has talked about the importance of the Perkins family to the life of Boston." Somehow Dad manages to imply that, in comparison with the Harvard history department, the Design School is about the level of Clown College. "I have some—what might one call it?—'inside information' about the true importance of the Perkinses. As a Junior Fellow at Harvard, I helped to research the life of Thomas Handasyd Perkins." Being a Junior Fellow is the ultimate Harvard honor, and one of the board, just about to object, closes his mouth. "That was quite some time ago," Dad says, "and when Harvard published the book, the decision was made not to mention certain aspects of the Perkins family history. After all, as my colleague has pointed out, Thomas Handasyd Perkins was a great benefactor of Boston. The Perkins Institute, named after him. The Athenaeum. The Museum of Fine Arts, founded in part from his bequests. This great city owes much to Thomas Handasyd Perkins. And so," Dad suddenly drops his voice to barely above a whisper, "there was a story we did not tell. No one has heard it, in all its details, until tonight."

Everyone on the board leans forward.

"My son," Dad says, and I jump. "My son knows a girl

named Katie. He once asked me why I call her Katherine. Why I do not like the name Katie. It happens that, at the beginning of his career, Thomas Handasyd Perkins owned a ship named the *Katey*. A two-masted brig. Her captain was Robert McGuire, a Scotsman. She had a crew of sixteen. She usually sailed between Africa and the harbors of the Southern states.

"The *Katey* carried slaves.

"I will not ask you to feel guilt about the slave trade, or to deplore the slave trade. Your ancestors deplored it, and a decade after the *Katey* was launched, the United States passed a great and humane law. From the first day of January, 1808, no man or woman or child could be brought into these United States as a slave. No captain could land them, no owner could sell them. The penalties for attempting to do so were severe and would have greatly diminished Thomas Handasyd Perkins's fortune.

"What would an enterprising man do? The importation of slaves would not be against the law until the first of January, 1808. An enterprising man, a businessman, would make as many trips as he could until the law was in force. I do not ask you to condemn him for what the law allowed.

"In October of 1807, the *Katey* set out on the last of these trips. At Cape Coast Castle she took on her final cargo as a slaver. One hundred eighty-three men, fifty-four women, and thirty-seven children.

"Thomas Handasyd Perkins had given Captain McGuire the strictest instructions. The ship must return to the United

States before New Year's Day. By preference to a Southern port, but to some American port.

"If the ship did not land these men, women, and children before the first of January, they would be good for nothing.

"We do not know how many died on the voyage. We know that it was a long trip; they were delayed by storms and blown far off course, and the ship was damaged. And the *Katey* sailed, not into a Southern port, but into Boston Harbor on the morning of New Year's Day.

"She could not land her cargo.

"I am no sailor; you will forgive me if I have this wrong. She put down anchor sheltered by one of the Harbor Islands. Out of the storms, but not in harbor. The food had almost run out. They were on the water in Boston in January. It was bitter cold. The water would have been freezing.

"Captain McGuire and most of the crew came ashore. Captain McGuire consulted with Thomas Handasyd Perkins. It would never be possible for the ship to land the cargo anywhere in America. The law would be called down upon Thomas Perkins.

"Most of the crewmen were given leave to see their families. Captain McGuire and two of his men brought to the ship only the most necessary of supplies. Food, you would think? A few loaves of bread, a bit of meat? No. They brought out to the *Katey* twenty-four barrels of brandy.

"I wonder," Dad says, "how many of you have been to that fine dessert restaurant, Finale?"

His audience blinks and looks around at one another. Margaret Dyson raises a tentative hand.

"Crêpes suzette," Dad says. "Pancakes, orange juice, sugar. Over it all the waiter pours brandy. And then—"

Dad looks round at all the white people, smiling to an inch below his eyes. His eyes are cold as the water on New Year's night.

"Then he sets the brandy afire. Because brandy will burn."

Dad makes as though to light a match and drop it.

"Brandy will burn. An old ship, her decks tarred, all her ropes soaked with tar to preserve them. Tar will burn. The *Katey* contained gunpowder, to put down rebellions of the 'cargo.' Gunpowder will explode.

"This is the story of the *Katey*, as Captain Robert McGuire told it afterward. He and the three crewmen he had brought with him were drinking brandy. They had stowed the brandy barrels on deck, lashed. One of the crewmen saw that the Africans had got loose and built a fire on deck. The crewmen and the captain tried to stop them, but the Africans menaced them. The white men retreated to the longboat.

"From the longboat, they attempted to warn the Africans of their danger. But only one or two of the Africans could speak even a word of English.

"From the shore, people saw the *Katey* burn. They heard cries and screams. One hundred eighty-three men, fifty-four women, thirty-seven children. Some must have died on the voyage. Some must have jumped into the water to escape the flames. Perhaps a young man, whose strength had kept him alive all during that long, punishing voyage, a man who had hoped that at least he would set foot on dry land and find some way to live. Perhaps a woman with her infant in her arms. Perhaps a singer like you"—Dad gestures at a horrified Dorothy Clark— "or a wise older man, or a boy like my son. Perhaps they jumped into that freezing water. Perhaps they stayed with the ship and burned. Perhaps they were caught in the explosion.

"They were all lost.

"Not a man was saved. Not a woman. Not a child.

"It was reported as a tragic accident. Thomas Handasyd Perkins and Captain McGuire were very sorry, of course they were. They had not meant this. I do think they did not mean it," Dad says, "because no man could mean it and keep his soul alive. They had left two hundred and seventy-four people without food, without drink, in bitter cold, without an inch of land to set their foot on. With nothing on the ship but brandy, a flammable cargo. But it was not the white men's fault. No, it was the ignorant Africans who had somehow found matches, who had got into the brandy and set it alight. It was the Africans who sank the ship and destroyed themselves. The board agreed, the insurers agreed. And Thomas Handasyd Perkins was compensated for the value of the *Katey*, and compensated for her cargo, and paid no fine.

"My wife—" Dad turns to look at Mamma, and I do too. Mamma's mouth is wide and drawn down, her eyes are full of tears and anger. "My wife treasures the legacy of Frederick

Law Olmsted, and so do I. He was an abolitionist. He raised funds to free the slaves. Thomas Handasyd Perkins was a great and generous man, a benefactor, a philanthropist. I am sure Olmsted saw that in Perkins.

"I am sure that it is historic to have a house at Pinebank. It has been associated with the Perkinses since 1806, and the Perkinses helped to shape Boston. I am a historian and I do appreciate the past.

"I have talked enough—" Margaret Dyson actually shakes her head; Dad has transfixed her. "My wife and other worthy people believe Pinebank should be preserved. I do love my wife and I treasure her opinion. But I cannot visit the Harbor Islands without hearing the screams of people burning alive. And I cannot look at Pinebank without wanting to see the last of it.

"Because in 1807, when he sent the *Katey* to Africa, Thomas Handasyd Perkins needed to raise money.

"To pay for Pinebank."

No one says a word.

No one says a word. Not even me. Margaret Dyson looks round the room. I turn and look behind us. There were hands raised besides mine, before Dad spoke. People tentatively raise their hands again, then lower them.

No one else is going to speak.

Not even me.

I can't speak for Pinebank. Not tonight. Sometime soon I'll be able to ask myself what the fuck he meant, telling that story now in front of Mamma and me, driving the nails into Pinebank's coffin himself. Then the story will be about me and Mamma and Dad.

But tonight it's about them.

At the door I see Katie.

She heard. She is crying, crying outright.

I hold my hands out: *Wait for me.* But she shakes her head. She turns away from me, fades back into the darkened corridor.

By the time they've taken the inevitable vote, by the time Hugh Mattison jumps up to protest, by the time I've shouldered my way back through the people to the doorway, she is gone.

KATIE

JUST BEFORE WE'RE SUPPOSED TO GO OFF to the Pinebank meeting, Lucy Ms. Understanding Rosen goes into my room and starts making my bed. So she says. No one asked her to make my bed. No one asked her to come in my room at all. My room's mine.

And so she finds them all, all my ghost roadkill pictures, but the one that's on top when they bring me into the kitchen is the picture of the guy hanging on the stairs.

"It's a lynching." I push some of the pictures around. There's the woman who put on her pretty shoes to jump. There's the guy with the cell phone. "Okay, so I'm awful. I draw pictures like this sometimes. Scary pictures. Like the slaves, Phil. It's gross, but it's not crazy."

"It's not a lynching," Phil says. "You remember."

"What do you mean?"

"You know what we mean, Katie," Lucy says.

I have no idea what she means.

"I mean your father," Phil says.

"What about my father?" I don't draw pictures of him. "He died when I was a baby. I don't even remember him."

"Katie," Phil says. "That's enough."

"Katie," Lucy says, "your father died when you were six years old."

"No. I don't even remember my dad." I made my dad up.

"My husband came back from the war dying," Lucy says. "Your father came back with a habit. He and Annie split up when you were one. Annie and I used to go out to lunch and cry together. Your father was on the street. There was nothing anyone could do. We tried. Phil tried."

"Phil?"

"We were all friends," Phil says. "Since college."

"This is stupid. I know when my own father died."

"Just a second." Phil gets up and leaves me with Lucy.

Where's the ice cream when I need it? He takes me out for ice cream when he thinks I'm stressing. I want ice cream, I want ice cream first and pizza later, I want to be bored and staring at Mrs. Morris's fat ankles, I don't want this.

"Annie tried to keep him away from you," Lucy says.

"You be quiet."

All of a sudden, I see something in my head like a ghost. I am at a second-floor window and a man is standing out in the front yard, yelling something up at the window and crying. It is far away, a story.

"He wanted—" Lucy closes her eyes for a moment and starts again. "He loved you, Katie, but he wasn't getting better. Annie had a restraining order out on him. He kept trying to get in to see you."

The man out in the yard. He's a ghost, needing something he can't do for himself. I have to do something for him.

"Here," Phil says.

I look at the snapshot of a gravestone he's put in front of me. Phil thinks I must be able to see the dates.

"Late one night he got into the hallway," Lucy says. "Annie had locked the door, of course, she always did, and she phoned the police. Then some man, she always said afterward *some man*, said outside her door, 'It's all right, he's gone.' And she didn't open the door. She was scared. She was relieved. She didn't think *gone*. She said she was just glad Mrs. Beal downstairs didn't hear him. The next morning when she was going to take you to school, you went into the hall first. You saw him," Lucy says. "You saw him first."

I see him.

His tongue is sticking out, his face is purple-gray. The rope is cutting into his neck, above the dirty old camo jacket. His greasy hair is sticking in all directions. There's a smell like shit, like vomit. The fingers of his right hand are halfway under the rope, bloody, trying to claw it away. He didn't want to die after all.

There's a packet of cigarettes in his jacket pocket.

I know him. I know him. I know him.

I turn and run from Lucy Rosen. I scoop my coat and my bag up and run down the stairs.

_9_

I run for blocks before I stop, panting.

I'm in a frosty little park: dirty snow, an abandoned plastic tricycle, a frozen, creaking swing. I'm out of breath. The rubber seat of the swing gives a loud crack as I sit down.

"You coward. *Talk to me.*"

I don't even bother not talking aloud. Dad almost never comes to see me outside my room, but he'd better come now.

"You wanted to see me. You said you loved me. Stop this crap about *It's better for you if I leave.* We have to talk now."

"I do love you," says Dad.

He sits down in the other swing, big in it. I've always seen him in a T-shirt, but tonight he's in an old camo jacket, his shoulders tensed, his hands in his pockets as if he's cold.

Are ghosts cold? Do ghosts feel the way live people do? Or is that something else they can't do, like open Christmas presents or tell sane people their story?

"Scaring me to death on the stairs? That's love?"

He ought to have an answer. He doesn't. He sits on the swing, rocking back and forth a little, looking down at the ground.

"Katie?" he says. "That isn't me."

"Don't you lie."

"Yeah. I killed myself. I hung myself on the stairs and you saw me after. I was fucking stupid. I'm sorry, I would have said sorry before except I didn't want to bring it up. But what kind of person do you think I am, Katie? You think I hang myself again and again in Mrs. Beal's hallway so I can scare you? And then I come visit you every evening so you can not talk to me about it?"

"So it's not you on the stairs?"

"Katie?" he says. "It's you."

For a moment I'm speechless at the sheer gall of him.

"That's you," he says. "Trying to deal with me. The trouble is, kid, you think you see ghosts? And you do see ghosts? But that don't make you normal."

I never talked to Dad about the man on the stairs. No. I told Dad stories about school, what I'd done and what the teacher said. I never told him that I was afraid of the man on the stairs. I never talked about ghosts at all, until George. I just said *I make you up* and he would say *You see ghosts.*

I never talked to him about what scared me.

He was the one who talked about ghosts.

"Why should I talk to you about stuff you did? You were so stupid, so stupid and so—you were so *addicted*, such a *drunk* and a *drughead*—"

I've never talked to him about the times when he stood outside crying and Mom kept me inside. I was old enough to remember. I just didn't. That was another man, not my Dad, nothing to do with me. La la la.

"Yeah," he says. "Drunk. Addicted. Off my head. Ever wonder if I passed it on?"

I shiver. "No."

"Sure you wonder. Kid, you don't even take aspirin. But—I don't know much about this," he says. He pulls out that endless cigarette pack from his pocket and takes his time lighting the same cigarette he's been smoking for years. "When they gave out answers, I was off having another time. Yeah, I coulda passed it on, all the stuff, the drink and the drugs and the nutcase stuff. You think I don't worry about that? Bad shit happened to you even before Annie died. Your bad shit was me. I could have passed that on." His eyes go unfocused. He looks off across the park, seeing things nobody else can see. "Too much stuff happens, it gets to you. Things fall out of the sky, things blow up, things happen and things happen and after a while they just keep happening. Maybe, Katie? Maybe you're a little messed up, you know?"

"My life is full of roadkill and people *lie* to me and you *haunt* me and *maybe I'm messed up and you're sorry?*"

Dad stands up. "Look," he says. He turns to me, and I see the face of the man on the stairs. The purple face, the thrust-out tongue. And behind it, like on the other side of a piece of glass, the face of my dad.

"Look," he says, "listen, listen hard. Nobody could have saved me. Not Annie. Not you. Not your fault. But you got to deal with it. You. That's your job. What're you going to do?"

The mask fades out. It's Dad again. It's not Dad that scares me, makes my heart pound, makes me so afraid that I feel like something like death is waiting for me, coming to catch me. *"I want to make you up."*

"I saw ghosts. I got to seeing body parts," Dad says, "people blown up on the sidewalk. But I never got scared. I was fine. Don't you be fine. Be scared. Be fucking scared."

You saw body parts on the sidewalk. "I'm not like you," I shout at him. "I'm not."

"You think it's easy for me knowing I'm your nightmare on the stairs? Knowing you're going through what I did? Listen to me. Get well. They offer you help, honey? Take it. Because it sucks being dead. Just about anything's better than dead. You live. Get to enjoy it. No matter how hard it is. Do it."

"*Go away!*"

He fades out and leaves me alone in the world.

I sit there in the park for a while until I realize how cold I am, and then I walk over to the T and wait for a rickety old D car. I see myself in the wavery glass window of the stop, my face all over snot from crying and chapped from the cold. Like someone who lives homeless. Like Dad.

I'm not like you.

I'm late for the meeting. I walk all the way around City Hall, looking for an open door, and finally find one in the back, underneath the stairs. I scrub at my face in the ladies' room mirror until I hope I look as if I'm just cold. Then I wait endlessly for the elevator.

So when I get to the right room, it's Law's father's voice I hear. I stand in the hallway in case Phil and Lucy are inside looking for me.

The Katey, I hear. *Not a man was saved, not a woman, not a child.* Yeah, they died but they didn't go away. *Because he was paying for Pinebank.*

I feel them around me. I smell them. I am in a crowd of them, all of us floating in a broken ship, in the January cold, and we can't land. I take a chance, look into the room, don't see Phil or Lucy, but the room is full of *them*. They are standing behind the folding chairs, behind the Landmarks Commission members in their padded seats; they are hunkered down beside the backpacks, wedged into every free corner.

There is Mrs. Perkins, sitting frozen-faced, half-hidden in a corner, and they are all around her like flies.

How could Thomas Handasyd Perkins trade in slaves *again*?

A terrible thing starts out being an accident. Then you get used to it, because you have to. Suicide. Murder. Never seeing your mom again. Seeing people blown up around you. Burning a whole shipload of people alive. Seeing ghosts.

How can you get used to things?

People do.

Maybe those things turn into something you know better than anything else. Maybe the stories you tell about them turn into the center of your life.

Maybe they haunt you.

What stories did George's grandpa tell himself on the golden sofa? Maybe, so as not to be scared to death, he had to say it was right somehow. He had to say it was their fault. Their own people sold them. Somebody had to buy them. They got into the brandy, they set it alight, they died. It was a terrible thing, but it wasn't his fault.

Maybe that wasn't enough. Maybe he had to say, this is so all right that we can do it again. Not the burning, of course, what a terrible accident, but the rest of it. The next time his captain would be careful. The captives would be treated well. He had sent them brandy, hadn't he? Everyone would see that. The next time everyone would see that the slave trade was so all right that people could do it again.

I can feel them all around me. They hate and distrust all white people. The burned, sea-eaten mother is standing near me, cradling her burned child. She turns her eye sockets toward me. For two hundred years these people have been lost here, prisoners alive and dead.

And George, who said the treasure was for them, George is a prisoner too. For a hundred and fifty years he has guarded the treasure meant to buy more of them.

This just has to stop.

I can see Law, too. He's looking across at me. He gestures to me: *Wait for me.*

"The motion is to demolish Pinebank," Margaret Dyson says.

What can we do? Tell the other half of the story Law's dad told tonight? Say that Thomas Perkins was going to do it again? Will any of that stop it?

Will anything help?

"The motion is approved," Margaret Dyson says. Law's mom gives a little cry and puts her head in her hands. Hugh Mattison jumps up to object.

I'm thinking of what George said about the secret place, about Leroy the thief putting his hand right next to it. *He could lean on it,* George said, *and it would open.* So can I. I can put out my hand and push, and I am being pushed, as if I were a planchette in the hands of ghosts. Now it is finally happening, it feels simple and natural. It was supposed to happen. I'm not scared.

I shoot one warning look at Law—*I love you, so don't you get caught in this too*—and I go.

LAW

FROM THE BACKSEAT OF OUR CAR, I text Katie, WAIT FOR ME. When we get back to the house, Mamma goes into her study and shuts the door. Dad looks after her for a moment and then turns and goes into his study.

I follow him. I have to say something before I go off and kill myself. "Dad."

"What, Lawrence?"

"Call me Law. Law is my name."

"You know how I feel about that."

"I know how you feel about that. You've said so. You knew how Mamma feels about Pinebank."

Dad sits down behind his desk as if I were a student making trouble during office hours.

"You know how I feel about it too, if you bothered to notice. Why did you tell that story tonight?" I go over and close the door; this is between the two of us. "You'd won. They'd decided to tear down Pinebank already. So why did you need to spring that story on Mamma?"

"It needed to be told," Dad says. "It is not about your mamma."

"Those people burned to death. I'm sorry. You have no idea how sorry I am. But you needed to tell it, Dad, to make yourself look good. Everything you said tonight was you doing your Ancient African Soul act. You whip out that bloody shirt, that Middle Passage, that diaspora, Dad, and you wave it, and it's so obvious the white man is wrong so you've got to be right, and then you're so fucking comfortable with the prestige and the Lexus and Harvard."

"Do you think I am comfortable, Lawrence? Do you think it was easy for me not to tell that story years ago? To pass Perkins Street and not spit on the ground?"

"I think you managed it, Dad." Around me, his office: Dad surrounded by other famous people. Dad's Big Important Man desk, his fancy little computer, his white-ass leather chair. And Grandmam's typewriter. "You're like them. You live like them. And maybe it isn't easy for you, because you'd like to live like that, too"—I point at the poor-but-honest typewriter—"you'd like to live both ways. If you can do it, you can have it. But, Dad? You know where you can't act all that shit out? You can't take your wife and my mamma, who just naturally thinks white because that's what she is, and you can't make her feel sad and uncomfortable because you feel uncomfortable. She didn't kill anybody. She didn't know the history of the house, so she couldn't make a decision about the house, because you didn't tell her. And you can't take me down like that either. I've got some big decisions to make about how I want to be black, and you can't guilt me out of them and make me feel the only way to act is like you. Sometime you've got to stop being the self-appointed head of the entire race and stand up for your family."

"Lawrence—"

"My name is Law. Call me by my name."

I slam the door and head upstairs to my room before he can tell me to go.

I'm not fooling myself. Yelling at Dad doesn't count. I should have said something at the meeting. No matter what story Dad told, no matter how shocked I was, I should have stood up, back at the Landmarks meeting. *Here is a wrong we can never fix. Here is another wrong that we can still make good.* It would have been a terrible speech. I would have done it just to make myself feel good.

Like Dad. Doing it to make myself feel better.

My name is Law. Call me by my name. Shit.

I pick up the phone and call Katie's cell.

She doesn't answer.

I text her, KT PICK UP.

Katie promised me she wouldn't go in alone.

WAIT 4 ME.

Okay, I think as I quick-change into jeans, okay, with John Wathne's pictures of that mantrap cellar clear in front of my eyes. Boots. Hard hat. If those beams come down on me when I'm in the cellar I might as well be wearing a paper hat, so let's just get lucky, huh.

Just the minimum. Hard hat, gloves, flashlight. Sweater and fleece vest and windbreaker because it's cold. All this time I'm punching Katie on speed dial until the bars sink on my phone.

If I had spoken, she'd have waited to hear me. I won't think about that now. I don't have time.

I leave a note under the fruit bowl on the kitchen table and let my car roll down the drive so no one hears me leave.

Even with layers of gear on, it's freezing. The car wheels slide on ice. Katie must have had to walk; she can't be here yet. Sleet crusts on my sideview mirrors. By the time I park in the lot by Perkins Street, the ice is slick under my boots and we're into a full-on snowstorm.

Up the path toward Pinebank, I turn on my flashlight to look for tracks. Some bicyclist has come up here, slipping and sliding; the tracks are blurring. I think about Katie's bike and my heart pinches.

Katie's bike is under one of the big bushes near the house, under the lowest branches, like a frozen body. Her footprints from there are hollows in the snow going toward the fence.

At the fence, the snow is broomed and agitated. She's climbed over. Beyond it, I think I see her footprints heading toward the house. The snow swarms too thick in the lights to see clear.

"Katie!" I cup my hands and yell through the fence. "Katie!"

She has to have taken a flashlight. I look up on the second floor to try to see a light.

She's not going to be there.

She'll be in the basement.

The basement windows are boarded up. I run toward the front of the house, looking for chinks of light.

"Katie!"

Nothing but the snow whirling through the light, thick enough to muffle sound.

The fence is a waffle of yellow plastic and ice. The snow is coating it, and when I kick at it with my boot toe, my boot slips away. I tighten the strap on my hard hat and turn on my headlamp.

"Katie!"

My cell phone rings. It's in the pocket of my fleece, under the windbreaker. I unzip and fumble frantically; it's Katie's home phone.

"Hello? Katie?"

"Do you know where Katie is?"

It takes me a moment to recognize Katie's stepdad. He sounds scared.

"Mr. Stephens? I think she's at Pinebank. I'm here and her bike is here but I can't see her. I think she's gone in."

"Wait there, Law, wait right there, we're coming."

Wait? No. I hook my gloves into the snow-slippery plastic, kick into the toehold of plastic fence, climb and take much too long to drop clumsily on the other side.

Where to get in, where to find her? I flounder along the side of the house, stumbling on the ice and the broken bricks. Boarded windows one after another. A window is losing its plywood, but on the windward side of the house; the bricks are slick with ice, no way to climb. I look up. Above the porte cochere, three open windows, disturbed snow on the windowsills. Trim missing on the right side of the porch, dark gaps in the brickwork. As good as a ladder.

I climb it before I can think and swing my legs over the windowsill, into Pinebank.

All I can hear is my own gasping. My headlamp lights a ruin of broken plaster. I swing my head to see more. A glint on the floor is a shard of lightbulb. A door hangs off its bottom hinge. My arms ache and my face prickles and itches from the cold. The darkness is thickened with dust and the smell of old burning, and with something more, a heaviness in the air, an intensity.

"Katie!"

The walls and the wind swallow my voice. *Katie, please.*

Footprints darken the floorboards. Fresh and new and wet with snow, heading unhesitatingly across the floor to the door and the darkness.

"Katie, answer!"

Under my feet the floor bounces suddenly, once and a series of aftershocks. In the cone of the headlamp I see the floorboards sag.

And then the floor rips like a piece of paper. The house screams. I throw myself up onto the granite windowsill, holding on to the quoins. I pull my legs over and slide down the slate roof and hit the ground and roll and run. I run into the yellow mesh and my face scratches against it and I hold on to it and turn my head round and see the chimneys of Pinebank swaying in the lights. Bricks thump onto the ground. A peak of the roof sags and leans sideways.

And then the whole roof slumps, the peaks are gone, and a wall of dust and grit hits my face like a giant's slap.

I had a girlfriend. She needed help. I didn't speak up when I needed to. I was too slow to speak, too slow crossing a room. I didn't stay with her. I went home with my parents.

She went into the house.

I spend the night at the hospital getting some stitches in my face. Then I go back to Pinebank.

In the morning the police try to send dogs onto the site, but more of the roof comes down.

So we get the materials-handling equipment after all, we get all the equipment we need. Tom Menino's men carefully start taking apart Pinebank from the roof down. I watch from the south lawn: Mamma and I, Katie's stepdad Phil Stephens, Ms. Rosen the art teacher. We keep vigil.

Mamma says, "I'm sorry, Law. I'm so sorry."

Sorry doesn't help anymore.

After school on Friday, when the word has got round, students come and stand here too and whisper and tell stories about Katie. I hear things about her I never knew before. She used to draw dresses out of fashion magazines. She could pop a yo-yo. People come up saying they were her friend. They talk about how she stood up to Petrucci last week. Somebody brings flowers. Shar and Darryl bring pizza. Somebody else brings a teddy bear. Teddy bears mean death. We're all waiting for them to find Katie's body.

Katie. Katie who I kissed in my parents' kitchen, Katie who I skipped school with and hunted treasure with. Katie who, one cold day outside Starbucks, told me she saw ghosts. The only girl who will ever tell me she sees ghosts. Katie: green eyes, curly hair, scraped knees from climbing on Pinebank, fingers smudged with charcoal. I never saw her pop a yo-yo. I never asked her to dance.

What did it matter she was white? She was Katie.

I wait in the cold and the snow.

The excavator machines rip at the inside of Pinebank, dipping their heads and coming up with mouthfuls of boards and plaster. They tear off the roof peaks and the tall chimneys stand gawky and desolate. The landscape is losing its focus. Dust and soot grime the snow and turn the trees gray as if they are vanishing away from inside. Mamma goes off and comes back with red eyes, and stands, head bowed, by the flowers and the bear that the kids have left for Katie.

The entire cellar is full of debris. The excavators dig down. We wait.

By the third day of excavations the cellar is half dug out. Nothing is collapsing any more. Two German shepherds and their handler show up and the dogs begin to sniff the site. Different dogs from before. Cadaver dogs.

"They should look for the box," I say. "That was what she went in for. That's where she'll be. Get them to find it."

I walk away from all of them, down toward the pond. Near the Hancock steps I lean into the bushes and throw up pizza, coffee, everything I ate.

And so we wait for something to be found that won't be Katie anymore. The machines butt at the brick exterior wall with the ruined windows. I look away, at Jamaica Pond, at the ducks and a cloud flowering in the sky, at a jogger in a red warm-up suit puffing past John Hancock's steps. My friends come and sit beside me. They go away. The sun moves in the sky.

I wait.

Where is Dad all this time? He brings food. He and Mamma avoid each other carefully, as if they're in adjacent universes that will destroy each other if they meet. He comes over to where I'm sitting on a rock looking out at the pond and sits next to me until I tell him to go away. He brings me back a sandwich and stands next to me while I don't eat.

He doesn't say anything to me. Doesn't have a word to say. That makes me angry, in a dull sort of way, and scared, in a dull sort of way, when not even Dad has words to help.

Sunday night Mamma makes me go home. The demolition men are going to work through the night. They're getting down to the level of the basement floor. "I'll call you," she says. "If— if anything happens. I promise."

I charge my phone and sit by it while it's charging. I look at my messages—there are a lot—and there's one from Katie.

For a moment the whole world flips over and turns bright, and then I see the date.

I don't want to listen to her, because when I do, that will be the last time I hear her voice.

I sit for maybe a half hour and then I push the button.

". . . what really hurts, Law, is Mom isn't here. No matter how much she cares or I care, she'll never be able to just hug me or give me a kiss on the forehead. Whatever she wanted to say to me and never said, I'll never know. I mean she isn't *here*."

I press the button to save the message, and then I slump on my bed, still wearing my parka, grubby from the site and with my chin all unshaven and whiskery with stitches, and hold my pillow against my head and yell into it until my stomach hurts and my throat and my eyes.

She isn't here.

Katie's gone, not here, maybe somewhere else with her dad and mother, with George; with Gordon or Peter and the victims of the *Katey*, with Thomas Handasyd Perkins and Walker and Frederick Law Olmsted. With Pinebank.

With history, which Katie could see and I can't. With history, not something that Dad or Mamma or I can study, but a slammed door. Katie has gone through it and left me on the other side.

I wake up in the black of night. I sit by my desk, still in my grubby coat, staring at the green letters on my phone, CHARGING COMPLETE.

Katie's on my speed dial. I snatch it up and speed-dial her and listen to the phone go to voice mail.

No hope, no hope.

But I get my car keys and head back toward Pinebank.

KATIE

DARK AS IF I WERE BURIED ALIVE; thundering as if I were inside a big brick drum in the middle of a tornado; shrieking and pounding and dust everywhere, dust and soot and things shaking down out of the chimney, and my eyes are streaming and I cough and wheeze and can't get my breath. For hours it goes on. I crouch and tuck my head between my arms, breathing through my sleeve. Giant monsters batter the bricks above my head and scream. It's so frightening I almost fall asleep, it's too much, too much, more than my brain can hold.

And when it stops, finally, it's really, really quiet.

"Hello," I say as loud as I can to see whether I've gone deaf, and the sound echoes, but it's muffled somehow. I can't hear anything from outside. No car engines on Perkins Street, no hiss of snow or muttering of wind, not even the little sound that moving air makes in your ears.

I can't see anything either.

I can still smell my coat, and my eyes are gritty and full of tears from the dust, so I guess I'm still alive.

"Hello," says George.

I feel my face, my ears, my mouth. I can feel myself breathing. I can feel myself about to panic, too, but I can't do that.

"George. What happened? Can you see?" I don't care what happened. I just have to get out.

I brought my flashlight that lights when you shake it, and when I turn it on it works. The dust is thick plumes in the air. I can barely see the walls, though the room is so small. A brick half-barrel of a room, low at both ends, arched in the middle. I'm crouched at one low end. At the other is a heap of blankets and quilts, old bedding.

It really is a secret place. George showed me how to open it. You press a brick on one side of the chimney arch, then go across and press another brick on the other side, which unlocks the false back. When I pushed it, the whole false wall rolled backward on iron tracks, shrieking from rust, but it rolled. The arch wasn't straight-sided; it was a barrel shape. When the door reached the widest part of the barrel shape, there was room on either side to squeeze through.

And then, just after I squeezed inside the secret room, things started falling outside, and I had to push it shut.

"Someone needs to let you out," George says. "You have to be careful not to close it and get caught inside, Uncle Eddie said. Because you can't get out by yourself. Someone has to let you out."

I'm trapped.

I'm not going to think that. I'll just think *Law knows where I am. I'm in the cellar.*

I heard him calling me. Just when George showed me how to open the door. Just before I heard that awful screaming and tearing, just before I pushed the door closed—

Law has to be all right. He isn't stupid or crazy. He hasn't spent too much time hanging around with ghosts. He wouldn't come in after me. He said he would, but when it came to it he'd know better. He's the smart one and the sane one. He'd tell his mom, and his mom would call the Parks Department, and they'd all look for me, very, very carefully.

Law wouldn't be fooled by a false wall. Not Law who knows about architecture.

He will find me.

Law didn't die.

I know it.

George is looking at my flashlight curiously. I shake it for him. "It's the kind that runs off magnets," I tell him, and George looks blank. "It means we'll have plenty of light." The light is LEDs, blue and spooky and dim, but it'll last as long as I need it.

Maybe longer. But I'm not going to think that.

"Law knows where I am."

At least it isn't as cold as outside. It's cold like a basement, but not snow-and-sleet-and-wind cold.

I wish I had coffee, though.

I could wrap myself in that old bedding, which is all stained and crusty-looking, but I could keep warm.

On the other flat wall there's a little chimney inside the

big one, and underneath it is a little fireplace of sooty bricks. I could shout up the chimney, but I can't make a good shout, just a chicken squawk and coughing. I could start a fire and get warm, if I had matches and something to burn. I wish I smoked and had matches.

If I could start a fire, I could make a signal.

I shine the flashlight beam around the room. I could burn the blankets, I guess.

I could burn the box if I could find it. A black chest, soaked through with tar. But I don't see it. That's the worst thing. It's not here.

"George, where's your box?"

I can see myself, breaking up the treasure chest, using the blankets to start a fire with the box. Law looking for me, looking up at the chimney, seeing smoke, understanding exactly where I am.

In the blue light from the flashlight, George is almost substantial. He is crouching by the blankets. Which I see now are not a heap but a few blankets, covering something.

"It's here, Katie."

Gold coins. Treasure. The last thing I am now is excited about treasure, but at least I'm going to know.

I put my flashlight down and pull at the blankets. They're stiff and they smell sour, in a long-ago-dead-animal way. *Mouse nests, ick. Don't be silly, Katie.* I pull them away.

And jump up, crying, and bang my head on the bricks. Something crunches under my shoes.

Blood is running down my forehead from my scalp. That's not why I'm crying.

"Oh, George."

"I'm sorry," George says. "I'm sorry. I didn't mean to scare you."

He didn't burn alive.

Here he is, scattered bones and leather, moth-eaten jacket and pants, cracked leather boots, a skeleton curled round a black wooden box.

I went in the secret place by myself.

Someone has to let you out.

"It was dark," George says to me solemnly, "and I was scared, and no one came to *find* me." He puts his face near the flashlight, still looking at it. He is translucent blue, smoke from a fire. "Don't worry. I'm not *there* anymore. I'm *here.*"

"Law is coming to find us," I tell him. "He'll find both of us."

"That's good," George says. "Katie?"

"What?"

"It was bad to be alone."

I wish I could hold his solid hand. "Will you stay with me, George? I'd really like you to stay with me."

"I promise."

I move those awful blankets to the other side of the room, and George offers me the jacket from his body, *gross, gross,* but I disentangle it from his bones and put it on. With everything piled around me, I'm really not so cold, just hungry and tired and beginning to be thirsty. I wish I smoked and had matches in my pocket. I wish I smoked and drank and even did drugs like Dad and got into every sort of trouble but ghosts, and I wish I was home, I wish.

I try my cell phone, which I ought to have thought of before. But it isn't getting any bars at all.

I try Dad. For all the good he could do. Where is he when I need him?

He isn't here.

Mom?

Not her either.

I ask George what I should have thought of before. "What was this room for?"

"For the people we don't talk about," George says.

"The people we don't talk about were here?"

A thick-walled secret room. A couple of blankets that were old a hundred and fifty years ago. A mingy little fireplace for a little fire. No windows.

And from the inside, no way to get out.

A prison.

In the corner of my eye, *I will not look*, a shadowy mother and child crouch next to George. George doesn't see them.

More of them hover in the corners like dust.

Who was this room for? Slaves? Would Perkins have dealt in slaves from here? Right here by Boston?

When the fire happened, George closed the door and locked himself in. The secret entrance would have been blocked by beams and plaster (just the way it is now, and I won't think about that). Uncle Eddie thought George had been burned. He didn't look for George after the fire. The family just went away.

But when they came back, why didn't they find George? Because Uncle Eddie didn't call attention to this room. He didn't think George and the box were here, he thought they had been burned. He wanted to keep the room secret. So he never even opened it. He rebuilt the house around the chimney with the secret room, and then he gave it away to his friend Olmsted. Who made sure Pinebank wouldn't be demolished.

So the secret room would be secret forever.

The secret room.

With the secret inside it.

With the explanation of the secret, inside the box.

I dig my way out of the scratchy blankets. The treasure chest is over on the other side of the room, next to what is left of George. His bones have fallen away from each other. I step carefully around. "I'm sorry, George." The chest is almost too heavy to lift. I drag it to the other side of the room, scattering bones.

Just as I've got it back into the low part of the arch, something hits the chimney, *bang*. "Oh, shit—" Bricks thud on the floor I've just left. I hear more debris slithering onto the pile outside. The barrel-shaped room makes echoes of everything, *bang* bang *thud* thud *thud* thud thud thud, until it fades to a mutter like ghosts speaking.

George and I look at each other.

"What's that, George? Can you find out?"

"And leave you, Katie?"

"I have the light. George? While you're gone I'm going to open the chest. Is that okay?"

My boy George thinks.

"I won't hurt anything that's inside. I'll take as good care of it as you would. You'll come back. I won't be scared. Everything's fine."

Sure everything's fine. But George believes me. He nods and fades out the door.

I'm alone with the chest.

And with the Other People who care about it.

What is in here was *for* them. Without George's safe presence, the dark eats up the little column of blue light. The echoes of falling bricks mutter in the corners. *Hikuja. Hey. Emgiboo.*

Above the light, an edge of eyeball gleams, a bit of exposed bone.

I'm doing what I can. I turn back to the chest.

Wooden chest, tarred black, with iron bands around it. Of course it's locked. I bring the light close to the lock. It's brass. It looks awfully sturdy.

If I had a big nail, or a hairpin, or anything that people in adventure stories have, I could pick it, if I knew how to pick locks.

If I had a crowbar, I could break it open.

Law would have brought a crowbar.

Law's all right, he's looking for me—

George is at my elbow, suddenly like he does. "Katie, big cranes—like the ones that load ships—" His eyes are wide, afraid, a little excited. "Katie, they're taking Uncle Eddie's house apart."

"They're going to dig us out." I hope. "And the treasure. We can take the box out. Then you can go home to Grandpa, George. Do you know, was there a key for the chest down here?"

George shakes his head.

"Then I'm going to have to break it open. I'll be careful."

I wedge my foot against the bottom of the chest to hold it still. I curl my gloved fingers around the iron-bound edge of the lid and pull.

And nothing happens.

In a hundred and fifty years near Jamaica Pond, the iron has furred and bound together. I tug so hard I raise the chest a little from the ground. Nothing.

But the rusty iron bands have thinned too, sharp and fragile as George's bones. I don't need to open the lid.

I bring my boot up and stomp on it.

Okay, not as fragile as it looks. I stand on it. I jump up and down on it. George dances around me. *Oh Katie, careful.* I stand on it and bring my boot down again and again, until I'm coughing and wheezing from dust.

Careful, careful, careful . . .

And then I hit it just right and hear iron and wood snap.

I tear off a strip of blanket and wrap it around my hand. I

bend the brittle rusty bands. Bit by bit I pick away the wreck and splinters of the chest lid and pile them by the fireplace.

The top layer of the chest is all papers, which is good because they're protecting anything underneath. I look at them as I pull them out. Old ledgers. Payments to people. A letter of thanks from somebody to Edward Perkins.

And just below them are three pieces of heavy old paper, headed in a brown scrolly handwriting: *Manifest of the Ship KATEY, October 1807.*

Around me I hear muttering.

And then a hand almost snatches it: a vapory hand with broken pink fingernails and cracked, burned skin. I can see that hand as if it were my own.

"Here. This is yours." I hold it out to them. They darken all the air around me, pinch me with cold, I half feel them elbowing me and scratching me with their fingers, I smell their terrible stink. But they can't hold the paper, their fingers slide through it.

"What is it, Katie?" says George.

"This is what the Other People were looking for, George." Their names. Their stories. Who they were. Their lives.

"Let me read it," I tell them.

Manifest of the ship KATEY, October 1807,
Cape Coast Castle.
1. Man, about 20, tall, tattoos on cheeks, broken
nose, bone ring in ear.

But that's all. Where is his name, that was taken from him when he was made a slave? Where is who he really was? I begin reading aloud.

"'Man, about twenty-five, medium, tattoos on hands.'" This one is lined out, with a note: "'Died on voyage.'"

"'Woman, about fifteen, scar like a *T* on cheek, and mulatto infant.'" Nothing but that.

"'Man, said to be thirty years, scars from whipping, limps, can mend sails . . .'"

Can mend sails is something. But their names are gone. Not a single name.

"This is all it says about you," I tell them out loud, like they can understand English.

Law said the slavers gave them numbers. It was me who thought the slavers must have written down the names. But there's nothing. Not their names, not where they came from or how the man with the limp got hurt or who the baby's father was, not anything. Why would the slavers care? These people would never be people again. They didn't need names. She was raped, I think, the girl my age with the baby. That man could mend sails. Maybe he was a sailor. But on the list they're roadkill, dead before their deaths, turned into one line of age-and-sex-and-distinguishing-marks and a number. Not people but things, cargo.

Afa. Hey. Hey. I hear words in the mutter of voices, but they don't mean anything to me.

"I wish I could do something. That's all there is about you."

Afa. Nem. Hey. Nem. A single voice separates itself from the muttering, a deep, angry man's voice. For a moment I see a man's face, as if out of the corner of my eye, but I could draw him. Dark skin, lines of tribal scars swirling across his forehead and cheeks. Nose burned away, eyeless sockets, bone. He is wearing a cocked hat like a Revolutionary soldier would have worn. He reaches out twisted black fingerless stumps, but he can no more touch the paper or me than George could touch the Christmas ball. *Nem. Mgubene.* He's only a shudder in this cold basement.

George is crouched down, looking at the broken chest that he guarded for so long. "George? Do you know what he's saying?"

Mgubene. Mgubene. There should be a language of ghosts. But George just looks at me, puzzled.

Afa. Nem. Mgubene.

"I can't help you!" I shout at the man. My voice is nothing but a rasp. "I wish I could." I hold up the papers, the cargo log of the *Katey*. "It doesn't have your names!"

The chimney rumbles again. I scuttle back toward the chest. My blue light is almost out. I shake it again, and something heavy falls across the ceiling. Near the chimney, a crack is snaking across the bricks.

Okay. Signal. Got to make signal. Now.

There might be something in the treasure chest. There isn't anything else in this place. Nothing for them or me.

They are muttering around me, angry, and I can't help them.

Carefully I pry the rest of the top off, and one by one I bring out what is in the chest.

Mostly it's paper. More records, more ledger books, paper after paper. After the *Katey* manifest, I don't want to read any more. But tucked in among the papers, in leather pouches and leather boxes, there are things. Stuff. A heavy, old-fashioned gold necklace set with green and white stones. Earrings as long as my finger, with great winking pink rubies. A huge string of pearls. When I pick it up, the string melts to dust and the pearls bounce and fall back into the chest.

Treasure. It's amazing how much I almost care.

Nem mgubene, says the man. *Afa mgubene.*

"I wish. I'm sorry." As I pick through the papers, I keep finding pearls. I put them in my other pocket, take one out and put it in my mouth to suck because my mouth is so dry.

Not a book of matches, not a lighter, not a Ghost-to-English dictionary, not a sandwich or a bottle of Coke.

Nothing I can use. Nothing.

With lots of time, I could find the letters that the Perkins Bequest men signed.

I don't think I have lots of time.

The crane or whatever it is starts to bump against the chimney, and soot and bricks fall down on the hearth, covering the splinters of wood from the lid and puffing gritty smoke into the air. The crack in the ceiling is widening. I fit myself down into the lowest, safest corner of the room, huddled in the blankets and leaning against the ruin of the chest, sucking at the pearl like it was a throat lozenge until I almost swallow it. I spit it out and put it in my pocket, and blink and shiver and fall asleep.

I dream I'm in a mall. The elevators are on fire. Smoke is coming out of the elevators, except it has eyes and teeth and is trying to speak to me. The elevators slide open and they are all fire. People come screaming out of the fire. I run outside. The smoke follows me, and I can hear bangs and screaming but I don't look back. Fiery people snatch at me. *Mgubene. Afa. Nem.*

I run and run. The fire people fall away behind me, and it gets dark. I stumble, I run, down a crooked path in the dark and the cold. Past pine trees that whip my face, past overgrown bushes, into a field with a baseball diamond and a park bench. My bike is chained to the bench. I could get on it and run but I don't have the key, and besides I have to bring George.

"Look," George says.

I look back and I see Pinebank in flames. George is looking back at it too, frightened, but he has to go back. We both do. Pinebank is burning, and the smoke is rising from it in faces and clutching hands and screams. In the middle of it blue lights shine straight up.

I struggle awake. My blue flashlight LEDs are almost dimmed out. I shake it again and the light brightens, a bar of light in the dusty air.

If I shine it up the chimney . . .

It has to be as dusty out there as it is in here. If I shine the light up the chimney . . .

If I am underneath the chimney and more bricks come down, they'll come down on my head.

I have to do this. I pick a couple of long splintered pieces of wood, maybe a foot long each, and hold the flashlight between them like with giant chopsticks. I'm cold, and the flashlight is slippery and heavy, and it's hard to breathe with all the dust and I have to stay as far away from the chimney as I can, but I stretch my arms out and balance the flashlight so it shines up.

No. This is stupid, I'm not thinking. My brain is all gluey. I pile bits of brick around the flashlight, balancing it so it shines up. That's better.

I crouch in my corner of the room, in the smelly blankets, and stare at the light. Every few minutes I have to pry it out with the sticks and shake it to keep it going, and then put it back.

For a long time there's nothing in my head, nothing in my eyes but blue light and afterglow. Not the Others, not George; I don't hear anything but the creaks and groans from the chimney and once a sharp crack.

I don't even hear the machinery anymore.

Have they given up? What time is it out there? What day? Is it day or dark? If it's daytime, will they see my light?

I look at my watch, but the dust has made my eyes blurry and I can't see.

Have they given up and decided to just tear Pinebank down? Are they tearing down the walls now, battering them into rubble, shoveling the rubble into the basement?

Burying me alive?

I've fallen asleep, I think. My feet don't have any feeling and the light has faded completely away. I can't feel my arms. My body is dissolving because I can't see it.

"George?" I scrabble and fall across the floor, but my invisible fingers touch the flashlight. I shake it and see myself again, my blackened dirty hand, my torn fingernails. I almost cry because I'm still here.

"Katie," George says.

I'm so thirsty. I could cry but I don't want to waste water on tears. *Stay with me, George.*

I promise.

I hear the vibration of the backhoe in the bricks of the chimney. Someone is out there. I shake the light and shake it and set it up in the chimney again, shining upward, a signal, and half roll and half drag my fallen-asleep legs away.

Am I just shining light up into the bend of the chimney? Will anybody see it, does anybody know I'm here? Maybe I should shine it through the crack in the door instead. Maybe there's a space in the rubble, maybe somebody will see—

And then it all collapses at once, an avalanche of bricks and pieces of tile down the chimney. I scream and hide my head in my arms and cower down in the low corner of the room. Soot and dust pour over me. I hold my hands over my nose, my eyes, my ears, I pull the blankets over me, and the room roars around me.

When it's quiet I open my eyes.

And see nothing.

❦

The light is gone and it's cold.

I feel one hand with the other. I feel my face and touch grit and dirt and blood. I'm fragments. Blood is coming out of my ear, my foot is scraping against bricks, there's nothing but cold and shivering between them where my body ought to be.

George—

I can't hear my voice. I listen for my own breath and can't hear it. My ears are throbbing, numb to sound.

If I scream and there's an echo, I'm still alive. But when I try, I only feel myself coughing until my throat hurts.

Katie. I can hear George but maybe not with my ears anymore.

I can hear *them* too, just as urgent.

Speeg. Speeg afa mgubene. Speeg nem. Mgubene.

Ndele, says another voice. *Ndele. Atu.*

Speeg nem mgubene.

George! Help me! What's happening?

Enfasu. Omelek, the voices say, the voices of smoke and dust. *O speeg,* the first man pleads.

Something makes me giggle, which makes me think I'm still alive. I think of *The Lord of the Rings* and the part where they're in the dark looking for a door. *Pedo mellon a minno.* Speak friend and enter. Then there is a light, and a door, and they're saved. Speak friend and enter. *Friend,* I think. I think this is the end. I won't be scared. Mom's on the other side of that door I hope I'll find. There will be Mom and Dad and no more ghosts. I won't be scared. But I don't want to die. *Speak. Friend. Pedo mellon a minno. Speak friend and enter—*

Speeg, the man says. *Speeg nem.*

Speak.

Speeg nem.

"Speak *name—*"

In my memory I see a man. A dark man, like Law but much darker, with crispy hair. A man I drew once, back when there was light and I had hands.

Walker.

Where he comes from, if you speak a man's name after his death, his spirit is healed and can go to rest.

Speeg nem. What is *mgubene*?

Speak name Mgubene.

He still knew his name.

"Mgubene," I croak aloud.

It is like the fire I wanted. He is light. He rises out of the middle of a light brighter than fire, a real person, a man dressed in a blue shift. He has short curly brown hair and big ears. He smiles at me, and behind him I can see a village, a palisade fence, houses, and people running toward him in the sun, and he turns in the light to meet them.

Titilayo, a woman calls out. "Titilayo," I say. A tall woman with big cheekbones and surprised, decisive eyes. She looks past me and bursts into laughter, seeing someone she loves.

Ufane. "Ufane." He is tall and very dark, and tribal tattoos swirl on his cheeks. He looks round him and holds up his hands, stretching out his fingers in wonder. Maybe he made sails.

This shouldn't work for all of them, they didn't all come from the same place and they shouldn't all have the same religion. But it's the only thing I have, to speak their names.

Memze. "Memze." He is a little butterball of a man and he blinks as if he is coming out of a dream.

"Fatima." She is tiny, with thick dark eyebrows and olive skin. She reaches into the soot and shadows, swirls a long white veil around herself, and stands proud and tall.

"Olongwe." He is a tall, thin boy with a pointed face and a runner's build. Cattle moo around him and a dog begins barking, hysterical with joy.

"Leandro da Cunha." A light man with an earring in one ear. He crosses himself and laughs and bows to me, catching his name like a ball out of the air.

Ndele. "Ndele." It is the woman with the child. She's so young, she is the one from the list, only fifteen: a black girl with springing black hair. *Atu,* she says, holding up the charred, armless, legless lump she carries, "Atu," I say, and she makes a little noise like a moan and cuddles her perfect baby. He nurses against her, paler than her dark nipple. She looks around: Where is their place together? She pushes out her lips. Not back in her village. Wherever. Together.

"Memet." He cries *Ashadu Allah ilaha!* "Imanewo." He scowls and pats his body as if he's looking for something in his pockets. "Anfande. Tupifanzu." He is wearing a spotted animal skin and looks as tall and broad as a king, like Law's dad. He

moves among the darkness, bringing people forward. "Atasha."
My tongue rasps in my mouth. "Mutu. Kande. Egibwe.
Ayesha. Gome." Two brothers, "Atuho. Amane." The light is
so bright, so various, from so many places: green jungle, yellow
grasslands and fields, a sharp seashore light, a muggy warmth.
I am still shivering and I can't see even my hands. But I see
the people. "Engibwe. Odulu. Amina." Children run toward
her. "Omafane." He puts his hands together and bows to me.
Bricks are falling into the chimney and the air is full of dust.
I suck at my knuckle to have spit enough to talk, and I taste
dirt and grit. A sailor climbs up, flourishing into the air as if he
is climbing rigging. "Zamir. Ngewayo." They fade into light,
toward a village, onto a boat. Their friends reach out for them.

Some hang back and shake their heads. One of them keeps
shouting angrily at me as people stream by him. Someone tosses
a woman a spinning reel. A man holds a monkey. A man kisses
his wife and swings his children high in his arms. A man makes
a joke and laughs at it himself. Someone is cooking fish on a
fire, and the smell is so good that my mouth waters and I can
keep calling the names. I hear birds.

And then they are almost all gone, and the light is gone, and
no one is speaking except the shouting man, and then even he
goes quiet. It's so dark and so cold. All I can hear is the thumps
of the machinery outside, the bricks falling.

"Katie?"

I can feel a little cold hand in mine.

Did you see it? That was Heaven, George.

"What's happening?"

I think they've given up finding me. I can hear the debris slithering and piling up outside the door. *I think they're tearing down the house.*

I think they're burying us, George.

Do you want to go to Heaven, George? And see your grandpa?

"I'm staying with *you,* Katie. I *promised.*"

You've watched long enough. You can go home. You'll see your friends and your family. Maybe there'll be a dog—

The sound is suddenly much louder, snapping and screaming; Pinebank is falling. An avalanche of bricks pounds all around us and I cower back into the smallest corner of the room. "George," I choke and call out his name. "George Perkins. George Handasyd Perkins," and I feel his hand slip away from mine. "Katie Mullens!" I call out. "Mom! Dad!"

And then for me too there's light.

LAW

MAMMA SENT ME AWAY LAST NIGHT because she expected the
demolition men to find Katie's body. What I'm expecting when
I get back to Pinebank is an ambulance that doesn't need a siren.

But there's no ambulance yet. Everyone is standing around.
Mamma is talking to Katie's stepfather and a man in a hard
hat. They haven't found her.

"They're down to scraping bare floor everywhere but by the
chimney," Mr. Stephens says. He's shivering with nerves.

"We sent in the dogs again last night," the man in the hard
hat says. "They're not finding anything."

"That might be good news," Mr. Stephens says, hoping, but
nobody believes it is.

Pinebank is open to the sky like a model of itself. We can see
all the rooms on the whole south elevation. On the left there's a
dining room with a built-in china cupboard, open and empty;
on the right a sitting room or an office. This is the room with the
fancy two-flue chimney, the room Katie said she was in. Now
the room has no floor at all; the floor is beams in the basement

and a mound of rubbish burying the base of the chimney. The sun is just barely up; the floodlights are still on.

"The dogs didn't find anything by the chimney," the man says. He must be the chief demolition man. "You're sure she's there?"

The man in the hard hat and Mamma and I look at the rubble round the base of the chimney.

I know buildings; I saw the base of that chimney; I know what the issue is. The chimney isn't stable, and sooner or later, while the heavy machinery is knocking around the base of it, it'll fall. If the equipment or the men are underneath, it'll fall on them.

"My son saw her footprints going downstairs," Mamma says.

"Yeah," the man in the hard hat says. "Okay."

Dad looks as if he's been here all night.

"Try taking it down from the top of the chimney?" Mamma says. Mamma, telling him how to destroy Pinebank.

"I figure," he says, and nods. "Start from the up-side, shave her off from the top. You folks all get back."

He's trying to keep us away from where we can see the base of the chimney and the pile of rubble. Mr. Stephens walks forward to get as close as he can, but he gets waved back. I stand by him. Mamma and Dad stand in their two parallel universes, near each other, not close.

The big yellow excavator grinds away toward the back corner of Pinebank. The jaws of the clamshell rise over the ruins of the roofline, and it picks at the ornate brick chimney crown as delicately as a giraffe lipping at leaves. The chimney shivers, and we hear bricks thumping and slithering down inside the chimney stack, cracking like shots as they hit the bend.

The neck bends toward the Dumpster, and the jaws open and vomit out dust and broken bricks.

Up, over the chimney. The jaws worry away at the bricks, and broken chimney liner avalanches down the inside of the stack. A whole section of the wall around the chimney spalls off. The digger rocks back and knocks the chimney top loose. The shortened chimney puffs soot and dust, as if for the last time someone has lit fires in Pinebank. Bricks pound onto the pile of rubble.

Mr. Stephens turns away.

Ms. Rosen puts a doughnut and coffee in my hands. I hold them, but I can't swallow.

The excavator stops and reverses away. The heavy backhoe comes in, scooping up brick and tile and frozen grass.

The giraffe-head moves in again. It bends down over the shortened, tottering chimney and begins to pick at the pile of rubble.

Around the base of the chimney, wooden beams mix with plaster chunks, ripped sections of wall and floor, bricks and stone. A big transverse crack runs across the base of the chimney where the stacks meet the square box of the chimney foundation. The debris piled against the foundation looks like the only thing keeping it from collapsing. That's what we're asking the demolition crew to pull away.

The big machines go silent. The chief demolition man comes round the side of the house and squats at the edge of the cellar, looking down. He walks over to us, looking at Mamma, not at Mr. Stephens or me.

"We're going to bring down the rest of that chimney. Have it try and fall straight down."

What he's saying to us is he's taking care of his men and his machines and not thinking anymore about Katie. Mr. Stephens nods, stiff as a puppet.

"Do you want to go sit in my car?" I ask Mr. Stephens. "It's warmer." He shakes his head, but Ms. Rosen takes his arm and leads him away. He and Ms. Rosen lean against each other like wounded soldiers.

"Do you want to go too, Law?" Mamma asks.

"No. I . . ."

"I know, hon," she says. "It would be better, though."

"I'll stay."

Sunlight is slanting in from the pond, down into the cellar. It hits the worn-away edges of the brick chimney foundation. I can see a part of the arch.

The excavator starts up with a roar and trundles round to our side of the house. It stretches out to the height of the chimney and grabs it in its jaws. It starts shaking the whole wall. The house isn't going easily; the whole machine rears back on its treads. One of the big granite lintels detaches itself, with a whole section of wall, and folds outward with a crash, but the chimney doesn't give.

I squat and look down at the brick arch. Now it's almost

filled with rubble, but there's something strange about it. It looks wrong.

"Mamma—"

"Get back, Law, you're too close."

"Does that arch look funny to you? It's bowed out."

The two machines are working in tandem now. The excavator pulls back, the backhoe lowers its scoop and lifts the lintel. It falls into the Dumpster and the ground shakes.

Arches aren't built like that.

Dad comes up behind us.

The backhoe reverses. The excavator stretches its steel jaws around the chimney and begins to tug. The chimney is swaying and the machine rears up, tearing at the whole wall to bring it down—

For my whole life, what happens next is going to define us as a family, the perfect Walker family moment, because we all see it at once. A crack opens all around the arch, all around the bricks that line it. The back of the arch moves. "That's—" I say, and Mamma says, "Oh, Charlie, look!" but it's Dad who runs toward the machines, even faster than me, Dad in his Brooks Brothers overcoat who runs waving practically underneath the jaws of them so Mamma has to run after us both to pull us back to safety, Dad who calls out to the demolition man in his biggest voice, "Stop!"

"What is it?"

"That," says Mamma, pointing—

But I'm the one who says what it is.

~

"It was a prison," Katie whispers when she wakes up in the hospital that evening, when we're sitting there holding hands. Every time I'm not off getting her more ginger ale, we're holding hands.

"It wasn't," I say. "It was a station on the Underground Railroad."

"Perkins?" Katie whispers. "Was a good guy?"

"When he rebuilt his house in 1848, Perkins built a station." A hiding place. For us.

"Reparations?" she croaks.

"For the *Katey*? I guess."

And Olmsted, going South? What was he doing for Perkins? Not handing out poisoned candy but spreading the word? Giving money to conductors on the Railroad?

Doing exactly what we always knew he was doing? Telling the white folks that slavery didn't pay?

People will be writing whole new biographies of Olmsted.

"Perkins locked the black people in," Katie croaks. "No trust."

No.

"Bring me paper? Please?"

"Now?"

She's asleep when I come back with a good sketchbook and good pencils, and the people at the hospital make me leave them and go home. But when I get there next morning, she's working, sheets of paper scattered all around her. Faces. People.

A girl in a white chador, a man laughing, a girl with a baby, a man with a tricorne hat. Katie has scrawled names on each one.

My girl who sees ghosts.

My girl.

KATIE

WHAT WITH COLD AND DUST and being hit with bricks and everything, I have to stay in the hospital for a couple of days. The weird thing is lots of people come to see me.

After Law and Phil and Lucy Rosen comes Mrs. Perkins. She looks like she's going to her own hanging. She brings flowers.

"I had hoped no one would know the reason for the Perkins Bequest," she says, to Law more than me. "And now everyone knows. What you must think of us."

"He did it because of the *Katey*?" Law says.

"It haunted him," Mrs. Perkins says, as if she's heard this from Thomas Handasyd Perkins's own birthmarked lips. "He gave and gave, he was very charitable, you know. And the story had been hushed up. He knew his friends would never mention it." She puts a little emphasis on *friends*. I guess Law's dad is off her Christmas card list. "But his conscience haunted him. He tried to make up for it with the Perkins Bequest."

Law and I lean forward. The whole basement of Pinebank has been declared a national monument or something, and archeologists are going over it with tweezers, which means nobody we know has seen the Perkins Bequest letters and nobody knows for sure what it was.

"He gave a third of his fortune, and risked the rest. You know there were tremendous penalties for helping slaves to escape. He got his friends together and helped finance persons like Mrs. Tubman bringing their people from the South. He hid escaping slaves in his own house, in the place where you were, Miss Mullens. After he died, his son kept it on. The money funded schools after the war." This is the Civil War she means. "We kept on until the 1970s. Ted and I sold my engagement ring to help fund Freedom Summer. And it was no good. I was afraid of what would be in that box, I was afraid of what it would say about my family's origins, about him." She looks around at us, half-angry. "Thomas Perkins was a good man. He did a great deal of good. Now he will be known only for the *Katey*."

None of us says anything for a moment. Mrs. Perkins stands up slowly and goes over to look at my drawings, which are all spread over the bottom of the bed. I've done the best I could. I'm not sure I've got them right. Was baby Atu's nose shaped like that? Do I remember Ufane's tattoos?

"Like wastewater over the side," Mrs. Perkins murmurs. "He told Robert McGuire, 'Get rid of them however you can.' He didn't mean . . . But I suppose it is only right he is known only for that."

"The *Katey*?" Law says. "Excuse me, Mrs. Perkins. But

things like the *Katey* happened all the time. Twenty million people were sold out of Africa. Millions of people died. They were murdered. Try the *Zong*. Everybody knows about that. Every African American knows that. There were lots of ships like the *Katey*."

Law looks at Mrs. Perkins, and Mrs. Perkins looks at Law.

"So everyone we helped knew that we were helping them out of guilt?" Mrs. Perkins says sharply. "I suppose they pitied us, or scorned us?"

I pitch in. I don't have much of a voice, what with the dust and everything, but I try. "You still helped." Some. Later.

"And how many did we help?" Mrs. Perkins says. "Not enough. Never enough. The only possible help would have been to prevent it happening."

That is so true.

Mrs. Perkins turns back to the people I've drawn. She says to them: "Forgive him. I hope you can."

They're only drawings now. They don't look murdered. They look alive. They all look free.

"I wish he had known them," Mrs. Perkins says.

When she's gone, Law excuses himself. He has to make some phone calls, he says. He's grinning like he has an idea.

Law's dad shows up. He looks at the drawings too. *This one is Fon,* he says, *this man is Ashanti.* "A white person seldom draws a black face correctly," he says. Law comes back and tells his dad I've been studying history. "Your heart is in the right place, Katherine," he says reluctantly, and points out a couple of places where I've got details wrong, although I'm pretty sure they're right.

When he's gone, some of Law's friends arrive. There's legendary Bobby Lee Portis, who was making films in grade school, bringing cameras and lights and a computer and a scanner, and an amazingly gorgeous black girl, and, of all people, Darryl Johnson, who's going to be Brookline High's star quarterback next year. I could be jealous of the black girl, except it's clear she and Darryl Johnson are together. "Dude, I can so make something out of this," Bobby Lee says to Law. "Katie, can I scan your pictures? Do you mind?" The girl pounces on one of the pictures, the Portuguese man: "My name is da Cunha too," she says. "Shar da Cunha. From Rio. Hi." Darryl Johnson is just looking at the pictures, one after another, people as dark as he is.

Bobby Lee starts scanning my pictures and pointing out things to the others, and they smile at me as if they all have a secret.

"Law, what's this about?" I croak.

"The Walker Prize!" says Shar. "Our Law has some plans for the Walker Prize."

And Law tells me.

LAW

THE BASIC RULE OF THE WALKER PRIZE: Finalists have to give the speech they wrote. If you write one speech and give another, you're disqualified.

But there's no rule that says once you're disqualified, you have to sit down.

The weekend before Martin Luther King Day, Shar and Darryl practice their speeches, and Dad wants me to practice mine in front of him too, so I practice the one he thinks I'm going to give, practice it until it almost sounds convincing. The rest of the time, I'm at Bobby Lee's house with him and his dad and all their media gear and Katie. Katie sketches furiously, and I spend a lot of time on the phone with the other finalists and a lot of time making sketches myself and doing PowerPoints, and just a little time, not enough, practicing another speech.

The person I'm on the phone with most is Mrs. Perkins.

Once upon a time the Walker Prize speeches were given in the African Meeting House, but until we raise that four million dollars for reconstructing it, we're in Tremont Temple, a huge

Victorian barn. Sunday afternoon all us finalists get a chance to practice in the space with the mikes. Bobby Lee and his father skulk around the hall and eyeball distances to the nearest wall outlet.

"Dude," Bobby Lee says, "when your dad's head explodes after you do this, I'm not going to clean it up."

"Yeah, well, just DJ my funeral after he kills me."

"This is really going to work?"

"Oh, sure."

When I see the crowd in Tremont Temple on MLK Day, I nearly lose it. Everybody my family knows is here. Dad's entire Harvard department, including the secretaries. Reverend Stith. Reverend Gomes. Liz Walker. Everybody from church, even old ladies in wheelchairs. A lot of kids from school are here, mostly for Darryl, but I can see just about everyone I know.

And in the third row front, where they're going to see and hear everything, are Mrs. Perkins and her ancient husband and a whole row of their friends.

The ten of us finalists are in the front row, in our shiny-best Sunday suits and dresses, in alphabetical order from Alvaredo, Juan, to Walker, Law. The one time in my life I'm happy to be last.

In the second row, in the middle, sit the judges. And just to one side of them, three or four seats away to make it clear he isn't a judge this year, sits Dad.

Deval Patrick makes his entrance and everybody cheers. He makes a little speech and we begin.

"Our first speaker: Juan Alvaredo. Topic: '*Yo Borinqueño*: Race, Ethnicity, Culture.'"

Shar goes second and gets a lot of applause, though the Puerto Rican guy has made some of her points. Darryl is fifth. He's the least polished of the speakers, slow and hesitant, but from his first sentence he has the whole audience. "Until tenth grade I couldn't read." He talks about what it's like to be big and black and so dyslexic that even his friends thought he was stupid. "Thought I was good for football and nothing else," Darryl says. "I got nothing against being good for football. I *have* nothing against being good for football. I'd like to spend my life with football. I thought I was happy with being stupid, too, until I met a girl who wouldn't go out with me until I learned to read."

I love that man. I remember what Darryl was like a couple of years ago, big and dumb and angry. I love Shar for making him go past that. I love her for nagging me. I love my friends' courage. They can do that, I can do this.

"Law Walker. 'The African Meeting House.'"

The lights are shining in my eyes at the podium, but not enough so I can't see the judges, and the audience, and Dad. At the back of the auditorium I can see Bobby Lee.

"I was going to speak about the African Meeting House," I say. "But I'm not going to."

The murmur starts in the auditorium. The judges sit up and whisper to each other. I don't look in Dad's direction. I've just disqualified myself. One of the judges begins to speak, but I've learned from Dad and I go right on.

"Because something happened a week or so ago. Something that made a big difference to me. I was going to talk to you about the African Meeting House, and ask you to give money to restore it. It's a good idea. You all know that. Give money. But today I want to talk with you about something else.

"Some of you know my family. My father is Charles Randall Walker, who writes those books about reparations that get everyone riled up. My mother is white. She's a historical architect. And me? For most of my life I've thought I'm too white to be black and too black to be an architect.

"I've spent a lot of time thinking about that. I wasn't even happy with the idea of competing for the Walker Prize. Was I black enough to stand up in front of you? How could I talk here as if I'd made up my mind about myself?

"Then last week my girlfriend was in a house that collapsed. You've read about Pinebank collapsing. She was in Pinebank. She was lucky. And brave. She got herself into a basement shelter, a hidden shelter, which the house's white family had built before the Civil War. A station of the Underground Railroad.

"Now I'll tell a story against myself. Just before we realized she was there and not dead, I was looking at the chimney, the house, the way the chimney was built. At that point all I could think about was missing her. I thought I would never see her again. And still, I was looking at the architecture.

"I guess that makes me an architect. Black or not. Good or not. That's what I am.

"That's my gift, and I decided I was going to stop apologizing for having a gift. I was going to stop insisting my life had to be typical, and simple, and easy to explain.

"And as soon as I stopped trying to be simple, I began to notice how complicated everybody else is."

That's Bobby Lee's cue. The house lights dim. In the darkness behind me, Bobby Lee's dad unrolls the projector screen. In 107 years of the Walker Prize, nobody has done anything other than stand up and talk. No media. But I'm disqualified anyway, so I might as well do it big.

The slide on the screen is us ten finalists. Bobby Lee took it yesterday in front of Tremont Temple.

"We, uh, sort of collaborated on this one. Come up on stage, guys."

You're sure we aren't all going to be disqualified? Shar asked me. *No. Just me. They can't disqualify us all.*

Here we are, ten African Americans, the candidate teen Voices of Our People, standing on the stage in front of our picture. Bobby Lee hands the mike to Juan Alvaredo.

"Juan Alvaredo. Spanish, African, Arawak Indian, and all *borinqueño*."

Shar takes the mike. "Sharona da Cunha. From beautiful Rio and Detroit, the land of hip-hop."

"Charles Eliot. My mum's New Zealand Aboriginal and my dad's black from Vancouver. Everybody thinks my family self-emancipated from the South, but my dad's white family came to Canada in 1780 because we were Loyalists. God save King George."

"Albert Foster. Obviously I'm part black and part Chinese, but both my parents are white because I'm adopted, and mostly I think about mathematics?"

At the end of the line, before me, Bobby Lee captures the mike and says, "My racial heritage is NASCAR." I grab it back from him.

"Law Walker. Georgia, Philadelphia, and Brattle Street." Yesterday Katie drew pictures of all the finalists, and now our faces flash up on the big screen, one by one. "We're African Americans. Or African Brazilians. Or Chinese, or Spanish. We're all here because we're supposed to be spokesmen—sorry, Shar, *spokespeople* for the race, and thanks for thinking we are, but our ancestors are British and Polish and Navajo and Venezuelan as well as Fon and Ashanti. We date Greeks and Irish and Russian Jews. Our race? When Martin had a dream, if he dreamed for our race, he was dreaming for every country and race on the planet."

Now Katie's pictures of the Other People are flashing on the screen.

"Even back in Africa it was that way. These are my girlfriend's pictures of what the slaves in one Middle Passage trip might have looked like. These people are from most of the tribes of West Africa. Different countries, different languages. We are one people. But we were never only one people."

And now they start to change. Katie and Bobby Lee were sketching and playing with PhotoShop until this morning to get this part of the show right. The Portuguese sailor morphs into a T driver. Two brothers are wearing Red Sox T-shirts.

"These people could be friends and neighbors. They aren't, because all of them died in the Middle Passage. Here's the man who did it. His name was Thomas Handasyd Perkins." He's on the screen, sitting among his gold and his stuff. "He owned a slave ship full of people and he couldn't sell them." Katie's pictures go back up on the screen. Once they were slaves, now they are a girl in a graduation cap and gown, a lawyer, a garage mechanic. "He let them be burned alive."

The audience gives a collective angry gasp.

"When we think like black people—and we need to think like black people, America has taught us that—that is race war. He was white and we were black and he could do it to us and he did. That is dead wrong, wrong to the depths of Hell.

"But if we really are from all over the world, from every country: It's not only wrong, what he did, it's a tragedy. A man couldn't recognize his sisters and his brothers. So he killed them.

"You're thinking something like, 'This man is my brother? My ass!' Thomas Handasyd Perkins thought so too. Thomas Handasyd Perkins gave a lot of money afterward to the freedom movement. He built a station on the Underground Railroad in his house. But he never thought he was doing it for his brothers and his sisters.

"How can we live with people like him? I've got white blood. Most of us do. How can we live in the same world, on the same streets, in the same houses with them? How can we live with the blood of people like that in our veins and in our family? How can we live with their violence without being violent in return?"

I don't say anything for a moment, because I really don't know. I think about Blue Hill Ave. on a Saturday night and Dorothy Perkins, sunk in her white privilege. In what country are we sisters and brothers?

"My dad," I say finally, "my dad, who gives a lot of speeches, you know my dad, taught me a trick to give a speech. You think of a house. You walk through your house in your head as you plan your speech, and when you give your speech you walk through it again. If you give an important speech, if you try to say something important and complicated in it, it has to be a big house.

"Our existence as black Americans, as heirs of our history together with people like Thomas Handasyd Perkins, is the biggest American idea there is. Our existence is the most profound fact about America. 'America is more our country, than it is the whites',' David Walker said. And so to talk about ourselves, to find ideas and speeches big enough for our importance, we have to build an enormous house. If we are to talk to our brothers and sisters, our house has to be big enough that we can fit all of us in. Then we can say, 'Come on into this house. This house is ours. Here we speak Spanish and Portuguese and Kreyòl and the Queen's English. We cook fried chicken and French cuisine and Chinese and Thai. Our house contains the kitchen, the barbershop, the church, the Masons, the army barracks, the lawyer's office, the university classroom. And whoever you are, our house has a place for you.' Our house has to be so big that we can say even to the most tragic and deluded of our brothers, 'This house has a place for you too. It belongs to you too. Come in. But it is not your house alone.'

"This is the house Martin built when he had a dream. This is the house"—I gesture at the rest of the finalists—"the house we're building, the house we try to build every year with the Walker speeches.

"Me? I'm not a speaker. Like I said, I want to be an architect.

"I'd like to introduce Thomas Handasyd Perkins's descendant, Dorothy Perkins."

It takes Mrs. Perkins a minute or so to climb the stairs to the stage, even with Darryl helping her. For that whole minute, in that whole giant auditorium, no one makes a sound. The woman has guts.

"My name is Dorothy Perkins. My ancestor was a slaver. He also helped to start the Opium Wars." She gives a brief nod to Al Foster, whom to tell the truth I haven't thought of. "Before his death he gave a large amount of money as, I believe one would call it, reparations." In the audience I see Dad shift. "He died believing that nothing he had done would make any difference to his guilt. He had done good, I suppose, and he felt he put himself in danger, but he did good *for* the black people just as he had done evil *to* them. I do not think he ever sat down to eat with a black person. Or an Irishman, or a Jew, or a Chinaman—"

Mrs. Perkins smiles, just like a pirate.

"I do not intend to do good.

"Pinebank was built with the proceeds of slaving. In 1892 our family gave it to the City of Boston so that it might become a restaurant. Recently, at Mr. Law Walker's suggestion, I had our lawyers look into the deed. It seems we gave it with a proviso. Pinebank was to remain a restaurant, open to all, or a public building. If it should cease to be either of those, or if the City of Boston should fail to maintain and use it, it would revert to our family.

"For the past thirty years, the City of Boston has had the money to maintain Pinebank and has failed to do so. I understand that they do not wish to do so. It seems that Pinebank belongs again to my husband and me."

Take that, Tom Menino.

But I've spotted where Hugh Mattison is sitting. I can see his bitter grin from here. Pinebank is in ruins.

On the screen, Pinebank appears as it was when Frederick Law Olmsted dreamed of it. Then as it was in its last days. Finally, a heap of rubble.

For a moment the screen goes black. *I am an architect,* I think. *I am an architect, I am an architect. This is my speech, these slides that are coming. This is what I have to give. This is all.*

I didn't have a chance to do more than sketches. But here it comes up on the screen, my speech, my gift. A house in its garden. A restaurant in its park. One thing is still the same: The fourth Pinebank fits into the trees and Olmsted's curving paths like a note into music. The new building is still on the same foundation, with fragments of the same walls and the chimney with the Underground Railroad station. The rest is glass. Out from the verticals of the other chimneys rise arches like trunks and branches, and everything between them is glass. The kitchen is the center, a place that feels like the kitchen you invite your friends into, a place where work gets done. There's a staircase down to the station in the cellar.

It looks a little like a church, or an open-air restaurant under trees. It looks . . . I think of Katie's picture of daffodils, the spring and curve of them, that she showed me the first time we really talked. It looks like that. Like jazz. I'm sort of proud of it, really.

"I own a house that should have been a restaurant," Mrs. Perkins goes on. "I would like to give it away again. This time not to the City of Boston, so formal, don't you think, but to the people who will use it. Not, this time, for reparations, but for— To have a house where we can invite each other. We are setting it up as a nonprofit organization. Anyone may buy a share in it for ten dollars or the equivalent in work. If you think that is too little, please pay more. I hope to live long enough to dine in our restaurant. Thank you."

"Thank you," I say into the mike. "What we all decide on probably won't look like this, but if you'd like to buy in, anyone on stage can take your name and your money."

"We all going to help you sign up," Darryl says, booming into the mike. "All us finalists. No waiting. We having us a little contest, see how many people we can get signed up tonight!"

"Big round of applause," Shar says, "for the restaurant and Mrs. Perkins and Law!"

Using all the finalists was Shar's smart idea; there we all are, at every exit, each of us at a folding table, primed to sign up members of the Pinebank Restaurant Trust. Everybody's family and friends congratulate them while the judges confer, and the names and addresses and e-mails fill up the sheets and the ten-dollar bills fill the buckets. All the old ladies from church come over to me, to tell me what a shameful thing it is to turn the Walker Prize into an occasion for merchandising, and don't I remember what Jesus did to the money changers in the Temple, and son, don't you know what the white man *mean* when they talk about brotherhood, and then they pay their ten dollars to get exactly the same share of the restaurant that Mrs. Perkins is getting fifteen hundred dollars for at the next table. "Darling, they're asking for our e-mail," an elderly white woman at Mrs. Perkins's table quavers to her husband. "Do we have an e-mail?" Maybe she thinks it's a black thing.

Katie's asked to draw portraits so often she turns her table over to one of Darryl's friends from the football team and begins sketching to fund-raise.

And Darryl? He has to give his table up too, because my man Darryl wins the Walker Prize.

Charles Walker's son didn't win the Walker Prize. Was losing worth it? No matter what Dad's going to say, yeah. Bobby Lee has kept my sketch of the restaurant up, and Mamma is standing looking up at it with a big grin on her face.

But it's Dad I have to talk to. I just give Mamma a hug and take a hug and keep going, to where Dad is standing near the judges, who are congratulating Darryl and his foster mom.

"Dad, I'm sorry. I know you'd have liked me to win. I'd have liked it." This is a little more true than I expected. "I didn't know what I wanted to say until a few days ago."

Dad shakes his head. "Pinebank," he says. "Of all places. Pinebank. To keep it going but not as a monument to them. To make something like a multicultural clubhouse and hot dog stand. Brotherhood? You should show those dead people's faces."

"Yes." Tiles, I think. Or etched into the glass . . .

"Are you comfortable with this? At all? Are you comfortable with the farce you made of the Walker Prize?"

"No. Shit no, Dad." I lower my voice. "I wasn't comfortable with disqualifying myself. Or bringing everyone else up on stage; that was gimmicky. Or using slides in a Walker Prize presentation. Or using all that glass in the building, because it's an invitation to breakage. Or having a white girlfriend, or fighting you all the time, when you're such a big person in my life and you have it so together. But if I'm going to have any kind of life at all, it'll have to be an uncomfortable life, because, shit, if I was comfortable, I wouldn't be doing anything at all."

"Comfortable," Dad says, and looks at me with the oddest expression on his face. "Comfortable. Let me tell you about uncomfortable, son. Freedom Summer. Nineteen years old and going to Alabama, back when Alabama *was* Alabama. Later on, telling my mamma I was going to marry your mamma. This new book of mine, it's going to make a lot of people uncomfortable. When it comes to uncomfortable, Law, I can give you lessons."

"I expect you can, Dad."

I expect he will.

Of course he will. And all of a sudden I realize something.

All right, here's something about my father.

Dad is always going to do a lot of things better than me. He'll always have advice for me, whether I want it or not. He'll always keep me running to stay out of his shadow. Always.

That's almost like being able to count on the man.

And he's not comfortable either.

He gives me his discomfort like a gift.

"What you should be doing," Dad says, "you should be trading mailing lists with the MAAH. The same people who are supporting the African Meeting House will— What are you grinning at?"

"Nothing, Dad. Nothing."

I've just realized my father called me Law.

KATIE

LOSING SOMEBODY, EVEN SOMEBODY LIKE MOM, is sort of sad and sort of reassuring. For a while you can't bear the idea that anything will ever happen again. How could I get nearly through eleventh grade, or get a real boyfriend, or start thinking about college, without her?

And then I did, without her. And it was hard. And I could.

It's a lot easier with Law and Shar and Darryl and Bobby Lee starting the college thing too. Law's dad and mom have enough advice for all of us. They don't really approve of me, but I'm not going away and they know it, so they give advice. Law's dad is a terror and a half, but once you realize that he expects everyone else to be as tough as he is and fight back, he's all right. Law's mom . . . She gives me books to read and feeds me whenever she sees me, and we'll let it build from there.

I have a new shrink. He's not Bruce Willis, but he's not Mrs. Morris either. He asks me how I feel instead of telling me.

I think I'm feeling okay.

The weird thing is that I'm actually sort of popular. When

I went back to school, people started talking to me. Sure, for totally idiotic reasons, like I was in a house that fell down. The questions they're asking me now are pretty much as dumb as the questions they didn't ask before. "You went in that house all alone? Wasn't it scary? Did you really find a dead body?" Dumb.

But people aren't dumb, you know? I like people.

Shar has decided Law is going to ask me to the junior prom and I have to be prepared, so now I'm her personal fashion project and we go shopping. I forgot I like clothes. And shopping. I've started doing fashion drawing again, along with the portraits.

We all hang out at Starbucks. I have non-imaginary friends.

I haven't drawn a ghost, except from memory, since Pinebank.

Right now they're leaving me alone.

Mostly. Except for one.

The rededication of Pinebank as a historic site is on a bright April day, strong sunlight and strong wind. Of course there's no building, there won't be one for years probably, so they're dedicating a hole in the ground with a tent over it. Still, it's a start. Everyone's there. I can see Dorothy Clark and the Mattisons. There's a fat kid in a hoodie and a tall thin kid, Tyler and Leroy. Phil and Lucy are holding hands on the edge of the crowd. Bobby Lee is prowling round with his video camera. Margaret Dyson has introduced Tom Menino and he's giving a speech, but the wind's blowing into the microphone and no one understands what he's saying anyway.

I'm wondering whether I'll see the shouting man from the *Katey*, the ghost who didn't want me to call his name. I wonder what he's doing now, without his friends. Whatever it is, he's not here today.

Law and I hold hands on the platform, next to Mrs. Perkins. Tom Menino introduces Mrs. Perkins, *mumble mumble mumble benefactor*, and she makes a speech too.

There's a tarp over the chimney base and the room where I almost died. The cloth makes a snapping sound like sails in the wind. I shiver, and Law cuddles me against him.

"Too close? You want to leave?" I shake my head. It's not the cellar that's bothering me.

It's what I still need to do.

Law and I have to give little speeches during the dedication. After we get through that, after the cakes are cut and Law and I each have a piece of each flavor, we go on my errand.

Mrs. Perkins and Mrs. Wilson are back by the trees by Mrs. Perkins's ancient Rolls-Royce, Mrs. Wilson standing guard and Mrs. Perkins in a ratty fur coat that must be eighty years old, with her hands tucked in a muff like the coat's tiny wizened grandmother. But her hair is blowing in the wind, piratical, and there's color in her cheeks.

"At least our George has come home," she says. She had a whole new funeral for George last week. I went. It was weird. "I would like to thank you for finding him and letting us lay him to rest."

"No problem." Laid to rest. I wish. The living people aren't the only ones who are here at the dedication. George is looking curiously at the flying lady on the hood of Mrs. Perkins's Rolls-Royce.

He told me, *I'll stay with you.*

George takes things literally. George is responsible.

"Mrs. Wilson, could I speak with you a moment?"

"Before you do that, I would like to give you each a gift," Mrs. Perkins says. "Miss Mullens, you first. Florence and I are in disagreement. I believe that young girls are fond of jewelry. You found this, at some risk to yourself. It should be yours."

Mrs. Perkins takes both hands out of her muff and hands it to Mrs. Wilson. Her right hand is cupped around something. "Hold out your hands, Miss Mullens."

And she pours what she holds into my hands.

Emeralds sparkling like spring in the sunlight, rubies and diamonds, a river of sun. A golden necklace. The pearls, restrung.

Wow. For one minute I hold it in my palms and it's mine. The pirate treasure of the Perkins Bequest. It's beautiful.

If I sold this stuff, that would be my college education right there.

I look at Law and Law looks at me.

"Mrs. Perkins, that's really nice of you." I hand them back to her fast, before they can stick to my hands. "That's really beautiful stuff, but if you're giving it away, it belongs to them." I nod back at Pinebank.

"That is admirable of you, my dear. I agree, it should go to the Trust. But I do wish to give you something. You will find this a very inadequate and old-fashioned gift, I'm afraid," Mrs. Perkins says, "but Florence says it is the right thing. It would please me greatly if you would accept it."

Mrs. Wilson hands Mrs. Perkins a paper bag marked HALLMARK that looks about ten years old. Mrs. Perkins hands it to me. There's something flat and square inside, wrapped in slightly crumpled tissue paper. "Be careful, it is glass."

I unwrap it. A picture.

It's George.

It's the picture of George, with the hundred-and-fifty-year-old dried flowers from his first funeral. Mrs. Perkins has tucked a new white rosebud into the frame. From George's second funeral.

I just hold it and nod at her, blinking back tears.

"And Mr. Walker," Mrs. Perkins says. On cue Mrs. Wilson hands her a second bag, and Mrs. Perkins hands it to Law. "Mr. Walker, you are a historian as well as an architect. The Athenaeum will have a great number of our possessions when Ted and I are gone. I do not think we need to give them this. Take it, and let your light shine."

In Law's bag there's a little tin box painted black. Law opens it. Inside the box, with a piece of paper, is a little brown stub of something that looks like a petrified thumb until I see the wick.

"I lit it once when I was a girl," Mrs. Perkins says. "Mr. Walker, I hope you don't take it ill that I give you something of Washington's. He owned slaves."

"Is that *Washington's candle*?" Law says.

"It is an ordinary candle," Mrs. Perkins says. "Lit by a fallible man, given to a fallible man in a fallible world. If you sell it, I imagine you will send the proceeds to Pinebank. But—I should like you to have something of Thomas Perkins's. Try to think well of him."

"Thank you," says Law. "I will." He will. My Law.

Back toward Pinebank, a band is playing dance tunes. Margaret Dyson is talking with Tom Menino, who's eating cake. Some people are dancing on the lawn in front of Pinebank. This is going to be a good place for music and dancing. I see Law's dad and mom gesturing at each other. They're always going to fight; they just do. Law looks at them and me and shrugs and grins.

"Go get them out of each other's hair for a moment," I tell Law. "Mrs. Perkins, thank you so much for everything. Mrs. Wilson, could I talk to you?"

Law tucks the tin box very carefully in his pocket. Mrs. Perkins heads with Law back toward his parents. Mrs. Wilson's eyes slide past me to a spot at the end of the hood of Mrs. Perkins's car.

"How did you know about George?" I ask her, like I don't know.

"There you were, spelling out *G-E-O*."

Oh.

"I used to be in the fortune-telling business," Mrs. Wilson says. "Before I came to Jesus and started working for Mrs. Perkins.

People tell you things. Then they're surprised you know."

"But maybe you had some, um, talent?"

We look at each other. Mrs. Wilson is good at staring people down. I do my best to look desperate.

"I might have had some inklings here and there," Mrs. Wilson says.

"Look, here's the thing. I asked George to stay with me," I say. "When I was in the secret room. And he sort of has this thing about rules and responsibility? He promised."

"I *promised*," George says.

Go somewhere a minute, George. Back by the house, okay? Mrs. Wilson and I need to talk.

George heads obediently back toward Pinebank, looking back at me worriedly as if I'm going to ask him to go away.

"He promised. So he's like—I mean, he's done with Pinebank now, the treasure is safe, he can leave. So he left Pinebank. But where does he come? To see me. Like all the time. My dad used to come see me at night when I was doing my homework? Now it's George. If I send George back here, he goes, but then he's all alone, and I feel like I need to come out here, and *I* don't need to haunt Pinebank."

How can I say no to him? But I want other things too. I like having real friends. I like being pretty sure that I can draw somebody's picture and it'll only be their picture.

And Law and me? We're taking things slow. But if George stays around like this, slow is going to be never. I don't want it to be never.

"You want to send this George away?" Mrs. Wilson says.

"I want him to— I want him happy."

"We're talking about you now. You want him gone forever?" she says, and her voice sounds weirdly sure, just like a woman who keeps a Ouija board over her stove. "You can do that. You can send anyone you want away. Forever. All you have to do is stop paying attention."

That's what I've been waiting to hear from Dad, from Mrs. Morris, from anyone. I can get rid of my ghosts. I can be normal.

I want so much to be normal.

And I think back to crying in Law's arms after I drew Walker, and Law telling me, *This is a gift*, and I think about those last moments in the underground room, calling out their names. I think of the ghosts.

Lose George? All I have to do is not see him. Not talk to him. Not think he is interesting or responsible or important.

Not think slaves are important. Be like Dr. Petrucci, zoom right through the causes of the Civil War and not be heartbroken by a single face.

She waits for me to say something. It feels like the moment I stepped out into the hallway with the knife, knowing I could saw that rope free, knowing I could banish that ghost. Not knowing what I was doing, but feeling my future in my own hands. Not thinking what I'd lose.

I am so going to regret this.

"I want to keep my gift. I don't want to stop seeing ghosts."

Mrs. Wilson nods once, as if I'm in a fairy tale and I have cast my own spell on myself.

"But if there's a kind of average between never seeing ghosts," I say, "and having them everywhere all the time, like cat hair . . ."

She considers. "Harder than never seeing them at all."

"Could you teach me?"

"There's folks you could learn from better than me." She thinks. "You come see me. I know a woman, a Spiritist doctor. She can maybe start explaining things to you. She hasn't accepted Jesus in her heart," Mrs. Wilson adds, as if that might be exactly what I need.

My life isn't going to stop being weird anytime soon.

"Right now, though, this George. No sort of work for a Christian woman like I am now, dealing with spirits, but I can take him in hand. Anything your boy likes particularly? Never mind, I've got grandsons his age. You come with me."

Mrs. Wilson moves away from the car into the woods, and I follow her. She looks under one bush, then another. She pokes her shoe into a culvert and squints up into a tree. "Call your George to come here."

Why did I ever think nothing dies in a park? Mrs. Wilson looks up into the trees, and the shadows of squirrels run along the branches. Birds sing and wings flicker. I call silently to George and he comes up beside me, at my elbow, as puzzled as I am. Something rustles through the weeds. The three of us come out onto the field by the baseball diamond. Right by the pitcher's mound, a deer with huge antlers is cropping the grass. It doesn't raise its head. It doesn't notice us.

"There," Mrs. Wilson says. "Look over toward that street, tell me if you see anything."

She purses her lips and whistles soundlessly.

I hear the squeal of brakes. I hear a shriek, cut off. The accident happened years and years ago; the car has fins. (I can see that accident, I could draw it, but I don't have to anymore.) From over by the road, running in fright from the car that killed him, there's a dapple of motion, a shadow, a substance, light on white and black fur, frightened eyes, a little spotted dog.

"*Oh,*" says my George, and he's running. George and the dog collide in the middle of the field. George throws his arms around the dog, petting him and soothing him and telling him he's a *good* dog. The dog shudders and wedges himself into the crook of George's elbow, and shakes, and then sort of pulls himself together and decides to redefine *things are all right* and licks George's face.

There's a shadow ball in George's hand, an old brown leather ball. The dog sniffs it and wriggles a little. The ball arches across the field and the dog barks and streaks after it, and George goes galumphing after, laughing, not thinking of me at all.

And then they're gone, vanished into sunlight.

"Is that it? I mean, is he *gone*?" I ask, suddenly afraid.

Mrs. Wilson shakes her head. "Sometime you'll need your George. You'll need all your haunts. Just won't be underfoot for a while, is all. You can take some time off." She pats me on the arm. "You come see me when you get a chance. You going back to the party?"

"In a minute. Um, Mrs. Wilson? When I come see you, will you teach me how to make your cookies, too?"

She smiles. "Why, child. Easiest thing in the world."

"You don't know how I cook."

She heads back toward the celebration, and as I look after her toward Pinebank, for a moment I think I see George's house restored and whole, transparent as glass; but then the light brightens and everything is gone for now.

I stand in the middle of the field, all by myself. No haunting. No ghosts. Tonight Phil and Lucy (*my parents*, I try out. My stepparents, anyway) and Law's parents and Law and I are all going out for dinner together.

Then it's back to high school. Life goes on.

I miss Mom. I always will. Dad hasn't come back since that night before Pinebank, and I miss him, too.

Maybe later on I'll see Mom and Dad again. I hope so.

I learned some lessons from ghosts. Don't kill yourself, even with pretty shoes on, it isn't worth it. Don't drive when you're talking on your cell phone.

But don't keep yourself locked in the past like Mrs. Perkins did either. Because this is the other thing I learned from ghosts: Once you're dead, there are a whole lot of things you'll never get to do again. Unwrap a Christmas present. Get a boyfriend. Make cookies. Find a treasure. Build a house.

Death sucks. Life is a lot more fun.

So live, huh? Even when it's hard. Like Dad says.

I head back toward the party. People are dancing, even in their coats. Law's mom and dad are doing some step that involves a lot of waving their hands at each other, or maybe they're still arguing. Mrs. Perkins is waltzing with her ancient husband. On the lawn in front of Pinebank, my boyfriend and his friends are dancing together, Shar and Darryl, Bobby Lee trying to teach Law some complicated dance move.

I have a lot to learn. People to meet. Life to live.

I run toward Law and he puts his arms around me. "Want to dance?" I ask him.

"Wait," he says. "I've got to ask *you*. Don't ask why—" He takes a deep breath. "No. I was going to invite you to a dance way back in seventh grade and I didn't have the nerve. It's been too long. So, do you want to dance?"

"*You* didn't have the nerve to ask *me*?"

"Katie Mullens, will you dance with me?" Law asks me again.

"Let's ask each other," I say.

We count, one, two, three.

And "Will you dance with me?" we say together.

And "Yes," we say. "Yes."

ACKNOWLEDGMENTS

THIS BOOK OWES ITS EXISTENCE to two people above all. Hugh Mattison, head of the Friends of Pinebank, introduced me to Pinebank and to Thomas Handasyd Perkins, and loaned me his copy of *Merchant Prince of Boston*, source of the story of the *Katey*. Dorothy Clark, another Friend of Pinebank, told me what that story really was. To all of them, to the Museum of African American History, the whole Boston preservation community, and Boston Parks and Recreation, thanks for supporting Boston's many heritages, and special thanks to all of you who allowed yourselves to appear in this book. Thanks to Mayor Thomas Menino for his support of *other* preservation projects.

Barbara Neely gave me initial encouragement. Caitlyn Dlouhy, my splendid editor, pushed the story to be much more than it was; Caitlyn, thank you so much. Lauren Rille designed the wonderful cover and the format of the book. Kiley Frank chased details with efficiency and dispatch.

Thanks for their patience to my agent, Christopher Schelling, and *The Other Side of Dark*'s first readers: Holly Black,

Cassandra Clare, Josh Lewis, Gavin Grant, Kelly Link, Ellen Kushner, Delia Sherman, Steve Popkes, James Patrick Kelly, Alex Jablokov, Vandana Singh, Shariann Lewitt, Jim Cambias, Brett Cox, Elaine Isaak, Marsha Finley, Andi Pascarella, Tempest Bradford, and Betsy Shure Gross.

My day job is with the Mastering and Customer Service groups at Pearson (MasteringPhysics, MasteringChemistry, and other fine products). For their encouragement, I am grateful to many more Pearson friends than I can mention here, and especially to Lewis Costas.

Heartfelt thanks to my husband, Fred Perry, for being my cheering section and for making many dinners and eating many leftovers while I was working on this book. Love you, sweetie.

This story is a combination of real persons and fiction. The Perkins Bequest is real; no one has ever found what happened to it. The real *Merchant Prince of Boston* was actually written by two other authors, who I hope treated their researchers better. Instead of Dr. Petrucci, Brookline has Malcolm Cawthorne and the Hidden Brookline Committee. For more about this book and its background, visit sarahsmith.com, where you'll also find links to Facebook, BookViewCafe, and other places where I hang out online.

Thanks to you for reading. Until you read it, no book exists.

RUNE MICHAELS

GENESIS ALPHA

"Dark, dangerous, and utterly riveting." —Kenneth Oppel

RUNE MICHAELS

Does anyone ever, really, die?

THE REMINDER

RUNE MICHAELS

NOBEL GENES

Does it matter where you come from?

FIX ME
RUNE MICHAELS

Praise for *Genesis Alpha*:
"An adrenaline-charged thriller. . . . dark, dang
riveting." —Kenneth Oppel, Michael L. Printz Honor-

Praise for *Nobel Genes*:
"Clever, intriguing, and captivating. I read it in
be thinking about it for a long time. . . . I loved
—James Dashner, au

Imagine you and your best friend head out west on a cross-country bike trek.
Imagine that you get into a fight—and stop riding together. Imagine you reach
Seattle, go back home, start college. Imagine you think your former best
friend does too. Imagine he doesn't. Imagine your world shifting. . . .

★ "Fresh, absorbing, compelling."
—*Kirkus Reviews*, STARRED REVIEW

★ "Bradbury's keen details about the bike trip, the places, the
weather, the food, the camping, and the locals add wonderful
texture to this exciting first novel. . . ."
—*Booklist*, STARRED REVIEW

"The story moves quickly and will easily draw in readers."
—*School Library Journal*

"This is an intriguing summer mystery."—*Chicago Tribune*

"*Shift* is a wonderful book by a gifted author."—teenreads.com

**Atheneum Books
for Young Readers**

TEEN.SimonandSchuster.com